PRAISE FOR EYS

"Carolyn Jack delivers   and the trauma of familial dysfunction that can span generations. In beautifully rendered prose, she reminds us of the essential role the arts and creative expression play in making us fully human. This tale of love, loss, and human frailty will stay with you long after the last page."

—John Grogan, international bestselling author of *Marley & Me: Life and Love with the World's Worst Dog* and the memoir *The Longest Trip Home*

"How she can write! Here are grandeur and piercing moral insight. A very promising start to what will be a great career."

—Benjamin Taylor, author of *Chasing Bright Medusas: A Life of Willa Cather* and *Here We Are: My Friendship with Philip Roth*

"A lush, elegant aria of a novel, *The Changing of Keys* will transport—with gorgeous, tender lyricism—the reader into the mind of a musical prodigy in search of meaning.... *David Copperfield* meets *Norwegian Wood*, this novel will break your heart only to mend it in startling and marvelous ways."

—Naheed Phiroze Patel, author of *A Mirror Made of Rain*

"Remarkable... I could hardly put it down. It's so infused with feeling, atmosphere, and texture, and the innovative way of transitioning from father to daughter is as surreal as it is captivating. I am completely gobsmacked by the poetry and pertinent detail of the writing."

—Donald Rosenberg, author of *The Cleveland Orchestra Story: Second to None*

"A wickedly smart and thoroughly engaging writer, Jack writes with verve. The enthusiasm she has for exploring the obsessions and desires that rule the lives of her characters is contagious."

—Elissa Schappell, co-founder of Tin House literary magazine and author of *Blueprints for Building Better Girls*

"It's precisely the kind of novel so many of us are pining for—a modern classic of a literary novel with an unexpected, glamorous setting and a devastating family history."

—Ira Silverberg, literary editor and consultant

"With extraordinary literary style, Carolyn Jack deftly weaves the complexities of brilliant talent, the intense pressure of the world of opera, and the dark repercussions of a mother's emotional neglect into a beguiling tale of heartache."

—Morgan Howell, author of *The Moon Won't Talk*

"Carolyn Jack's *The Changing of Keys* is a bold and riveting story, told by a brilliantly unreliable narrator who both charms and dismays as he rises to fame in the world of classical opera. Chained to ambition, haunted by the past, he is a stunning character, tangled in complexities, surprising the reader at every turn."

—Megan Staffel, author of *The Notebook of Lost Things* and *The Causative Factor*

"No word is out of place in this riveting portrait of a man trapped by his past and the ghost of a cold and wounded mother. Jack writes with elegance and clarity, and with a clear-sighted emotional force that compels us to care about an intractable character who demands love he cannot return and is gifted with a great talent he fails to nurture, but who remains unfailingly human in the midst of his consuming and lonely grief."

—Thérèse Soukar Chehade, author of *We Walked On*

THE CHANGING OF KEYS

Carolyn Jack

Regal House Publishing

Published by
Regal House Publishing, LLC
Raleigh, NC 27605
All rights reserved

ISBN -13 (paperback): 9781646035175
ISBN -13 (epub): 9781646035182
Library of Congress Control Number: 2023950835

Cover images and design by © C. B. Royal

Regal House Publishing, LLC
https://regalhousepublishing.com

For Jean

This night a Child is born,
This night a Son is given;
This Son, this Child
Hath reconciled
Poor man that was forlorn
And the angry God of heaven.

I sang at Advent and wondered that one boy could be so spoiled and another so spurned by the same fathers. And then I ceased to voice at all what I'd no gift, and they no heart, to hear.

I

There was a time when the world was nothing but blazing sun. Other people measured the passage of days in terms of wet season and dry, cane planting and burning, but none of that meant anything to me.

What I knew was sun and dark, the latter a nothing, a time in which I slept and did not exist, but the former an invasion by God's eye, his blinding, relentless eye, which illuminated everything, turning the water in the bay a strange graphite blue and making every object leap from its background as if outlined in ebony pencil. The sun-world was extra-dimensional, unnaturally bright. A world of holograms. I used to think the sun could see right through me, exposing the bones inside, like Mother's X-rays. Mother said God's eye was everywhere.

She never said his ear was everywhere. Maybe because she didn't like to remind herself that hers were dying. That's how I thought of them, anyway—fainting, withering little cochleae in the twilight chamber of her head, coughing their last in the penthouse sickroom atop her thin, tough, indefatigable body. Nothing else about her ever stopped. Certainly not her expectations. But the ears languished on in a kind of permanent invalidism that only made her vision sharper.

We lived in those years on Duke of Gloucester Street, near the end where it almost touches South Cove. Ten feet beyond our hedge, the pavement turned to sand and became a path through the scrub palms that cluttered the shore nearly to the water's edge. The palms weren't tall enough to provide shade, but because I was so small, I could hide behind them and peek through their spiky fronds as if through my own fingers, sheltering a little from the prying sun when we went to bathe. I would watch Mother and my father sitting on a blanket with the radio they always brought down to the beach: my mother impassively upright in the wooden chair she preferred to sit on, small and unyielding, just like her; my father sprawled on his back with his shirt unbuttoned, exposing his soft, always-pasty stomach, his arms crossed over his face.

They listened to opera. Mother could barely hear even the loudest voices, but in spite of that, she could tell when my father was humming along and would shush him curtly, as if seeing him enjoy the music offended her. She would guess at the names of the arias and he would grunt very softly—an almost imperceptible laugh in the sound—if she were wrong. She couldn't detect it; it was his refuge, for no one wanted Mother to hear that she was wrong.

But if she guessed right, he would reach up and pat her knee, and there was still tenderness in the touch. I remember that he patted her very gently.

We went down to the beach nearly every weekend, as soon as my father had dismissed his last class and carefully dusted the harp and two pianos, locking the room behind him. He wouldn't permit the janitor to touch the instruments; instead, he kept a stack of soft cloths in a cabinet and polished the smooth black wood, the yellow keys, and the ornate, gilded harp frame himself, singing a little or stopping to strike a few chords. When I was finally old enough to attend school, I would report to him at the end of the last day each week and watch him do this, impatient to get home and change and sink my feet into the sand at the water's edge.

I was eight when I stopped being able to remember his face.

Before her hearing took to its bed, Mother had been something of a singer herself, a soprano with a small, clear, Christmas-carol sort of voice. She and my father met when she was twenty, after he became choirmaster of her church. I have always imagined them eying each other over their sheets of music, their want heightened by the film-score effect of the hymns and motets pulsing around them. I frankly don't know what the attraction was, at least on her part, probably because I can't recall him clearly. All I see of him in my mind anymore is those moments on the beach and in the schoolroom. He remains now too shadowy to exude any sexuality perceptible to the adult me. A mood is what he has become—a mood of reassurance that has irrevocably disappeared.

Most likely, Mother was drawn in part to his musical gift and to his position of relative authority. I asked her once why she had married him and this is what she said: "Conducting." That's it. Conducting. I feel pretty sure she wasn't implying that he conveyed any electricity.

I never heard her say she loved him. I never heard her say she loved me, either. It seemed to be one of those things she thought no one needed to actually say, such as why it was important to practice scales. If you had to ask, you were an irredeemable ninny for whom an education was a waste of her effort.

I did hear her say once that she missed him. Or something like it. I had wanted her to explain, shouting as I had to, how to count the 5/4 rhythm of a passage I was practicing. I was eleven, I believe. She started to reply and then stopped. "Your father would know," she finally said. It's the only time I remember her even obliquely admitting that she didn't have every atom of the ability necessary to raise me to manhood.

It gave me a curious feeling, half triumph, half terror. Even though I deeply resented her know-it-allness, even then, and knew it to be a dominating, arrogant pretense that she maintained through sheer, implacable, unpleasant will no matter how often we both confronted her fallibility, the sham had gradually become as dependably normal as it was irritating to me, and surely sustaining to her.

To admit of a chink in this titanium armor was to suddenly face the possibility that the sun could burn out or that playing the piano could become boring. It was startling and unthinkable. Mostly unthinkable.

I practiced a great deal after my father died. Mother didn't have to urge me, although she did, of course, constantly. Playing accomplished a number of things at once: kept me on good terms with her, made me feel near to my father, allowed me to stay out of the merciless sun. I wouldn't go to the beach anymore, which suited Mother as well. She now sat in that small wooden chair just outside the parlor door, on the screened porch, pretending to read scripture. Mostly, she listened to me endlessly play exercises and recital pieces.

Well, listened. *Felt* me play was probably more like it, although I think, for a long time, she could pick up some of the *forte* right-hand tones. She had lost the left-hand ones years before, but for their vibration.

When I was angry with her, I would play lightly, so she couldn't feel them.

She was determined that I would be a prodigy, I guess, and I obliged her by becoming one. A pale enough distinction—there wasn't a lot of competition on our island, naturally, although the church had a good boy choir, most of whose older members had studied with my father. Still, even most of those boys practiced football a lot harder than they did their music. I might have, too, had Mother permitted me to play sports.

I suppose you could say that I had an inclination for piano at that age, and it certainly helped me later. It was something I could do that Mother couldn't. Not well, anyway. And it wasn't singing, which she could. Once.

I was taught by Simon Brownlea, the man hired to replace my father. By the time I was fourteen, I could play better than he and we both knew it. Mother would invite him home to dinner occasionally and he would play for her afterward, his graying blond hair falling over his spectacles as he thumped his way through the Grieg—again—or some Mozart. If he hit a wrong note, I would call out the right one and the sound of my voice always made him flinch.

Which I enjoyed, of course. Oh, it wasn't that I didn't like him, exactly—I rather did. He was a good, encouraging sort. I learned a great deal from him. But he had the inescapable misfortune not to be my father, and by the time I surpassed him, I had begun to feel contempt for the smallness of his life and ambitions.

I suppose I was beastly to him. I always teased him about his great success with the ladies. He wasn't married, and as far as I knew from my teenaged snooping, had never even taken a girl to the movies. Of course, I hadn't either, yet, but I was certain I had the potential, whereas he lived alone on the second floor of an old house owned by an old lady and took most of his meals with the spotty young biology teacher at Tantie Rhetta's Tea Room, a fusty place that served stew and scones no matter how hot the weather. I had no use for such a pathetically dreary existence and let him know it.

He was in love with my mother, you know. Maybe because she couldn't hear how bad his playing was.

Whenever he came to dinner, he would always bring her a bouquet of hibiscus that he'd probably pulled off his landlady's hedge, or a packet of the dark chocolates she liked from the chemist's, and she'd smile a tiny, dry smile at him and say loudly, the way she did, "You're too good, Simon," and he'd blush. I found it unbearable.

Once I said, "Oh, he'll spare no expense to make you happy, isn't that right, Mr. Brownlea?" and he blushed in an altogether different way. Mother just looked at me. Her look could chemically alter bone marrow.

Between her gaze indoors and God's eye outside, I felt more and more like a lab creature in mid-dissection, held fast by two pins. I took to practicing at school every afternoon, even on Saturdays—there was always a match of some sort and the door nearest the shower room would be open. Brownlea was often about, performing odd chores in the music room, but he left me alone, generally.

One afternoon, after he had gone out for his dismal daily tea with Mr. Dampson, I started poking about in the cupboards and found a stack of yellowed song books with my father's name written on each one. They were all tenor arias, many of them ones I suddenly could remember my father singing at home. After I had gone to bed, as a small child, I would hear him singing at the piano—bits of *Messiah*, Rodolfo's "Che gelida manina" from *Bohème*, Almaviva's parts, some Verdi and Donizetti. I had forgotten that. I had forgotten the tunes until I saw them on the moist, rippled pages, the notes immediately singing for me what I had known before only by ear.

So I took the books to the piano and played them all, all my father's songs. I found I knew every bit of the Bizet, "The Flower Song." It must have been his favorite, I knew it so well. Even when I tried the words, in bad French, I recognized them. I had not sung at the piano since my long-ago lessons with him, had not sung at all, and was oddly surprised to hear something like an adult sound exit my mouth in place of the boy soprano I had been expecting.

I sat there in the sterile, humid choir room, as the light grayed with a pending rainstorm and the atmosphere thickened to the consistency of porridge and sang "The Flower Song" over and over in a voice like a balky transmission—now stalling out, now cracking and skipping into an unwanted higher gear, the brittle waver of it disappearing into the smothering tropical air and the sticky wood of chairs and walls—and what I heard were the voices on the radio and my father humming along.

I didn't tell Mother I had found the books. And I didn't sing at home—home, where the predatory sun endlessly forced its way through every slit in the shutters and Mother sat with wire-tight sinews, seeming to sense every quiver of motion in the room.

Very rarely now, I look at pictures of her from that time and realize all over again that she was pretty, fiercely pretty, with no soft, embraceable loveliness to her, but a taut intensity of angled bone and burning gaze, of sharp black lines of eyebrow, hair, and iris against the white of skin and eye—the kind of girl who would gladly go to the stake for what she believed. A dark Joan. And though she believed all too much in God, music was her real religion and the piano was the altar on which she sacrificed me. There was no singing in her house anymore.

She made her announcement right after my third-year recital,
when we were back at the house with Brownlea and a crowd of
other boys and parents, drinking lemonade. It had been rather
a grand day, as these things go. The hall at school had been
packed: men in pale jackets, women in their silks and linens
and hats, hushing the squirming, noisy, younger brothers and
sisters—all of them sweating like cane cutters in the April heat,
even though the drier winter was only just turning back into the
swamp of sultry air that, by late May, would have everything on
the island coated in tacky moisture. The hall, with its fissured
plaster and dark, scarred wooden seats, usually looked somber
in spite of the light that came through its arched windows, but
the mums had all donated bouquets from their gardens and so
the place looked positively festive. There was even a bunch of
oleander sprays from Mother, in a vase beside the piano.

Five of us performed: two singers, a violin player, a cellist,
and myself. Mother had seen to it that Brownlea put me last
on the bill. The others weren't much to speak of—oh, the
violinist did all right and the tenor was passable, I guess, even
though he flatted out most of the low notes in the Schumann.
I didn't bother to listen much. I remember sitting in the room
backstage, playing my piece over and over on the tabletop
and wiping the sweat off my face with brown paper towels.
I was performing the Beethoven *Appassionata*, and my fingers
constantly repeated the relentless, tricky arpeggios of the last
movement. I had good pianist's hands—large, even then, with
long, slender fingers. Rather like Mother's, but ringless. I never
could bear the feeling of anything on my hands.

She came backstage a few minutes before I was to play,
appearing at the door like my own personal Roman legionnaire,
marching imperviously across the room full of boys and teachers to ask, in her very *haute voix* while she straightened my tie
and collar, if I had pared my fingernails so they wouldn't click
on the keys.

She, whose radar could pick up the slightest tremor of
human movement, appeared not to notice the convulsions of

snickers this produced. I flung her hands off and walked out to the corridor, where the next-to-last recitalist was just coming off the stage, followed by an entourage of parents and aunties and toadies. I remember his name: Colin Atcheson. One of those graceful, good-looking, all-round boys—his family let him play football as well as violin, despite the danger to his precious hands, and he did both pretty well. And here he was, surrounded by mates and his healthy father and his soft-spoken mother, calling, "Good luck, then," to me as I walked past and I wanted to impale him on his own rosewood bow. I muttered, "Piss off!" under my breath as I climbed the stage stairs.

Brownlea was waiting at the door and he immediately looked alarmed at my expression. "Here now, what's wrong? Can't you tell me? Well, you can't go out there with that ferocious look on your face, you'll frighten the tots."

A man of humor as pallid as his personality.

"Come on now, manage it a bit. Use it for the music, you know? Give Ludwig a good, controlled kick. I emphasize controlled."

I looked at the floor.

"Oh, come—no sulks. You're good at this. Go show them."

He tried to pat my shoulder. I jerked away from him and threw open the stage door, hurrying to the piano bench. I barely bowed to the collection of mediocrity watching me and seated myself at once, almost simultaneously crashing out the first chords as if the keys were the triggers of so many guns.

I played with vicious precision for the next twenty-five minutes.

When it was over, I just sat there until some of the crowd ventured a timid handclap or two, and then I was on my feet and the audience was, too, looking a little windblown and stunned, as if I had diverted a hurricane through their tea party, but applauding madly as I took my bows. I finally went off and Brownlea thumped me on the back, saying, "Marvelous!" over and over and even Colin Atcheson came down the corridor and whispered, "Bloody great job" in my ear and I could tell he meant it.

Mother said, "Shall we go?"

How Mother. But at the house, she picked up her glass of lemonade and tapped on it with a spoon and I scarcely dared to breathe for hope and disbelief that she might compliment me at last.

"I welcome you all to my house," she announced. Her voice had never sounded so toneless. "Especially the boys who performed today."

Polite applause.

"I can think of no better occasion to tell you all that I have decided to send my son to the States at the end of the term. He will be studying piano in Chicago with my husband's friend and colleague, Gunter Hellman, and beginning what I am confident will be an unsurpassed professional career."

I think there was a gasp. I think it might have been my own. I don't really remember. I know that she sat down without looking at me and that people crowded round to shake my hand and offer ever more puzzled congratulations as they saw my face. I suppose I said thank you.

Brownlea finally got close enough to take my elbow and pull me into the kitchen. He scraped his hair away from his glasses with an oddly helpless gesture and stared at me.

"I begged your mother to tell you sooner, to talk it over with you, but she wouldn't and she made me promise not to, either. She said she wanted it to be a surprise, but I was afraid it would be a bad one and I can see that I was right."

I didn't say anything.

"I know you're shocked now, but after you've had a chance to think about it, if you really don't want to go, perhaps I could talk her out of it."

A gate seemed to fall open inside my head.

"Don't you speak to her! Don't you ever speak to her at all! Why would I want her to talk it over with *you*?"

My voice cracked, making me even more furious.

"What have you got to say about it, anyway? It's up to me, isn't it? To decide my own future? I should think! I'll be the one who says if I go or not, but I'll tell *you* something, if Mother thinks I should go, then perhaps I should, because she's a lot smarter than you, a *lot* smarter, and so am I!"

Brownlea took a deep breath.

"I didn't say you shouldn't go, only that if you didn't want to, I would try to reason with her. Of course, it's not my decision."

"You're completely right, it isn't! It's none of your business and my mother is none of your business! And she never will be!"

Drops of pure hate ran down my cheeks. Brownlea's face contracted with an anger I had never seen in him before.

"Here now, that's quite enough of that. In fact, I've had quite enough of your wretched temper altogether and you'd better belt up right now. I'm trying to help you, you know? I've always tried to help you because I think you're very talented and very lonely and you need someone to stand by you, but all you've ever done is jeer at me like a nasty little sod. You keep that up and all your fears are going to come true—no one at all will care what the blazes happens to you. So go to the States or don't go to the States—it's all one to me—but at least think rationally about it before you decide. And talk to your mother yourself."

He slammed out the back kitchen door. Through the window, I could see him striding up the street like a frumpy, middle-aged Horatius heading for the bridge.

Talk to Mother.

I don't believe I had ever talked to Mother, just shouted and listened and watched. It was all she had ever seemed to allow.

In order to be talked to, would she not have had to hear what I was saying? And I do not refer to her Camille-like cochleae.

I dried my face with my sleeve and got some ice water from the refrigerator. No one else had come into the kitchen and it occurred to me that they all—well, Mother excepted—must have been able to hear the quarrel and were either afraid to enter or had fled the house entirely. I hoped they had. I didn't want to see any of their alarmed, stupid pudding-faces ever again. Let them all run away from this house, this appalling, silent house that I, too, must leave, evidently. Well, the sooner the better.

I suddenly wanted to go after Brownlea. I still don't know why. Not to apologize, certainly, and not to ask his opinion. What would he know about plotting international success? And I didn't want him ever again to mention my mother. But I wanted to walk with him.

There was still no sound from any other part of the house. I quietly stepped out the back door and went round to the road. In an instant, my white dress shirt began to cling to me and my skin to sting from the violent sunlight and the fine mist of sweat it produced all over me. I had forgotten a hat.

I slowly passed up the line of bungalows that led toward town, feeling separated from myself and curiously objective. Would I miss these houses, after living here nearly all my life? This was all the home I'd got, after all—I barely remembered the mother country we'd come from. Sand and heat and salt and rank vegetation were what I knew, sticky piano keys and the slight carbon smell of the heater inside the piano case that was supposed to keep down the damp. Mold that grew on shoes and belts in their closets. Coarse weeds that grew overnight through the pavement and insects that fell out of books when you opened them. A crawling, seething, primordial world whose prim, manmade structures secretly rotted under nature's relentless attack.

I knew no temperate places. Even as I put one foot in front of the other, stirring up the bleached earth, the sun crushed and disoriented me; all color, sensation, thought became both painfully heightened and enervating. The sight of thick, fleshy leaves on a vine irritated me beyond endurance. The smell of the sludgy ponds that simmered everywhere on the island offended me to the point of madness with their bacterial stink. And the ocean—I could no longer look at it, nor wished to.

No, I would miss nothing. I would go to a bitter place and thrive.

I had reached the center of town. It was the hottest part of the day and few people except the bazaar merchants and some tourists were about. The cobbled street appeared to undulate with the slow-rolling waves of steamy air. The usual cacophony from the wharf echoed off the stucco walls of shops—conch vendors, their small boats piled high with huge, spiral shells, shouting at each other as they vied for position near the market stalls, the pilots of pleasure craft calling out for people to board their catamarans and glass-bottomed boats, the shrill laughter of the locals who hawked pineapples and bits of coral and whatnot to the hungry and the souvenir hunters. There weren't many travelers on the island this time of year. Most came in the winter, when the weather was relatively cool and dry. By mid-spring, the heat could slay anyone idiotic enough to spend all day shopping, climbing the falls, or sunning on the beach. And yet some still came after Easter, intent on tans and loading up a year's supply of duty-free rum and Royal Doulton.

But ours was not the main island, where the casinos and nightclubs kept the night air throbbing with hideous noise until dawn. Ours was dull—picturesque and terribly authentic, if decaying colonial buildings and a dirt-poor indigenous population were the authentic you wanted. It was popular with the artistic crowd, hence the ready availability of good teachers for the school. You could spot them instantly—they tended to go native a lot, or what they thought was native, wearing bright cotton clothes and straw hats and abandoning their shaving habits. The women, too. Many were seasonal folk who returned home in the summer and, to them, their time here was simply a biggish holiday.

Not so for the year-round residents, the Anglo ones. Our little society rigidly preserved the standards of the old life back home, as terrified of contracting island ease and indolence as if those were blood diseases. Arrayed in the armor of leather armchairs and church services and, apparently, underwear that pinched, my group vowed stern, silent oaths of social rectitude and cultural purity, to embalm the dowdy, reserved, middle-class existence it had known since the war and to cling to it as if to a holy era that must be honored unceasingly by repetition. Time seemed to have stopped for our parents twenty-five years ago and on another continent. They wore cardigan sweaters and listened to the old songs on the radio in the evening, complaining when their deliveries of digestive biscuits and knickers from Marks & Spencer didn't come through on time and threatening to write letters to the royal governor.

Mother belonged to all that. Yet she remained apart from it, as well, and not only because she was isolated by her inability to hear. A ferocious otherness possessed her, a sense of mission that surrounded and separated her like an electrical field from the ordinary folk in our community. She wandered into the grocer's and the wool shop like the others, nodded and smiled at her neighbors in church of a Sunday, was as thoroughly English as they.

But theirs was the England of eel pie, while hers was the England of Excalibur.

I turned into a small lane off the Queen's Way, at the far end of the marketplace. It connected the more elegant main street with the wharf side along the curve of the Bay Road. In it, a row of shabby wooden cottages sat close to the stone curb, with bits of overgrown garden behind, crammed with metal bins and broken pots, hurricane shutters askew at the windows. For a block, the world on the cottage side of the street from earth to sky was solid brown and green and gray, like a section of strangely configured jungle, with vines made of clotheslines connecting one tree house to the next.

Across the lane, as if across the border of a tropical Oz, lay the rear grounds of the bay-front hotels, their thick pink- and yellow-painted walls and expanses of stone terrace barely visible through the fiery cumulus of poinciana, bougainvillea, and oleander, the rainbow striations of hibiscus and allamanda, the dark spires of banana and royal palm trees.

Divided by their no-man's-land of pavement, these worlds opposed each other like reality and subconscious. I wondered if Brownlea sat on his landlady's porch in the evening, staring out from the framework of peeling clapboards that would blinker his peripheral vision, and yearn for the color and mysterious privilege of the life on the other side of the street.

He was just turning into the garden of the block's largest and most dilapidated dwelling, walking less fiercely now, with more than the usual slump to his shoulders.

"Mr. Brownlea."

He didn't turn. I jogged a few steps. My clothes were sodden with sweat.

"Mr. Brownlea!"

He stopped then and looked at me without replying, simply waiting for me to catch up.

"You didn't...you never told me whether you thought I'd managed that bit in the last movement all right."

A spark of something—amusement?—flicked across his spectacled gaze and burned out.

"That was a long walk in the sun to ask a question I think you already know the answer to." He raised an eyebrow. "If you walk back now, you'll get sunstroke, judging from the color of your face. You look like a geranium. Come inside and have some water."

I had never been in his rooms, had never desired to see them. The thought of entering them now was still far from enticing, but I nodded and followed him up the creaking stair.

The walls were covered in grimy paper printed with cuckoo clocks, the expanses broken here and there by framed photographs of long-ago people whose images were too dim to make out in the half-light. At the top of the stairs, a short corridor ended in a flimsy wooden door that Brownlea opened, gesturing me inside.

The place was, in most ways, quite what I had expected—a threadbare settee, a narrow bed in an alcove by the window, a small table near a gas ring and kettle, dusty stacks of sheet music—but not entirely. On nearly every surface—every bookshelf, on the windowsill, the chest of drawers, even on top of the tiny refrigerator—were rows of brightly colored toy cars, miniature racing and sports cars.

I picked up a red one and looked at Brownlea.

"Model cars."

"Yes, I was absolutely mad for them as a boy and have collected them ever since. My mother made me take every last one with me when I moved out of her house. Said she couldn't bear to have them underfoot, like a lot of enameled mice. That's a '59 Corvette you've got there."

I spun the little wheels with my finger and replaced the car in its spot.

"I didn't know you liked cars."

Brownlea's glance was dry.

"There are rather a lot of things you don't know about me. You're welcome to look at those, if you like. I'll get us some ice water."

I went round the room examining the flashiest and the most curious of them while Brownlea removed his jacket and filled two glasses from a bottle in the fridge. He handed me one and sat on the single wooden chair near the table.

"One of the things you don't know about me that I'm sure will amuse you is that, when I was growing up, I wanted more than anything to be a race-car driver. I imagined myself going to America and driving the most exotic formula cars and breaking land-speed records and all sorts of rubbish. Of course, I didn't think it was rubbish then. And I still like the cars."

I sat on the arm of the settee. "Why didn't you try?"

He paused for a moment and seemed to decide that I was not being scornful but truly wanted to know. He nodded once or twice.

"I did. For a while. I actually did learn to drive and used

to lurk about a small racecourse not far from where we lived. There were some great chaps there; they all treated me well. They'd even let me get behind the wheel once in a while to drive the cars off the track and into the shed. Very slowly."

He laughed.

"But my mum and dad wanted me to go to university. They never had and I was the great hope of the family, you see"— again that quick and quickly gone spark of humor—"and I couldn't disappoint them. And by the time I went down after all that music study, racing cars seemed a bit outlandish, even to me. But I still enjoy following the sport. Ever been to a race?"

"No."

"No, I guessed not. Have you ever collected anything?" He indicated the cars.

"No. Well…when I was little." For some reason, I didn't want to tell him.

"Well, what was it?"

I struggled with myself. "Bird feathers," I finally blurted. "And American baseball cards. After my…after my mother and I were on our own, she made me throw it all away. She said it was a sin to waste time and money on such nonsense…that if I wanted to collect anything, it should be something useful."

"And do you?"

"Do I what?"

"Collect anything useful?"

I laughed, just for a second. The sound was ugly to me.

"No, I don't collect anything at all now."

"I know you like sports. I've seen you on weekends, before you come in to practice, watching the footballers and cricketers play. But why bird feathers?"

I shrugged and picked up another car. "They were pretty."

Neither of us spoke again for a while. Brownlea slowly finished his water. Bored with the cars, I poked through the books on his shelves. He favored Dickens and detective novels and someone named Wolfe whom I'd never heard of.

I turned to him. Brownlea, not Wolfe.

"Do you think I ought to go?"

He didn't answer immediately. Instead, he reached into his pocket for his handkerchief, took off his glasses and slowly polished them. His face looked surprised and blank without them, as if he were a rabbit down whose burrow someone had suddenly shone a light. He sighed as he put them back on.

"I would like to ask you a question," he said.

I nodded.

"Very well, then: Before you heard this idea of sending you to Chicago, what had you planned for yourself?"

"You mean, for my life?"

"Yes."

"I really hadn't thought much about it."

Brownlea waited.

"Well, what I mean is, I've thought about a career in music, of course. A real career. But not so much how to go about it, actually. I suppose I thought I'd return to England for university and start getting engagements at the Albert Hall straight away."

"So you saw yourself staying here for another three or four years?"

"Yes, I guess."

"Studying with me?"

The words startled me. I didn't know how to reply—my impulse to say "of course" was shamed by my acute awareness that he knew how little I now respected his ability.

"Well, who else?" I finally answered.

"Aha. Who else, indeed?"

He stood up and gathered the empty glasses, placing them in the tiny sink beside the refrigerator.

"Did you want more water?"

"No, thanks."

"Right. Well, that's the real crux, isn't it? The fact is, if you stay here to finish school, you'll have to keep on studying with me because there's no one any better in the islands. And I'm not saying that I have nothing more to offer you—though I suspect our opinions differ on that—but my immodesty is not so great that I believe I am the best teacher you could have. I'm not. And your gift is so remarkable that it deserves the very best teacher you can find.

"So. You must think about whether staying here is so important to you that you are willing to waste four years in which you could be making brilliant progress with another instructor."

He picked up his jacket.

"But…"

"But what?" Brownlea continued inserting his arms into his jacket sleeves.

"But *Chicago*…it's… I know nothing about it or about this Hellman fellow. It's so far, and what about my…my family?"

"Your family"—Brownlea put just the most microscopic emphasis on the word—"can best advise you about that."

He opened the door. "The sun's started down and you look a good bit less inflamed than you did. Think you can make it home all right?"

I nodded.

"Good. I'm off to have my tea, then. Mr. Dampson gets fretful if I delay his plate of stew too long."

We creaked down the stairs and stepped from the house into the long shadows of the royal palms. Brownlea paused before leaving me for Tantie Rhetta's, squinting at me through the orange and pink light of a sunset so vivid, it gave everything, including him, an atomic glow. He shielded his eyes.

"I know this won't be an easy decision for you. There's a lot to consider, for and against. But if it all seems too confusing, just think about this: You don't want to grow up to be me, now, do you?"

He smiled at me with a faint, sweet malice and walked away. I made my way home under a sky indistinguishable from the indifferent blue sea.

II

Only one light was on in the house when I arrived home, although it was by then fully dark outside. It was the light over the piano.

At first, I thought Mother wasn't there and I was briefly confounded, trying to imagine where she could be—she who no longer went anywhere in the evening except to the monthly church supper. And it wasn't church-supper week. But then I saw her rise from her chair on the night-filled screened porch and place her Bible, which she could not have been reading, on the table next to her.

I waited, hoping she would speak. She didn't. She stayed in the shadows, looking down at the book.

"Mother."

Nothing. I didn't believe she couldn't hear me.

"Mother!"

She turned around briskly then and entered the living room. "You don't have to shout," she said. "Where have you been?"

"I went for a walk."

The tortures of Hades could not have wrung from me that I had sought Brownlea's advice.

"Well, it's long past teatime. I'll fix something to eat. Cold beef all right?"

"I'm not hungry, Mother. I want—"

"You may not think you are now, but if you go to bed without a bite, you won't sleep well. Now, what would you like? There are sardines and some—"

"Mother, I don't want food! I want to talk to you!"

She stopped as if I had switched her off, gazing away from me at some distant point in the dim room, gathering herself. After a moment, she turned her head a little toward me and said quite calmly, "Then we had best sit down."

Neither of us took the chair that had been my father's.

I turned on another lamp and sat next to it at one end of the sofa. She did not choose to sit next to me, perching instead on the piano bench. The light behind her made it hard to see her face.

She waited. She was not going to help me start.

"Mother, why?" My voice cracked, angering me. I spoke more loudly. "Why?"

"Do you mean, why am I sending you to Chicago? I should think it would be obvious—you'll need a teacher of the first rank if you're to have a career."

"But you've never asked me if I wanted a career. And why Chicago? Why not New York or London? Why should I study with this Hellman geezer? Who is he, anyway?"

"No slang, please. And I'll thank you not to inundate me with questions."

Her mouth tightened and she folded her arms over her prim blue-cotton blouse. She shook her head as if a gnat were besieging her.

"My dear," she said tentatively, trying out a foreign expression, "Gunter Hellman was at university with your father and, unlike him, went on to a distinguished international career. He plays with all the major European and American orchestras and is on the Chicago Conservatory faculty. The fact that you have not heard of him signifies only that you are fourteen, not that he is inconsequential."

"But—"

"I beg your pardon. I was about to say that I had written to him two years ago to ask if he would take you as a pupil, and he said that when you were old enough to go to an American high school and if you were truly devoted to piano, then he would.

"I have prayed every night for the last year, hoping that God would grant you the passion and ambition to match your talent, so that you would not let it go to waste. It is a sin to waste great talent or to thwart it in any way. A sin."

She wasn't looking at me.

Her fingers gripped the edge of the bench, turning her knuckles livid and making the pale blue veins strain against the skin of her hands.

"Gunter last wrote me a month ago to say that, if I thought the time was right, you could come to him this summer. After I heard you play today, I knew you must go."

"But why didn't you tell me? You never tell me anything! Why does everything have to be a secret?"

"You are told as much as you need to know. I can't have you distracted from your music by details and half-formed plans that do not require your worry."

"There's nothing half-formed about this! You've been plotting the whole thing since I was twelve, you just said so! Why won't you let me decide what my own future will be?"

Mother looked straight at me. Her eyes were as hard as jet beads.

"Your future is entirely up to you. I can't earn your success for you or prevent your ruin. You must decide which it is to be."

She stood, as if ready to quit the house and me with it, to stride off with her sword and take up the cause of some worthier supplicant. I was angry and strangely terrified that she would leave altogether, who had never really come close. I held out my hand to stop her. She didn't take it—she hadn't taken my hand in years.

"But why aren't you coming, too?" I said, suddenly pleading. "Why do I have to go by myself?"

She looked away. Was she crying? I had never seen her cry.

She turned back to me, dry-eyed. "You will learn faster on your own," she said quietly.

"What? About playing?"

"About everything."

She coughed and stood up, pushing the piano bench in and turning off the lamp.

"You'll be able to come home for the Christmas holidays," she continued, already halfway to the door of her own room. "If you wish."

She called goodnight without looking back.

I sat for a while, gazing around the room where I suddenly did not belong. I was to go; I was already gone. The knowledge of my impermanence had, in an hour, made me a ghost in my own home. Another member of the family who would leave nothing behind but his habitual imprint on a cushion.

Oddly enough, I now wanted my tea. I went to the kitchen, unearthed some bread and cheese, and finished them off, along with the rest of the lemonade. A kind of excitement was growing in me, conjoined to the lump of dread. I was going to study with the best, *be* the best. Everybody would know my name. I would never again be locked away alone in silence. I would be surrounded by cheering audiences, blazingly visible in stage light far friendlier than the sun. I would succeed.

I rinsed my glass and knife, switched off the lamp in the living room, and brushed my teeth. The dark of my room seemed to drown all my hope. I lay in bed and listened to the waves in the cove, breaking against the beach.

Three months later, Mother and Brownlea and I took the boat to the main island. I was bringing very little, really, although the longer I carried it, the more burdensome it seemed. My few clothes and sundries went in the larger bag; the other held a few magazines—mostly to amuse me on the long plane trip—and my piles of sheet music, including the arias that had belonged to my father. Brownlea had brought them to me one day when Mother was out. Had simply tapped on the screened door, stepped in as far as the end table, and plopped them down.

"Thought you might want these," he'd said. Sort of waved his hand and went out again. I didn't even have a chance to offer him a glass of water. I would have.

He also said next to nothing on the way to the airport, just helped my mother on and off the boat and in and out of the taxi we took from the wharf to the airfield. Mother was—no surprise—not highly communicative, either, merely fussing about whether I'd got my money and passport and visa safely hidden away and if I remembered that Gunter ("Mr. Hellman, unless he invites you to call him otherwise") would meet me at baggage claim in the O'Hare Airport.

I was the tiniest bit uneasy about the flights. I had never in my conscious memory been on a plane and, above that, I had never clapped eyes on Gunter before. ("He used to be rather stocky, with thick brown hair. Of course, that was fifteen years ago.") And when you came right to it, I was leaving everything I knew for a strange country and a strange school, to be kept and taught by strangers until I was of age.

I got a bit snappish with Mother after she asked me for the third time to check for my plane ticket; Brownlea silently handed me a pack of chewing gum, cadging a stick for himself and popping it into his mouth.

I was to fly on one of the island puddle-jumpers to Miami and then get on a proper jet to Chicago. Mother spent a good deal of time catechizing some hapless airline official at the gate about what the company was doing to alert all of Florida that I was inbound and would require assistance in getting my bags, getting through customs and making my connecting flight.

"He's only fourteen," she announced at least five times in her most penetrating tones.

I tried to ignore everyone in the tiny terminal and stared out the window at a propeller plane taking off into the ocean wind. It dipped and rolled as it rose. I thought it would surely flop over like a kite and impale itself on a palm tree before it eventually buzzed out of sight. I felt queasy and resorted to chewing some of Brownlea's gum. I was surprised to find it was cinnamon. I actually liked cinnamon.

When it was time to board, Brownlea shook my hand and wished me luck. I don't think I said more than thanks in return—I mostly remember the queer look he gave me, half wistful and half relieved, the kind of look you'd give to a good old friend who was finally going home after slightly too long a stay.

I didn't try to hug Mother. She hesitated a moment, then

briefly kissed my cheek, saying, "Call me when you arrive at Gunter's." Then she stepped back from the doorway and watched me pick up my bags. She looked as tautly resolute as ever in her plain navy-blue dress and brimmed hat, like a sentry at the border of the no-man's-land that lay between us. But I thought I sensed, as I walked across the tarmac under the fiercely shining eye of God, that grief had blurred the edges of her small form like a watercolor, as if the tears she refused to let fall had seeped into the very air.

III

Gunter Hellman was a short, square, balding elf as wreathed in smiles as a German Santa Claus. He had a tonsure of thick brown-gray hair and a smooth-shaven face tanned nut-brown from, as I discovered, a serious softball habit. Despite his round, dense middle, he had powerful shoulders and unusually large hands for a man his height and could hit and field almost as well as he could play piano.

That took me a while to figure out, of course, because I didn't know beans—Gunter's favorite expression—about softball until I had lived in his house for some time. Likewise for his position within the piano-playing world. His skill as a pianist, though—that I recognized within minutes of taking up residence in the third-floor room of his Winnetka house—a teen suite, they called it—that had, until two years before, been occupied by his youngest son, now off at college.

Gunter—he insisted I call him Gunter—had dropped my bags in the middle of the attic floor, heartily clapped me on the shoulder and said, "Closet's there, bathroom's there. When you've taken a few minutes to settle in, come downstairs."

I hardly gave myself a moment to look round—paneled walls under a high, steep roof, two dormer windows, bed, desk, a small but recently installed tile bathroom—and wash my face and hands before quietly descending and peering into rooms, unsure where I should go. I found Gunter in the kitchen— Gunter was nearly always in the kitchen when he wasn't practicing, as it turned out—with his wife, Debbie, an even smaller, equally smiley person who had welcomed me into her home only a quarter of an hour earlier.

"Oh, honey, it'll be so nice to have a boy in the house again," she had said, embracing me with a warmth I found startling, but quite liked.

Now she urged on me an amazing array of snack foods—
chocolate biscuits, crisps of some sort shaped like dunce caps or
maybe trumpets, cheese puffs, nuts, little iced cakes with cream
in the middle. My mother never bought party food—her idea
of a snack just for us was tinned fruit or the leftover potatoes
from dinner. Also, I had been allowed fizzy drinks only on rare
outings and here the Hellmans must have had eight different
kinds in their pantry ("What would you like, honey?"). I chose
one that Gunter said was orange flavored and was allowed to
drink the whole thing before he beckoned me into another
room.

It was their living room, or at least a room for people whose
living was music. I saw two pianos—one a baby grand, the
other some sort of antique pianoforte, I guessed—three or four
guitars, a string bass, a cello, a mandolin-looking thing, several
violins in a rack on the wall, and a drum kit. The drum kit and
guitars belonged to their sons, and so did the mandolin-like
instrument, which was actually a lute, something the oldest boy,
Steve, had taken up during a folk-music phase.

"They've been in and out of bands since they were old
enough to care about impressing girls," Gunter said.

All the other stringed instruments were Debbie's. She was
primarily a violinist who played with a respected quartet, but
also taught viola, bass, and cello. I couldn't imagine how such a
tiny woman managed a bass.

Gunter sat down at the piano and played a few modernistic-
sounding phrases that I didn't recognize. On the keyboard, his
thick, utilitarian fingers suddenly had grace and intelligence.

"Come, let us hear you," he said, rising abruptly.

He sat in a soft chair while I adjusted the bench and gingerly
explored the keys. I didn't know what I should play; I wasn't
in the mood for the Beethoven, but everything else seemed
frivolous or stuffy. Finally, I decided to risk a bit of Chopin I'd
been working on for a few weeks. It was a little on the sappy
side for my tastes, but it demanded solid technique. Brownlea
had seemed happy with my results.

Gunter let me play it without interruption. When the silence continued after I had finished, I turned around to look at him. He had his fingers laced together with the tips of his forefingers pressed against his lips.

He raised an eyebrow at me and smiled, but his eyes stayed thoughtful behind his round glasses.

"You are a pianist, young man," he said slowly. "Do you wish to be a great pianist?"

I was taken aback. Wasn't that why he had invited me to America?

"Yes, I think…I mean, yes."

He sighed almost imperceptibly and paused. "Do you remember much about your father?" he asked gently.

I liked Gunter already, but I didn't want to talk about that. I shook my head without speaking.

"Your father had a way of leaning over the keys and tilting his head a little—so—when he played *pianissimo*, as if he were listening to something far away," he said. "You do the same thing."

He practically jumped to his feet. I would never entirely get used to seeing such a solid oak cabinet of a man move with so much energy.

"You are tired, you have come a long way. We will have a good dinner now and chat about things you like and go to bed early, and tomorrow, if it doesn't rain, we'll go for a drive in the convertible and show you *everything*."

Before I went to my room for the night, I called Mother. She generally avoided talking on the telephone but, in one of her rare concessions to her ailing ears, she had had an amplifier installed on the receiver a couple of years before and could probably understand anything said over the phone better than she could the discourse of someone in the same room with her.

She asked if I had met with any difficulties on the trip and I told her no, although I had, in fact, gotten turned around in the Miami airport and nearly missed my connecting flight.

Then she asked to be remembered to Gunter and his wife and reminded me to write her every week.

I could imagine her standing just outside the open kitchen door with the light over the sink spilling its greenish fluorescence onto the polished wood floor near the phone table and giving an eerie glow to half her face.

It would be so silent for her once I hung up.

Mother, do you miss me?

Do you, Mother?

You never told me I play like my father.

Did you think I didn't need to hear, either?

I wished her good night and climbed up to my attic. It took me only a few minutes to put my belongings away; soon, I undressed and lay on the bed in the dark, listening to the alien sounds of children still running about and shouting in the long northern twilight and of cars passing by. The air that drifted through the screened windows smelled sweet, from what I didn't know, but it was surprisingly cool and I pulled the sheet up and then the blanket. From downstairs, I felt more than heard the rumble of Gunter's voice, listened to the rush of water in the pipes and Debbie's quick footsteps, the quiet opening and shutting of doors.

The random notes and rhythms of sound moved through me as if I still weren't there, who had never been there before. There seemed nothing left of me but an echo floating through the close rooms of a nearly empty house on an island two thousand miles away.

IV

I made a friend the first day of school and that seemed to be my quota for the whole year.

Gunter and Debbie had spent a month showing me Chicago and getting me signed up properly at school, with many anxious calls from my inexorable mother, who insisted to Gunter that I not be enrolled in any injurious sports classes and that I instead be given a special tutorial three times a week in theory and composition. Gunter soothed her patiently on every occasion, reassuring her that my after-school studies at the conservatory would naturally include both theory and composition and that he would speak to the high-school administrators about excusing me from football and wrestling, at least. He didn't mention that he had begun teaching me softball and that I continued to practice with his team twice a week until the weather got too miserable. I wasn't much good at it, although I ended up being able to pitch fairly well and was allowed to by the physical education teacher during classes in the spring.

That was, I believe, the only time I was made to feel rather like one of the boys, one of America's hearty, hulking, school-ruling jocks, in my entire four years there. I got on better with Gunter's teammates, who were all musicians of various ages and not in it to prove the superior quality of their testosterone so much as to just get out of the dark concert hall once in a while.

Still, it was a ball game and not music, that won me my single friend. Debbie had dropped me at school the first morning; I was already pretty familiar with the place from our summer explorations and paper-signings, so I knew where I was to go and I managed well enough, although I had never seen so many teenagers together in one place before and couldn't imagine how I was to tell them apart. They all seemed to fall into one of two categories: short-haired or long-haired. As virtually all of them wore jeans or corduroys, they at first had no more individual distinction for me than would the members of a particularly large herd of antelope.

Several of the ones in my morning classes expressed some interest in my accent and origins. Of those, I was at least able to distinguish (I thought) between males and females, but their faces—which inevitably featured hair parted in the middle (usually girls) or nascent mustaches (usually boys) and dental appliances—simply ran together into a composite portrait of pasty youth.

When lunchtime came, I had no one to talk to while I ate, so I finished quickly and went outside. Some boys were running wind sprints and making practice passes with a football on the field across from the cafeteria. I walked over to the fence, trying to look nonchalant and feeling as if every single being on the campus were sniggering at me. I stuck my hands in my pockets and stared at the gym class's ragged and fumbling maneuvers. Another boy was leaning on the fence a few feet away, arms folded across the top bar with his chin resting on them. One sneakered toe thumped the ground behind him, rhythmically pulverizing a patch of clover. Just another nondescript, blue-jeaned body topped by another mass-produced shaggy head.

He caught me examining him and grinned.

"Suck, don't they?" he said.

"Rather."

"Rather? I don't think there's any doubt about it. Look at that!"

He doubled up laughing as one of the footballers got his feet tangled, clawed frantically at the air, and fell over. It *was* pretty funny.

"Do you play?" I asked him.

"Me? Hell, no!" He grinned again. "I got a full-time job here just making fun of the idiots who do. Besides, I prefer to get my concussions from really loud music. You like AOR?"

"Um, is that a band?"

"No, man. AOR—album-oriented rock. It's what some

radio stations play—not just the hit singles, but other cuts off rock albums and sometimes the *whole* album. Like WQME?"

I suppose I looked as vacant as the vicarage on Saturday night. He cocked his head.

"Would you be new here? Like, new to the USA?"

"Yes."

"Cool. Where you from, England? You sound English."

"My family's English. I mean, yes, I am, but I didn't come here from England, we live in the Caribbean. We…I've lived there since I was four."

"The Caribbean? Cool! Like, you're from Jamaica or something?"

"No, not—"

"But an island, right? Palm trees, blue ocean, naked babes?"

"Well, you're two-thirds right. I think we had laws against naked babes."

"Bummer. But even two out of three sounds damn good when you've lived on Lake Michigan all your life. Been through a winter here yet?"

"No. I hear I'm in for a load of fun."

"Well, you might like it, actually, since it'll be, shall we say, very different from what you're used to. But you better get some serious cold-weather clothes. Like three or four walrus hides and a team of huskies to throw on your bed at night."

He laughed again and pressed his foot against the fence in front of him to tie his shoe. I studied him hard as he leaned over his knee, hoping I'd be able to remember which one he was if I saw him again. He had straight mousy-brown hair that fell to his jaw line on the sides and lengthened below the neck of his Jethro Tull T-shirt in back. Pale skin, brown eyes with a sort of inquiring look about them, a bit of a turned-up nose, small mouth that had shown nice, even white teeth when he smiled. Odd—the nails of his right hand were rather long, while those on the left were short.

That was all I had time to notice before he stood up straight, pulled a pocket watch out of his jeans, and opened it.

"Uh-oh. Got five minutes to get to biology." He picked up some books that had been lying in the grass. "Oh, I'm forgetting my etiquette."

He stuck out his hand. "Name's Rob. Welcome to beautiful Winnetka High. And you are...?"

I introduced myself as we started walking and told him that I was boarding with my piano teacher.

"Wow. That must be great. I mean..." He gave me a careful glance. "I'm sure you must miss your folks and all but, man, I sure wish my parents would let me board with a guitar teacher. 'Specially if I could find one in San Francisco or New York or London. Or even Indianapolis." He grinned.

"Don't you care for Chicago?"

"Well, sure, it's a great place. But it's my home, you know? I already know what's here."

"So, are you a freshman?"

"Yeah. You?"

"Yes."

"What do you have next?"

"Um..." I checked the paper in my pocket. "Right. European history. Do you play guitar?"

"Yep. Been officially taking for two years, although I've been messing around with guitars for a lot longer than that. My brother plays, too. He's a junior here."

"Classical?"

"Not much. I play a little Spanish stuff sometimes, but mostly blues, R & B. Uh, rhythm and blues, that means. Ever heard of Jimmy Page?"

"No."

"No kidding. And he's English, too. Shoot, maybe I should lend you a Led Zeppelin record sometime—that's his band. Who knows, you might like it. Well, I gotta get upstairs fast—my brother says Mr. Ahrens makes you wear this stupid cardboard clock around your neck if you're late. See ya."

"See you."

As it happened, Rob and I found we had the last period

together, geometry. We were both rather terrible at it but managed to eke out Bs with emergency help from Debbie, who had real mathematical talent and seemed to remember everything she'd ever been taught about cones and congruent angles.

I had no time after school, of course, but Rob and I occasionally got together on Saturdays at the Hellmans' or at his house, and tried to educate each other about our favorite kinds of music. Rob played guitar quite well already and could imitate Page and some others he liked with pretty impressive accuracy. I'd lie on the bed in his room in his peculiar-looking, one-story house—like a stucco and glass-block flying saucer among the Winnetka colonials—flipping through his museum-quality collection of comic books while he put *Led Zeppelin III*, or *Thick As a Brick*, or *Tales from Topographic Oceans* on his stereo and played along on his red electric guitar that he cranked up to full volume and then slowly turned down to whatever level made his mother stop shouting at him.

At Gunter's, I'd play on the piano for Rob whatever I was currently working on and play records, too—Beethoven and Mozart, of course, but also Liszt and Chopin and Ravel and Bartok, things I was only just getting to know myself and wanted to toss at him, to see what he thought. He liked quite a lot of it, I think, especially the Liszt. He said Liszt was like a nineteenth-century piano version of Hendrix.

Gunter and Debbie even invited Rob to mess around with the guitars and drums their sons had left at home, and would come listen for a few minutes when Rob or I would play something.

One day, when they had gone to the store and left us alone in the house for an hour, on impulse I pulled out one of my father's songs and sang it for Rob, accompanying myself on the piano. I found I was nervous; I had never sung for anyone before. I had only gotten the idea because Rob knew nothing about my father or opera. I could sing some for him, I thought, without it meaning anything.

Mother appeared as soon as I struck the keys, hovering

somewhere behind me—a small specter of disapproval—but I defied her and poured out "The Flower Song" with as much expression as I could invent. My voice didn't even crack, although it wasn't altogether steady, either.

"Hey, pretty good," Rob said when I'd finished, appraising me with obvious surprise. "How long you been singing?"

"Actually, I don't sing at all, officially. Just a little practice on my own once in a while."

"Well, not like I know diddly about opera or anything, but that sounded okay. Maybe you oughta join the school chorus."

I made a face. Rob cracked up.

"They're not all *total* dorks, you know. In fact, two of the, shall we say, hotter girls I knew in junior high are singing in it this year. I'd join for that alone if I could carry a tune from one tonsil to another. Mom always says my singing in the shower would make a rubber ducky cry."

I closed the music. "No, I don't think so. I'm supposed to be betrothed to my piano."

"It's just another form of music. What could it hurt?"

I didn't know what to say, so I didn't answer.

After Rob went home, I practiced for hours.

Gunter came to the living-room door once or twice, but he didn't come in and didn't speak until it was time for dinner.

"Come on, now. We will have to put your hands in slings if you play any longer and then how will you scratch your nose? Come eat."

Debbie had made barbecued chicken, which had become one of my favorite foods, but I didn't seem to want much. I saw them look at each other.

"Honey," Debbie said to me, "is something bothering you?"

"No. Thanks. I expect I'm tired."

"Well, I'm not surprised, after all that practice. I just hope you're not coming down with something."

"I'm perfectly fine. Thanks."

My tone was sharper than I'd intended, but I didn't care. Bitter anger had suddenly enveloped my brain and heart and gut in blackness, as if they'd been dropped into a coffin. Nobody understood. Nobody could. Here was a woman with two healthy ears and more real concern in her eyes than a dozen of my mother and I couldn't tell her anything. What was there to say? For most of my life, the piano had been my medium, like an interpreter assigned to a foreign visitor. It was my voice. Who knew I had any other? There had never been anyone to listen when I wanted them.

I opened my mouth and shut it again, then stood up. I forced myself to say, "I have homework to do," and fled to the attic.

V

The conservatory wasn't much to look at. It consisted of a tall, narrow stone building full of dingy class- and practice-rooms; a small recital hall on the first floor and a bigger one in the basement; and a sort of common room that looked through large windows out the back, where a few trees and shrubs had been planted in a tiny courtyard walled in on the other three sides by other tall stone buildings. The courtyard could be quite pleasant in the summertime—they set a table or two under the trees and on sunny days, it offered something like a peaceful respite from the high tension thrumming through the school itself. In the winter, it was just bleak, like the rest of Chicago, a view of dirty ice and bare branches from an eating room littered with crumbs and wrappers courtesy of the cheap snacks in the machines.

But there was always something worth hearing.

Bits of other people's wretched practice sessions, which were excruciating, but fun, especially when accompanied by staccato bursts of swear words. Brief, sharp rows concluded by slamming doors and running feet. Occasionally, singing or playing so beautiful that it made me ache.

After school, Debbie would drop me at the El station and I'd take it down to the south end of the Loop and then jog three blocks to be on time for Gunter at 3:45. He had one of the best rooms in the building, on the third floor, with a view of South Michigan. He was even allowed to have his own coffeemaker, although I generally preferred to get a soda out of the machine downstairs or a cocoa when it was horridly cold out, which was often.

Sometimes, one of his other students was still there when I arrived, and I would have to stand about in the hall enduring the sound of whoever it was laboring through whatever measures were giving trouble. Not that most of Gunter's pupils weren't pretty good—they had to be, or he wouldn't have accepted them in the first place. But many of them still stumbled over the stupidest, easiest pieces. It would have been a laugh if it hadn't been so irritating.

I always got things quickly, even Gunter said so. I wouldn't allow myself to show up for my lesson without being able to play perfectly whatever I was to have worked on. Of course, living in Gunter's house meant I could consult him while I was practicing after dinner, but I didn't often. I didn't need to, frankly, and besides, I had my own ideas about interpreting the music. All I needed Gunter for, really, were matters of physical technique, fingering and attack and so on.

I did learn a good deal more from him than that. He was a marvelous teacher. But a lot of it I could have learned on my own in time. Gunter just helped speed things up a bit.

A great man, really. He had his own quirks as a pianist, as I soon realized—never could produce a truly perfect glissando and always stood on *ritards* so long I thought my teeth would decay during the wait—but he had a glorious dynamic range that reflected his tremendous feeling for the music. From the first, I felt we had that in common. The passion, you know.

He would work with me for an hour at the keyboard and then send me along to Mr. Dixon for a half-hour of theory. Dixon didn't let me start composition right away—insisted that I be more familiar with all the "tools," as he called them, before I dared actually to create anything with them. Pompous sort. In any event, it was all right with me—I had no particular wish to invent music, just to perform it.

When I had served my time with Dixon, I was grandly dis-missed, feeling as diminished as one of his pet seventh chords, and went to meet Gunter in the lobby for the ride back up the North Shore. It was my favorite part of the day. We usually didn't talk much—Gunter had to concentrate on his driving, with all the rush-hour traffic, which left me free to stare out the window as we went up Lake Shore Drive, gazing at the water, sometimes blue in early fall, later frozen solid in strange white ripples and slabs, most often gray under a gray sky. Once it began getting dark by 4:30, there was little to see but the lights in the wall of skyscrapers that lined the drive and the inky nothing of invisible lake that bordered its eastern edge.

At home, the nighttime had always turned the ocean surrounding our island into a vast void in which we seemed marooned. But beyond the blackness of this lake, as Gunter and I drove, I could sense the world.

I didn't think much about it, though. There was too much to absorb in the course of what passed for a normal day. I became accustomed to the routine of the house, of course, to Gunter and Debbie, their schedules and moods. Even school, where I felt vaguely uneasy or worse all of the time, became a habitual nuisance, like a low-grade headache that you cease to notice until you have an idle moment. And I had few enough of those—after school, practice and homework, what few minutes were left to me before bed I usually gave over to working on my weekly letter home, including adding up what money I'd spent on necessaries and accounting for it to Mother. Unsurprisingly, she demanded accurate sums and I got into the habit of saving receipts and grudging extra pennies. Mother sent $50 a month for such expenses as she thought I deserved—new socks or a shirt, a ticket to something, sweets.

She was paying Gunter for my board and lessons, naturally, though what that amounted to was something she was no like-lier to tell me than she was to divulge, say, the circumstances of my conception. Neither of which I desired to hear. I'd decided the day I stepped into Gunter's house that I was glad she had sent me and the only further piece of information I wanted from her was that I could stay on. There was some cold gratifi-cation in making that clear to her—I wrote and phoned only as often as she expected me to and had gone so far as to ask the Hellmans if I could spend Christmas with them before Gunter mentioned that Mother had already purchased my ticket home for the holiday.

Another secret. It was rather like being a character in Dickens, finding out the pieces of my own life only when I pried or surprised them from the conspirators around me.

Gunter didn't willingly withhold things from me, nor did Debbie, and their discomfort was evident when either felt obliged to impart some fact that Mother had obviously insisted they conceal. But their complicity, forced or no, sent me into a rage that I didn't always labor to hide from them. It was unfair to them and I knew it and would remember to save a scrap of my wrath for the twice-monthly call to my Miss Havisham, alone in her house with what I hoped were thick cobwebs of regret.

She registered no dismay when I told her that I would rather have stayed in Chicago than make the long trip home, merely noted that I had better get used to international travel if I were going to perform with orchestras around the world.

I said, at least then I'd be heading somewhere I wanted to go.

She didn't reply and I waited for a long minute, wanting viciously to hear her sigh or sob or hang up—wanting any kind of feeling response, anything, and fearing it while I hoped.

I couldn't outlast her, finally giving in and asking if she had heard what I said.

"No, you must learn to speak more distinctly on the telephone. Simon will meet you at the airport on the eighteenth. Give my regards to Gunter."

She rang off. I walked upstairs to the attic and threw myself down on the bed.

The shadowy room slowly grew darker. I heard Debbie call me for dinner, but I couldn't seem to answer or move. She called again a few minutes later and almost immediately after, I heard Gunter's reverberant steps coming up the staircase like crescendo-ing tympani. I didn't respond when he knocked and said my name before gently opening the door a crack.

"Are you all right?"

"Yes."

"Dinner is ready—will you come?"

"I guess not. Thanks."

My face was to the opposite wall, but I felt him standing there looking at me before pushing the door all the way open and coming to the side of the bed.

"My boy, I think you are not ill. Did your call home upset you?"

Part of me wanted to tell him, wanted to tell him everything, how shut out Mother had always made me feel, how managed, how all the warmth in us both had seemed to die when my father did. I wanted to say my father's name to Gunter. His name, that Mother never uttered. But I knew I would not and tears spilled out of my eyes and ran across the bridge of my nose and down into my ear and I knew I wouldn't reach for a tissue, either.

Gunter pulled my desk chair close to the bed and sat down with his hand on my shoulder.

"My boy," he said and that's all he spoke for several minutes. I lay there with his hand warming my back, for once not intent on flinging myself away from everyone and everything, but suddenly willing just to lie there in silence and let my fury relax into weariness.

He spoke again. "When your father and I were at university together, we had a kind of game we played. We were the best of friends, but neither of us was much at talking about things that disturbed us or moved us, the deeper things. You know, I could go on all night about a great pint of beer or some instructor who had annoyed me, but I never could bring myself to talk about anything like love. Or fear. Or hurt. Your father was the same. So we got in the habit of playing music when we had something on our minds, some piece that spoke for us what we did not want to say.

"We had rented a piano together for our rooms, an old upright. It wasn't good enough for serious practice, for that we went to the studios at the music school. But when we were at home, we could work out new pieces or just mess around, you know? And when I was angry or sad, I would play, oh, Shostakovich or a *lied*, whatever suited my mood. And your father would try to guess the piece and why I chose it.

"Sometimes, we would wind up laughing—I would crunch the keys and he would say, 'Oh, Bruckner—well, your shoes must hurt and you want to throw them in the river.' Or he would bang through some hair-raising Liszt and I would say, 'Massive indigestion. Too many sausage rolls at dinner.'

"But I remember one time in our last year, I had proposed to Debbie and she had said no—did you know she turned me down twice before she finally said yes? Didn't want to marry a man who was planning to go back to Germany, so I decided to move to America instead—and I was crushed into little fragments inside, like a bag of potato chips that someone had dropped a big rock on. It was all I could do just to walk home and fall into a chair. That's where I was when your father came home from class, just sitting and staring at the floor. And he saw immediately that something was very wrong, but he didn't speak. He just sat down at the piano and played the march-to-the-gallows section from *Symphonie fantastique*. But he was not mocking me—even in my coma of distress, I could hear the sympathy, the kindly humor, in his playing. I finally was able to look up at him and he was smiling sadly at me. He said, 'Come on, then. Let's have it.'

"So I got up and played the *Das gras ist verdorret* measures from Brahms, from the second movement of his *German Requiem*, because it was the most brokenhearted piece I knew and because that's what I thought my life would be, that my future without Debbie was like brown, withered grass. I played the whole thing and when I was done, I looked up and your father had tears in his eyes. But he jumped up and grabbed my jacket and threw it at me and said, 'You'll win her yet. Let's go get drunk.'"

Gunter rumbled out his rich, dark chuckle. "I thought he was a mind reader."

He patted me again. "I am not a mind reader, but I can listen and I will answer questions as best I can."

He stopped again. The room was nearly dark; a thin strip of light from the doorway formed a silvery bar down the wall near my head. The arch of my shoulder made a strange, humpy shadow at the bottom of it and the raised pattern of the bedspread rasped against my fingertips, irritating them. The only times I could remember being in bed at twilight were when I was ill, and I felt ill now, disoriented, with the lamplight seeping into the room from downstairs making the gloom even darker and the sounds from the kitchen seem remote and alien. The whole room felt surreal, as if I had a fever.

I couldn't find the energy to speak or turn over, though I heard Gunter getting to his feet.

"Why don't you sleep for a while?" he said softly. "We will keep your dinner warm for you."

He stepped to the door.

"Gunter."

I hadn't meant to speak and the name came out in a sudden croak.

"Gunter, I think…I think my mother did not love my father. I think she doesn't love me, either."

I still faced the wall. I couldn't bear to turn round. Tears were sliding down into my ear and hair again and I tried desperately to keep them out of my voice.

"She's never treated me like anything but a…a project. She never cares what I think or feel about anything, just yanks me about like a pony that has to be put through its paces. My playing is the only thing that matters to her, not…me. I don't want to go back there. I want to stay with you and Debbie."

I covered my face with my hands to stop my words. I sounded like a pathetic sniveler to myself, a hopeless, whinging infant betraying its own weakness by bleating for attention. I could feel Gunter despising me like everyone else, despising me and my awful family and our failure to be anything resembling normal. I knew he'd want me to leave.

Gunter sat down on the bed next to me and gently pulled at my elbow.

"Look at me."

I shook my head without turning.

"I must insist," he said. "It's important for you to see me when I say what I have to say."

I didn't want to. I never wanted to look at anyone ever again, but the firmness of his tone forced me to try to recapture some dignity and I half sat up, wiping my face with my sleeve and turning toward him, although I couldn't bring myself to look in his eyes.

"I know that your mother's ways have hurt you. You don't understand them and she has not explained herself to you. But"—and Gunter gently pushed my shoulders back until my gaze met his—"I also know that your mother loves you very deeply. I see you don't believe me, but after you have thought on this, maybe after you are grown, you may come to agree with me. You are young and have not yet recognized that, even though she seems cold and unbending, your mother is a sensitive woman, a woman who has been damaged and frightened by life. Your father's death, her own deafness, things maybe that even I do not know. She has changed much since I first met her and I do not pretend to know her well anymore. But I know this, she married for love and she wanted you and she sent you here to us because she believed it would be good for you and I don't mean just musically. I know it was painful for her to send you.

"Debbie and I love you like another son, but you must go home to her. There is much that only she can tell you. You must begin finding out."

He patted my cheek and left the room.

I sat on the edge of the mattress with the streak of light striping my rumpled shirt and bitterness stabbed through me as if the light were a blade.

Mother could keep her secrets, keep them until she went from her silent life to her silent grave. What difference did it make if I knew them or not? The effect would still be the same. I could be in her house or on another continent—she would always keep me one thin white arm's length away from her.

I was not going to beg her or anyone else for love, ever. I would keep my own secrets and need no one.

I stood abruptly and grabbed my jacket from the hook. If I was going to have to leave anyway, it might as well be now. I opened the dresser and took out the envelope of money I kept under the pile of handkerchiefs I never used. There was almost seventy dollars in it—Debbie and Gunter bought me so many incidentals that I had had little enough occasion to spend my allowance. I zipped it into my coat pocket and opened the window.

Gunter had told me that his boys used to try to sneak out by climbing down the tree outside when they thought their parents were asleep, to lark around the neighborhood in the summer. They never got far, apparently—Gunter said Debbie was always waiting for them at the base of the tree before they got low enough to jump—but it was nearly winter now, the other windows were closed and they wouldn't be likely to think of me as a tree climber. In fact, I had never climbed one, but I hardly cared. I would do it somehow.

I unlatched the screen and carefully tugged it free of the window frame, nearly falling over the chair Gunter had moved near the bed as I backed up to pull the screen inside. I had to move the bedside table, too, for fear of knocking into the lamp as I put my leg over the sill. I hadn't been able to force the sash up very far and had to bend nearly double to get my head under it, digging my nails into the wood of it in terror of falling. The tree did not stand right up against the house—the trunk was a good five feet away, but fairly sizable branches reached nearly to the wall, even up this high. I would have to lean out far enough to try to grasp one and swing from it until I could get my feet on another below.

Way below. The frosty grass, a strange orange in the ground-floor lamplight, looked like the surface of something about as distant as Venus and my stomach jangled with electrical shocks of fear. I was only half out of the window, afraid to let go the sill with my left hand long enough to stretch it toward the branch, afraid to launch myself into the void and find I did not have the strength to catch myself. I needed to free my other leg so I could push off, but the window opening was so narrow that I wouldn't have room to sit on the sill in order to jump. I was going to have to slide down the house until I could get my toes on the top of the next window down and then dive sideways for a handhold on the tree.

I leaned far forward to ease my inside leg out the window behind me, bumping my head on the frame and getting hung up briefly on the lamp cord, but I got my foot into the opening and slipped down the bricks, gripping the sill with aching fingers while I pulled my leg through. My fingers were breaking—what if I damaged them? I wouldn't be able to play!

And thought, "To hell with playing, it's only Mother wants me to play," and scraped my hand hard scrabbling along the sill as I fought viciously for a foothold. I wasn't tall enough to get a good one; I inched one toe onto the ledge below and knew I'd have to let go with one arm and reach for the branch all in one motion or my other arm would give out and I'd fall for sure.

Out of the corner of my left eye, I could just glimpse a sturdy-enough-looking branch a little above my head—I would have to fly up to it. My foot was starting to cramp from being extended so far and the muscles in my right arm felt as if all the living fiber of them had begun to rip. I couldn't wait another second.

A shower of paint chips and dirt fell into my eyes as I tore first my left hand and then my right from the sill and launched myself into the tree, blindly clutching where I thought the branch would be. My left hand grasped the thick part of the limb and slipped, scaring me so badly that when my right hand touched leaves, I nearly swam up the slender end of the branch like a lizard up the palm fronds at home. My feet found support and I clung to the trunk with one arm while the other bent the branch in frantic embrace.

As I hung there, panting, I saw a figure—Debbie or Gunter, I couldn't tell—come to the downstairs window, casting a long shadow that paused as if listening. Maybe they would guess what I was trying to do. Maybe they would check my room to see. I had to hurry.

The shadow disappeared and I slid down the trunk, landed on a root, and twisted my ankle. I swore silently for a long moment, all the nastiest words I'd ever heard, until the pain lessened and I thought I could stand up. I had to limp a little, but I could walk and was creeping into the neighbor's yard when I heard Gunter shout for me from my bedroom window.

I ran, hobbling. It was cold, made colder by the usual strong wind, and my ears stung as if grazed by shards of ice. The bare trees, intensely black in the harsh pools of street lighting, waved and rattled. With friendly, glowing windows in all the houses, the night was hardly frightening, but to be out at this hour and in these circumstances was undeniably queer and I felt, if not scared exactly, then certainly discomfited, as if I'd wakened in a strange room.

I listened to the soft thud of my trainers on the sidewalk, watching each panel of concrete as I passed, objectively noting the cracks and the bits of ice in them that were all that remained of the snowfall we'd had a week earlier. I had stood outside in it for a freezing hour, watching the flakes—the first I had ever seen—blow around me, shifting and swirling in synchronized harmony like a vast school of tiny white fish. They were fascinating and dizzying and damp and I had come back into the house with my hair coated in frigid drizzle that Debbie had toweled off, laughing. The next day, Gunter had ordered me into my new boots and parka and shown me how to make snowballs that I pitched for him to smash to powder with his softball bat. We shoveled the driveway and the walk and put down salt to keep the ice from forming. The neighbors must have done, as well—there was very little ice on the pavements, just streaks of dirty sand, mostly, rather like the island pavements. Rather like the pavement that went past our bungalow and ended near the sea.

I wouldn't think about that. I would *not* think about that. I got to the corner and turned down Green Bay, cutting through the parking lot of the ice cream shop to get to Rob's back yard. All the lights in his house were blazing—I could see his mother at the kitchen sink and was careful to stand well beyond the patch of garden that she could have seen from the window. Rob's room was on the side opposite, fortunately, but he wasn't in it. I stood for nearly half an hour in the bushes by his window, hoping he would appear alone and huddling myself smaller and smaller into my coat until I thought nothing would be left of me but a stump the size and consistency of one of those petrified logs out west.

At last, he came into his room and picked up a guitar. He looked like leaving again and I quickly tapped on the glass. I must have tapped loudly—he jumped and spun around as if I'd fired a cannon. In fact, he looked so bug-eyed with fright that it crossed my mind he might run for his parents, so I waved my arms over my head, hoping he'd be able to see through the curtains that I wasn't holding a weapon. What would I have, piano wire?

He must have realized that it was someone he knew—he sort of sidled up to the glass and cupped his hands round his eyes to try to see into the dark, staggering back in mock shock when he saw it was me. He quickly opened the window.

"What the hell you doin' out there?"

"Shhh. Keep it down, would you? Can you sneak out?"

Rob stage-whispered elaborately. "Why don't you come in?"

"I don't want your parents to know I'm here, but I need to talk to you. Can't you get out?"

"Well, yeah, maybe. It'd be better if my folks were in bed. But maybe I can fake 'em out—I'll go tell 'em I'm gonna close my door so I can study."

"Will they believe that?"

He grinned hugely. "They'll be so happy, they'll leave me alone till next weekend."

He walked out of the room and I heard him announce grandly that he had a big biology test coming up and was "not to be disturbed." He came back guffawing and grabbed a coat.

"All my dad said was, 'Just so you aren't practicing on any girls.' Step aside there, Van Cliburn, and let me defenestrate myself."

"That sounds painful—are you going to end up a soprano?"

I grinned back at him. I suddenly felt less desperate, though the fleeting thought of Mother seemed to drop like a cold rock of anger into my stomach.

Rob slid like an otter out the window and stuffed his hands in his pockets. "Shit, it's cold out here. So what's up?"

I told him what had happened as we cut through gardens, heading toward the lake. The wind grew stronger.

"So you gotta go home for Christmas. But that was the plan all along, wasn't it? I mean, isn't it kind of normal that your mom bought you a ticket?"

"Yes, but you see, she never talked to me about it, not even to ask when it would be most convenient for me to leave. She probably just asked Gunter what day my classes would be over for the holidays."

"Yeah, well, I can see how that might make you mad. I get really pissed off when my folks just present me with some scenario, you know, like I have to spend the day cleaning the garage and then we're all going to my aunt Ruth's for dinner and they haven't even asked me what I want to do. The old *fait accompli*. Yeah, that's a bummer. But I get the feeling you're mad about something besides having to go to a tropical island for Christmas."

We had reached the beach park and were sitting on the swings on the bluff above the water, looking out at the lake's lunar stillness in the bluish light from the streetlamps. It was so cold that Rob had pulled his arms out of his sleeves and wrapped them around his chest inside his ratty red ski jacket. I couldn't feel my feet or fingers anymore and the sling-type seat of the swing bit into my thighs. I didn't want to be out here any longer in the freezing Midwestern night—I teetered on the verge of tears again, wanting to be found and yet imagining how I would refuse to speak or come along should Gunter and Debbie appear and try to persuade me. Would they be looking for me? No one really cared about me, no one. All the adults schemed and bossed and manipulated, but that wasn't love, just meddling. I would not go where I was told anymore, would not be kept in the dark like a three-year-old unable to comprehend the world or choose his own path.

A car drove by slowly, lighting up the playground briefly as it turned the corner. What if they had called the police? Didn't police patrol these parks at night?

I jumped up, stiffly, and looked behind me. Rob raised an eyebrow.

"Come on, let's go to the pancake house," I said. "I have some money."

I loved the pancake house. There had been nothing like it in the islands. A festival of warm wood paneling and old-timey, stained-glass windows, with tables crowded together in a warren of little rooms, it glowed with a particularly American kind of welcome, scented with the hot, comforting smell of sugar and cinnamon. It was the kind of place in which you wanted to get stranded during a blizzard.

We jogged back along Green Bay, Rob with his empty sleeves flopping back and forth across his lumpy red middle, I with my deadened fingers pressed to my throbbing ears. It was a weeknight, so there was no line at the restaurant. We got a table right away.

"O-o-o-o-oh, baby."

Rob kicked my shin under the table—the waitress was coming, a tall, pretty girl with long dark hair and a snug pink uniform.

"Are you ready to order?"

Rob looked up at her soulfully. "Yeah, but I bet what I'd like isn't on the menu."

She rolled her eyes and I kicked Rob back. "Be nice, you little git."

"Sorry. Sorry, sorry, sorry. I guess my senses just kinda got overloaded, you know, going from cold out there to hot in here. I mean…" He gulped and grinned at the girl, whose mouth had begun to twist, despite the severity of her folded arms.

I fanned him with my menu. "He means he'd like a glass of ice water and a strong cup of coffee to *sober up*. And I'd like a large hot chocolate with whipped cream."

She smiled sweetly—"Sprinkles, too, right?"—and headed for the kitchen. Two softly disgusted syllables floated back to us in her wake: "Freshmen."

Rob's eyes widened. 'Now how did she know we were freshmen?'

"One of us gave it away."

"Well, you hadda go and order a kiddie drink just as she was starting to succumb to my charms."

"Oh, that was charm? It looked a lot like self-humiliation to me."

"No, man." Rob shook his head of shaggy hair in mock-exasperation. "That was *artless repartee*. Don't you read?"

"Well, I'll be surprised if she comes back. Besides, she isn't that great. Nice ass, though."

I nonchalantly picked up the saltshaker and examined it. I had never used that word in conversation before.

"'Nice *ahss*?'" Rob cracked up. "'Nice *ahss*,' your lordship. She may have one, but we're a couple of 'em—look what she's bringing us."

I jerked around to see the waitress approaching with a tray. On it were two big plastic clown mugs with paper parasols in them.

She smirked at us. "Here you go, kids. Any food to go with them? Maybe some Teddy Bear Hotcakes? I'll be right back to take your order."

Her pink uniform undulated away. Rob shook his head in admiration.

"That was amazing. What a putdown. What a totally cool putdown. I'm impressed. Beauty and balls, too… What are you frowning about?"

"That insulting…*bird*! What is her problem? Treating us as if we were babies. Just like a female, always implying that you're thick and contemptible, just good enough to do as you're told."

"Whoa. What?" Rob goggled at me.

"Girls. Women. They're always trying to lead men around by the nose, make them feel small. I'm going to speak to the management about her."

Rob was still staring. "She was just kidding around with us. And I had it coming to me, pretending to hit on her like that. No big deal."

"Well, maybe you don't care, but I've had quite enough of females acting superior and having some kind of private laugh at my expense. Besides, it's her job to treat customers properly and if she doesn't, she ought to lose her position."

I could feel my lips compress into a hard line and I couldn't look at Rob anymore, didn't want him to see the fury in my eyes, didn't want to read the wary surprise in his own. I stared at the table.

"You are really getting yourself worked up over not much, you know?" Rob said quietly. "Do you really want to get her, like, fired because you're mad at your mom?"

I glanced up, wanting to hurt him, wanting to smash in that well-meaning American face. "You obviously don't understand. Perhaps you're just not bright enough to get it."

His gaze darkened. "I'm bright enough to see that you got a seriously messed-up way of looking at things and you got a mean temper, too. Why are you acting like such an asshole? I'm your friend, you know? That's why I sneaked outta my house tonight, cuz I'm your friend. Friends don't insult each other for real. So if you're not one of mine, just tell me and I'll be happy to walk outta here."

I felt a stab of panic. Without Rob, I'd be completely on my own. I'd had no idea where I was going to go for the night to begin with and now it struck me that, unless Rob let me creep into his room to sleep on the floor, I would probably have to take the train downtown to find a cheap hotel in some awful neighborhood. And trains didn't run that often after six p.m. And I had money for probably only one night even in the worst fleabag in Chicago. What then?

I picked up my menu and studied it.

"I'm...I guess you're right. I'm not being much of a friend. This whole day has been rubbish and the waitress was just the last bit. I...didn't mean what I said. About you."

I pushed aside the lukewarm mug of chocolate and drank some water. My stomach had stopped growling ages ago and now just ached like every other part of me. Probably I needed to eat something, although the thought of asking that mocking witch of a waitress for anything sent bile into my throat.

My words seemed to satisfy Rob. He watched me for a few seconds and then the line between his eyebrows faded. He muttered, "Forget about it," and opened his menu, too.

The waitress returned. "Are you—"

"I'll have the French toast and bacon," I said, ignoring her and looking at Rob. "What are you having?"

"Just a short stack. I had dinner only about an hour ago. And some more coffee, please."

He smiled slightly and humbly at the girl and she smiled back, a real smile this time. She didn't look at me again.

Once she left, a heavy silence fell, but Rob didn't let it last long.

"C'mon, let's play table chess."

"What?"

"Table chess. Don't you play that on your island? Here, take the salt and pepper and I'll take the sugar and the bowl of creamers and we each have a mug and a water glass. Okay, make a move."

"Where? Why?"

"Anywhere on the table, just so you don't put the object where it's supposed to be. Go on."

I slid my water toward him a little.

"Timid, man. You gotta be bold."

Rob took the sugar and shoved it right in front of me. Half

angry, half amused, I shoved the pepper right in front of him. He moved his clown mug to the end of the table, right on the edge, and waggled his brows at me suggestively.

"Dangerous, huh?"

I moved the salt between the pepper and his water glass, making a tight row of vertical glass.

"Hmmm, trick-ee, man, but watch this."

He took the creamer bowl and deposited it with a flourish between the sugar and my mug and opposite my water glass.

"Ta da! Isosceles right triangle!"

"Is *that* the point?"

"No, there is no point. Table chess is random—it's just a dumb-funny way to kill time until the food shows up. And here it is."

The bird distributed plates and cups, commanded, "Enjoy!" and disappeared.

I didn't think I could eat anything until I took the first queasy bite of bacon and then was instantly convinced I'd starve to death before I could inhale everything in front of me. Rob had finished his small serving by the time I started to slow down and he watched me spear the last few bits and then scrape the remaining drops of syrup onto my fork.

"Maybe you should get seconds."

"No, actually, I think that was just enough. I'm starting to be sleepy."

"Yeah, we oughta get back. My folks'll freak if they figure out I'm gone. You think the Hellmans will check on you?"

"They already know I left. Gunter was calling for me just as I was walking out of the yard. I suppose if they were worried, they would have come looking, but they're probably just as glad to have done with me."

"Oh, come on. They're okay. For all you know, they've called out the Marines. We'll probably get nabbed on the way home. You know, it's like you always assume people don't like you and so you act like you don't like them. And I know you really like the Hellmans, so that isn't gonna work here."

"My, that was a lot of likes."

Rob squinted at me. 'You do have friends, man. You're not such a sorry case."

"Well, there aren't very many people I care to be friends with, anyway."

I frowned at my empty plate as faces seemed to appear one by one within its gleaming porcelain circle like slide projections on a white screen.

"People are stupid or haughty or both, generally. They're not even worth looking at, so I don't. I'm in better company when I'm alone."

I came to myself. "Except for you, I mean."

Rob kept on carefully tying knots in a straw wrapper and didn't look up.

"I don't think most people are haughty," he said slowly. "I think some of 'em just don't act friendly 'cause they're afraid of making fools of themselves. Afraid everybody else'll sneer at 'em and blow 'em off. So they, like, snub others before the others snub them, you know?"

A corner of his mouth tightened into a sort of half-smile as he glanced at me. "I get the feeling you don't realize you're using a good offense as your best defense."

"What does that mean?"

"Nothing—never mind. Hey, we better get going." Rob stood up. "Oh, and thanks for the pancakes."

We hurried through the darkness as quickly as full stomachs would allow. Rob had said I could stay with him overnight, but when we got close to his home, we could see Gunter's and Debbie's car in the driveway and I froze (only metaphorically, for the first time all night) where I was, abruptly scared instead of aloof and disdainful, as I'd planned. I didn't want to face them. I didn't want to go home to Mother and now I'd ruined any chance of being allowed to come back here ever again. I'd have to stay on the island until I was old enough for university and by then it would be too late. I would never get another chance. I was going to end up nothing, giving lessons for my living to loutish adolescents with less talent than I once had.

Rob nudged me. "C'mon, gotta face the music."

The irony of this expression barely registered.

I stuck my hands in my pockets and stumbled after him through frosty, uneven tufts of grass to the front door. It flew open before Rob could even touch the knob, and his scowling father pulled him into the house.

Debbie immediately took his place and did the same to me. She made no sound beyond an exasperated "oh!" and hugged me before giving my shoulders a couple of hard shakes.

"What on earth possessed you to run off like that?" she finally demanded in a breaking voice.

"Darling. Debbie." Gunter came up behind her and gently placed his hands on her arms. "Let us have our talk at home. Everyone is tired."

He gave me an enigmatic look and turned to Rob's parents, who were subjecting their son to a quiet but furious rant in the corner. "We will go now. Thank you for letting us wait here and, again, my apologies for this whole situation."

Rob's mom took her hands off her hips long enough to wave slightly and say, "We're sorry, too. Thanks for alerting us," and instantly rejoined her husband in their *sotto voce* harangue. I thought I saw Rob wink at me before Gunter discreetly but irresistibly propelled me back out the door and into the car.

We made the trip home in utter silence. I would have liked the ride to be a lot longer—all I wanted to do was stay in the back seat and close my eyes on everything and wake up far away from myself and my life, but after Gunter pulled into the garage, he opened the rear door for me and waited until I felt forced to get out, as if he knew I wanted to hide and wasn't about to let me.

We walked into the kitchen and Debbie said, "You sit down," without looking at me and went to hang up her coat. The room still smelled of dinner, but I wasn't hungry anymore and said only "no, thanks" when she came back and said she would heat up some food, if I wanted. She didn't seem much inclined to coax me.

Gunter had already sat at the table with me, and when Debbie joined us, he pulled an envelope from his pocket and put it in front of me.

"Go ahead, open it," he said.

I ripped open the paper and removed a small folder. It was my airline ticket. I saw that it was round trip.

"Before we talk about tonight, I want you to know that you will be returning in January, if you care to," Gunter said. "Did you think you were never coming back?"

I looked at him without speaking. Debbie started to reach across the table toward me, then stopped and wiped her eyes.

"We don't want you to leave for good, honey." She pressed her fist to her mouth for a moment. "We like having you here. We hope you've liked it, too. The idea was always for you to stay until you finish high school and we want that more than ever now that we've gotten to know you. So I don't understand why you ran away tonight, as if you thought we wouldn't care. Or as if you didn't like us."

Tears were collecting in her eyes again. "You put yourself in danger and you scared us badly. Why did you do that?"

Gunter's face was grave. "Please try to explain."

I stared with unfocused eyes into the short space between my still-zipped jacket and the table's edge. "It isn't that I don't like you," I muttered and fell silent again.

"Then what?" Debbie quavered.

"Are you angry with us?" Gunter asked slowly.

"Yes!" I burst out. I hadn't been for hours, but suddenly I was, all over again. "I'm angry at you and I'm angry at my mother and I'm angry at everybody! Everybody seems to have a say over my life but me! Everybody always turns out to be in league with my mother, carrying out her schemes for me, keeping her secrets from me, never listening to what I want for myself. It's my life, not hers! She had her own and I guess she

messed it up and that's her problem. But she doesn't deserve
to mess mine up, too, and neither do you! What do you really
know about me, anyway? You don't know how I feel or what I
want or what I…what I've been through! She sent me to you
so I'd have to be a pianist! Do you care that I don't *want* to be
a pianist? She doesn't! She doesn't know or care what I want to
do! She thinks God chose me to play piano and she's making
sure that piano is my *only* choice! It's nothing to her that I want
to sing opera, like my father!"

I broke off, aghast, hearing my own words naked and
screaming in my ears as if they were actual beings who had
found themselves brutally stripped in public. I wanted to grab
them back, grab them and hide them away again where they
could be safe and mine again as they ought to have stayed, my
own secret.

Gunter's and Debbie's faces seemed to reflect the shock they
saw on my own and, for a second, they simply stared at me.
Then they both rose, carefully, as though not to frighten me,
and put their arms around me.

"It is all right, if you want to sing," Gunter murmured. "It is
all right. You can study voice as well as piano, like your father.
We will not tell your mother—if you become sure that a singing
career is what you want, then you can tell her."

"She'll know somehow," I warned them in a whisper. The
voice I wished to sing with had vanished.

I couldn't explain it to them, about Mother's God and his
eye, the sun that relentlessly sought entry to our house like a
prison-yard spotlight, no matter how tightly Mother fastened
the shutters around her own shadowy, unspoken life. I realized
then that I believed she regarded singing as a sin.

"I'm sure I'll end up paying," I finally said. I didn't mean for
the lessons.

VI

My father was born in Wales, in Caerphilly, where an ancient castle looms aloof and bleak over the town like a scarred specter of mysterious times and where everyone is always singing. The people of Wales sing the way other people dream or make love—to fill the darkness with magic.

My father sang with them, from almost his first breath—with his family, with the wireless that was always on in their tiny parlor, at church and at school, in Welsh, English, Latin and, much later, in Italian, German, French, and Russian. His father had been a teacher, too, not of music but of science, in one of the grammar schools. And yet, in spite of a clear love of the natural world that kept his house full of curious insects, birds' nests, stones, plants and varieties of fungi, preserved on pins in boxes or cluttering the shelves and tabletops, it was nonetheless music that was my grandfather's true passion and he taught his two sons to need it as much as he did. They joined him in the glee clubs to which he belonged and learned to savor opera from attending local music-society performances and from the annual trips to Covent Garden that were the family's much-saved-for and anticipated holiday treats.

I remember a photograph of them all from one of these pilgrimages: my grandmother, in her cloche hat, with her hand on the shoulder of her tall eldest; my father, a solemn six-year-old in a belted jacket and short pants, in the arms of his own dad, who smiled and gazed at his child instead of at the camera. The noble columns and pediment of the opera house rose behind them like the palace of heaven, as if this were where they would choose to come after death.

In the days before I was to fly home, Gunter told me, as my mother never had, that piano had come second for my father after singing. Yet he had had such a gift for it that he was admitted to university on a double scholarship as a member of the college choir and as a student of the legendary Basil Higgins, whose long lionization as the premiere pianist of his day had come to include growing renown as an opera and orchestral conductor.

Gunter had studied with Higgins, too—that was how he and my father had met. Gunter had been sent by his parents to Britain as a ten-year-old to escape the growing power of the Nazis and he had lived with an uncle who had immigrated years earlier. The uncle had become director in a lucrative chemist-supply business in London and was able to send Gunter to university when the time came. That bit of luck was considerably offset by the death of Gunter's Jewish father in one of the camps and the destitution of his German Protestant mother, who arrived on her brother's doorstep after the war with a few framed photographs and some documents showing her husband to be the owner of two shops and a house in Dresden, which had first been seized by the Reich and then demolished by Allied bombs.

Gunter was two years older than my father and, from the first, had looked after him like a protective brother, Gunter said one lightless afternoon at the conservatory, where we had paused during my work on a Rachmaninoff concerto to look out the window at a howling snowstorm that was making the air look like horizontal static on an old black-and-white telly. My father was shy and rather serious, but not at all difficult, apparently. Diffident, if anything, masking his intensity with a quiet, noncommittal air. Gunter said he'd had an unexpectedly creative sense of humor, though: When my father found out, a few months after first meeting Gunter, that his new friend's birthday was coming up, he'd organized their musical mates into a sort of bell choir at their favorite pub, with pint glasses filled with beer to ring particular tones, like a harmonium. They'd tapped out "Happy Birthday" with butter knives and then helped Gunter quaff down all the beer.

That story was a tangent—what Gunter had actually been

talking with me about was which one of the conservatory's voice teachers I should study with. It meant about an hour's extra lesson and practice time each day and more later if I really meant to go on with it. And he wasn't about to let me neglect piano—he'd made that clear right away. Said he wasn't going to let my mother and my talent down by easing up on me, even though he had agreed to my clandestine singing.

"Your father managed to do both in school and perhaps he would eventually have been able to create a sort of combined career for himself," Gunter had mused to his reflection in the snow-whipped glass. "There are some singers who have become conductors, too, though not many who have been both singers and world-class pianists. Perhaps he would have decided to concentrate on one thing or the other, in time."

"But he really wasn't doing any of those things anymore," I'd protested. "He was just teaching. Except for a piece or two he played on a school program once when I was six, I don't remember him having a performing career at all."

"No." Gunter had glanced at me in a way that seemed apprehensive. "No, he had stopped for a while. He told me he did not want to have to travel a great deal while you were so small, or to leave your mother alone. It can be very hard on families, a musical career. Ask Debbie—I was gone as much as twenty weeks a year for most of our marriage and I could easily have been gone forty. It is important to take as many engagements as possible, but it is also important to be at home as much as possible. Compromise is difficult."

Actually, Gunter had begun to be absent from home more often as the season progressed. He was trying to travel less in the summer, when he and Debbie were likelier to get long visits from their boys, which meant limiting himself to a few choice festival performances. But during the main concert seasons in Europe and the United States, he had closely scheduled flurries of appearances every three weeks or so and had to leave his students under the supervision of his graduate assistant, Wei Ling. This dour fellow always insisted, in a soft, polite, relentless voice, that I repeat the rhythmic complexities in my pieces over and over until I thought I would shove his head into the piano case and drop the lid on it out of sheer vexation.

Gunter had said that he would begin taking me with him on occasional concert trips, maybe in the next year. But until then, I had to put up with Ling, whom I preferred to call Ding-a, though not quite within his hearing.

I would add voice lessons to my schedule in January. Gunter had recommended Annalise Taylor, a rather famous mezzo who sang at the Met, but I didn't care to study with a woman and had decided on Ralph Ennis, a youngish baritone who had just debuted at the Vienna Staatsoper and had a leaning toward Donizetti and Bizet. Gunter had no real objection; when I told him, he raised his eyebrows, but said nothing.

I was surreptitiously working on my voice at home, humming vocalises from my father's books in the privacy of my attic room and occasionally attempting a song or two when the Hellmans were out. Letting them hear what I sounded like, even accidentally, was absolutely out of the question. I had no idea if my voice was good—or even promising—and I was not about let them judge that before I had judged it for myself. I would not have them comparing my singing ability with my father's, even though I'd had no qualms at all about them measuring my pianistic skills against his. Piano had always come easily to me. I knew I was good and what people thought about it didn't concern me much. Piano didn't...*matter*. Singing did and I guarded it as I would a wound.

My father had loved to sing for others, Gunter said, and sang more readily than he would talk in company. It was the side of him that people who came to love him fell for first, before they knew anything else about him. Except for Mother, if I am to believe her own words. Or word. Conducting had drawn her to him, choral conducting, which, according to Gunter, my father had done merely to earn a living and stay in shape artistically while trying to find success as a singer and pianist. At least at that point, he'd had no intention of following Higgins's footsteps to the podium, Gunter was quite sure. He'd had some singing engagements with smaller opera companies and with orchestras in Britain and on the continent and was constantly auditioning for more. Higgins's influence had also gotten him on a variety of important piano-recital series and festival schedules that had him quickly gaining on Gunter who, having graduated first, had a head start on the professional circuit.

And then he had met my mother. Gunter, by then married to Debbie and living in the States, said he had gotten an overseas call one night, very rare in those days. My father had rung him up to say that he was getting married, too, and soon, to a girl who had been singing in his choir for only five months. Would Gunter be best man?

He had sounded blissful, Gunter said. And when Gunter and Debbie had flown to England for the wedding, they found my mother to be very pretty and rather quiet—though it was not the untroubled quiet of my father, but an intense kind of reserve she had, as if she were constantly holding back some passion that would have burst from a less self-willed person.

They had seemed to be very happy together, in spite of the hearing problem that had recently beset my mother, Gunter said. He remembered that, at the wedding dinner, a small but elegant party at a hotel near the church, Mother and he had talked a long time about my father's career. She had been quite enthusiastic about it and had wanted Gunter to tell her as much as he knew about Higgins's progress from piano virtuoso to conductor, as she thought my father was brilliant on the church-choir podium and would end up as music director at Bayreuth or Vienna. The idea of living abroad, she had said, had always appealed to her.

Well, that desire, at least, had been achieved, though perhaps not in the way she had hoped. I looked out the porthole of the plane as we circled the islands, dropping lower and lower toward the vivid green and white stepping stones they made across the turquoise sea.

Everything about them looked strangely just the same—the same catamarans bobbing in the water, the same sprawling hotels and clusters of shacks, the same ceremonial guards in pith helmets and jaguar skins at the foot of the drive leading to the royal governor's mansion that Brownlea and I hurtled past in a cab on the way from the airport to catch the boat home.

Certainly, Brownlea hadn't changed much. Perhaps the shirt was new. He was standing at the gate when I came through the door from the tarmac and gave me sort of a quick once-over as he extended his hand. He seemed a bit surprised when I shook it and asked how he'd been.

"Well enough, thanks. Classes a bit smaller than usual this year—government rotated some ministry families home and the new ones have only tiny children, generally, so less work for me, I'm happy to say, for a while."

"Who left?"

"Let's see, the Hurleys and the Haverfords, Atchesons, McGees and Denisons."

"The Atchesons? So Colin's gone?"

"Yes, and there's been a great taking on about it at the school, too. Well, Colin is a nice, smart boy and will be missed, but he's not God himself."

Brownlea gave me a sidelong look. "And how are you?"

"Well enough."

He didn't pry. On the boat, he asked an offhand question about or two about Gunter's playing style and repertoire and wondered how I'd taken to the Chicago weather, but he seemed determined to let me be, overall, and I was relieved to be allowed long silences. At last, one of our little island jitneys dropped us and my luggage on the pavement in front of Mother's house.

Even before we stepped out of the car, I saw her dim form on the screened porch; it disappeared and a moment later the front door opened, but she didn't come out. Simon grabbed the bags and went up the steps first, entering only long enough to greet my mother and tactfully decline her invitation to stay to dinner. He put down the bags, gave her his customary kiss on the cheek and set off walking home, cheerfully calling to me, "See you in a day or two" before striding away.

I thought it was good of him not to break into an actual run.

God's eye glared down on me from above the oleanders. I forced myself to walk into the house, where the unspoken past, and my mother, waited.

It took my eyes a moment or two to adjust to the shadowy room and she continued to wait until I had focused on her before stepping forward with her hands tightly clasped in front of her and kissing my cheek fleetingly, as if afraid to leave a mark.

She spoke my name, overloud, and added, "Welcome home."

"Hello, Mother."

She smiled slightly at me. I don't think I returned it.

"Did you have a good flight?"

"Fine, thanks. Not as bumpy as when I left. Shall I put the bags in my room?"

"Yes, all right."

She must not have moved in the five minutes it took me to carry my luggage to the rear of the house and unpack my few stacks of clothes. One whole case was filled with music and the Christmas presents for her and Brownlea for which Debbie had helped me shop. I shoved it under the bed, reflexively checking for scorpions, and returned to the hall to find her standing in exactly the same place.

"Would you like a fizzy drink? Gunter tells me you enjoy the orange sort."

Without waiting to hear my answer, she hurried into the kitchen and began filling a glass with ice and hissing soda.

I wandered into the living room, startled at how small it felt, and stood with my hands in my pockets. I didn't want to sit down.

Mother brought me my drink. I said thanks and was startled again—there were a few lines of gray in her hair. I suddenly felt as if I had been away years, on another planet, and that everything around me now was old, old and dusty and petrified in time, unchanged but for a creeping decline, while I had been moving at the speed of light and was altered totally, yet had hardly aged a second.

"I thought I'd make snapper for tea. Does that sound all right? You can't have had much seafood in Chicago. And for pudding, I got ice cream and those chocolate macaroons you like. Are you hungry yet or shall we eat at six, as usual?"

"I can wait."

I explored the room, knowing that if I sat and looked at her, I would have to ask all the questions that had been hiving in my head like angry wasps since November, and I didn't want to let them out just yet. I was afraid I'd lose control of them, lose the advantage of my justified wrath if I simply let them burst forth in a mass. I wanted to aim each one of them.

It did not even cross my mind that she might confide in me. I expected to have to startle and shame the information from her, sting her into revelation.

I sipped my soda and examined some magazines that had come while I was away; some were music publications I'd want to look at later. Mother's quarterly church bulletin had a largish picture of Colin Atcheson on the front with the caption, "Our head altar boy is to return to England with his family. Rector Parry calls the loss to St. Peter of the Sea 'a great sorrow.'" Colin looked rather pleased with himself.

"There's a bit of post for you on your desk," Mother announced. "It will be out of date now—it was an invitation to the Atchesons' farewell party in September. Everyone knew you couldn't come, of course, but all the church families and schoolmates were invited. It was quite a nice send-off for them."

"No one gave me a nice send-off." I couldn't help it, it just popped out of me.

"You were coming back at Christmas."

Our mutual awareness of my not wanting to return pervaded the air and remained there throughout tea. Conversation continued to be sparse—it was easier to eat five or six macaroons than to make disingenuous chitchat.

After our meal, she excused me from helping with the washing up—"I'm sure you're tired"—and I walked out of the house to look at the sunset. Huge pink clouds hung in the sky and all the vegetation glowed as if it had been irradiated and would soon vaporize. The bungalows, the sand—all were beginning the transition from orange-pink-red to violet-gray.

I had a sudden desire to see the water. I don't know why. I had a weird sensation in the back of my head as if an alarm had gone off and were silently shocking me with tiny jolts of electricity, as if I knew I was going to be sorry, but I couldn't stop the slow scuffing steps my feet were taking into the sand at the end of the pavement. The palmettos came only to my shoulders now, but were denser, and the sketchy path was interrupted by enormous weeds and emerging sea grape. Surely, other people came here—and yet the sand looked printless all the way to the shells and debris that marked the high-tide line.

I hadn't stood here for six years, hadn't thought I ever would again. I stared at the spot where my parents used to sit, tried to see my father lying there, the pattern of the blanket, the shape of his hands, his face. The details eluded me; I remembered only white skin, dark hair, white sand, shadows. He was gone, dissolved. The graying turquoise and gold water rippled into the little cove, the small waves breaking into bubbles and swirls of sand upon the beach. There was nothing on the water, no distant shape or sail or floating bit of wood to arrest the ocean's smooth, blank regard. It admitted nothing, had left no evidence of what it took.

Had it been that calm when it filled my father's lungs, that impassive as he writhed and struggled, clawing at his throat as if his desperate fingers could draw the fluid from it as they had drawn music from lifeless wood and wire? Had tears come to his eyes in his last panic, the first few molecules of himself to become indistinguishable from the medium of his death?

There was no mark on that unimpressible surface. Was that how it would always be for us, him and me, to be stilled by this flat silence, this cold, killing refusal to respond? We had to make it feel, make it acknowledge us, what it had done to us. I picked up a stone and threw it as hard as I could, awkwardly, threw another and another, scarcely waiting to see the brief injury each caused in the shining infinity of glass. I ran into the water, kicking it with my shoes, but it wasn't enough, it wasn't enough, and I raced up the beach, frantically stripping a palmetto frond from the stalk, slicing my hand, which poured blood down the green spikes as I tore into the sea, thrashing the dark water, thrashing it as if I could force it to cry out. And it was only I that cried out, instead.

VII

What was it she told me?

Not much. Not then—very little that I hadn't guessed at, really. There was a lot of shouting that night, starting with her hoarse and desperate calls as she ran down the sand, terrified—it turned out—that she would find me drowned as the police had found my father. Her relief and fury at discovering me on my feet, with no worse injuries than a cut hand and squelchy shoes, wrenched fierce sobs from her, the likes of which I had never heard her utter before. And tears. Real, actual tears that streaked her face and made her nose drip. I could hardly make out what she was saying over and over as she pulled me up the beach and onto solid pavement; it sounded like "not that," punctuated every so often by a clear and enraged "what were you doing?" which seemed to indicate somehow that it wasn't enough that I was alive, but that I also owed her a satisfactory rationale for my madness.

Not that she stopped for an answer, or for anything more than to wipe her face with her hand before half-dragging me into the house. And there we stood, both of us red, breathless and running with different kinds of saltwater, as at odds with the cool, impassive order of home as if we had been a couple of feral cats suddenly pulled indoors out of a hard rain. For a moment, I felt a strange kinship with her.

"Kick off those shoes at once and come to the kitchen," she ordered in a more normal voice, and strode around me to arm herself with soap and towels. Her examination revealed that the cut on my palm, though long and painful, was shallow, and after cleaning and bandaging it for me, she sent me off to change clothes. Neither of us said much. I realized that it hadn't even occurred to me to worry whether or not my injury would affect my playing and I felt certain that it hadn't occurred to her, either. Another first.

I stripped off my clothes and left them in a sodden pile. I felt…good. Oddly good. Being in no hurry to return to my mother, I took a long bath and enjoyed the sensation of salt and sweat dissolving in the cool water—cooler and glassier than the ocean, and yet not my enemy. I lay there watching a brown moth beating its wings in arpeggios of sixty-fourth notes around the overhead light before soaping myself as best I could without getting the bandaged hand wet and submerging myself completely, arm held aloft like a periscope, to rinse. I dried off, dressed in shorts and a shirt I had bought in Chicago, and strolled into the sitting room; Mother was dead ahead on the screened porch, as usual, but standing with her unopened Bible in her hands, looking toward the cove that she couldn't actually see because of the overgrown vegetation and the darkening sky outside. Her body in its trim cotton dress seemed tiny and stooped, tired. It had never looked so to me before. I wondered suddenly if I had grown since the summer.

A kind of power filled me. "Mother, there's something I want to ask you."

My voice startled her—could she have lost her extra-sensory ability to detect my presence?—and she dropped the book, pressing her fingers to her mouth before picking it up and facing me. She held it to her the way a naked woman would clutch the slip she had just let fall before an intruder entered. I addressed her boldly.

"Mother, why were you crying before? That's the first time I've ever seen you truly cry."

She stared at me without answering. I frowned.

"Mother, I know you heard me."

"Yes," she said a little raspily, and cleared her throat. "I heard you. I should think the answer would be obvious."

"Maybe to you. But I'd like to hear it."

I could see her trying to be herself, to muster her usual cold dignity and command, but that spell seemed broken for now.

She pulled the Bible in tightly. "I was...afraid. I couldn't find you and I was afraid that you had...that you were drowning."

"And what difference would that make?"

She looked at me as if I had struck her.

"What? How can you—"

"No, stop playing all innocent, Mother! What real difference would my drowning make? Father drowned and you've never seemed to miss *him*. You never, ever talk about him. Why would you miss me any more than him?"

"Your father," she started, and couldn't seem to utter another sound. Tears ran down her cheeks—twice in one day!—and she covered her mouth with her hand, bending over her book as if she were ill.

An icy little thrill of triumph corkscrewed through my solar plexus, transforming into alarm as she staggered. I pulled over a chair and she sat, still soundless and folded over, while I found a box of tissues, putting it at her feet when she wouldn't release her hands to take it. I had no idea what to do next. Waiting hopefully for my mother to regain control was an entirely new experience for me. My brief, predatory satisfaction at finally cracking her curtain wall was coming with an aftertaste of unease, as if her illness were catching.

"Mother."

She straightened up a bit and laid the Bible on her lap, reaching for a tissue and taking a couple of deep, ragged breaths as she patted her eyes and turned them to me.

"Is this what you want so much to hear?" she whispered. "That I wanted to die when your father did? Well, I did. I did. But I lived, instead. I lived for you."

I broke in, suddenly angry. "For me? Or for my glorious career? If I'm so important, why won't you talk to me? Why do you plan my life for me behind my back? Why haven't I ever heard you say you"—and I had to push the word out—"love me?"

"*Say?*" Steel had reentered my mother's eyes and frame. "Saying you love someone means nothing, nothing at all. You have to live as God intended, cherish his gifts, serve his will in deeds, not words. Only then does love become something more than sinful selfishness."

Her gaze dropped to the book in her lap and, with her forefinger, she traced the gilded cross on its cover.

"After your father…I knew I could raise you to be the man and artist you were intended to be only if I loved God first."

"So loving God first was your way of being an affectionate mother? I didn't need hugs or kisses or kind words because God was going to make everything all right for me as long as he was top of your list?"

I stood over her, arms flung wide, incredulous.

She lifted her chin with regimental precision.

"Yes, you have been wanting to punish me for that for a long time, haven't you? You've wanted to provoke me into telling you my feelings and my reasons. Well, you are a child still and you think like one. What are hugs and kisses when God has given you genius? What greater task could there be than to make sure that genius grows and succeeds? Everything I do and have done has been to carry out that task. Not for me, for you. It's a sin to waste genius. I have to see that you rise as far as you can and I've had to do it alone. I had lost your father. God took him from me, his judgment. I couldn't risk failing you, too."

She was on her feet now, too, shouting into my face, reckless and unfamiliar. "I needed God's help to raise you! I had to deserve God's help."

And that was all. The God she had shielded us both from so vigilantly had made his way in, after all, and long ago.

In the silence, I examined her flushed skin and sweat-dampened hair curiously.

"Why wouldn't you deserve God's help?"

Mother turned and picked up her Bible. "Pride," she said curtly.

But her eyes flicked away as she said it.

VIII

Doing the Mahler Eighth at Usher Hall proved regrettable. Certainly for Usher Hall. But also for me. Of course, our reasons differed somewhat.

I was actually rather excited when the invitation was extended. I was only five years out of Juilliard at that point, and though I'd been a winner of the Metropolitan Opera National Council Auditions and had already sung a number of roles in Washington, Chicago, and San Francisco, I hadn't made more than a handful of concert appearances, mostly with small oratorio groups. So to be approached by the Boston Symphony to sing "Pater Ecstaticus," first at Tanglewood and then in Scotland at the Edinburgh Festival, quite set me up: I'd be making my European debut in a showy gig with a top orchestra at one of the world's greatest arts events.

The Eighth is an enormous piece; its nickname, the "Symphony of a Thousand," exaggerates, but it feels like 1,000 musicians when you're wedged onstage with two large choruses, seven other soloists, and over 150 instrumentalists, while facing a sizable children's choir outposted in the seats of the upper balcony. It would be a claustrophobic experience in Times Square, frankly, but at Usher Hall, where the audience outnumbered the performers by only about three to one, it was an exercise in slow asphyxiation.

It took nearly twenty minutes just to get us all in our places. While crammed with the other soloists in a hallway leading to the stage-right wings, I struck up a conversation with one of the sopranos, who told me she'd overheard the festival-chorus manager, a stout Scot, inform his nearly 500 charges that he'd figured out mathematically how many of them could occupy each step of the staircase where they were to wait before going on. "Ay've done the sums," he'd announced before distributing them vertically in their predetermined numbers.

We smirked enjoyably about this, she and I—she was a replacement who'd caught my eye at rehearsal the day before, a tall and beautiful brunette with a general air of amused sarcasm about her that I found enticing—and then we were on, striding to our chairs near the apron of the stage, where at last we sat like a line of penguins caught between the cliff's edge and the restless mob of our black-and-white fellows teetering in tiers on the iceberg behind us. The precariousness of all those bodies in so few square feet added to my unease. Singing in a fully staged opera is stressful in a different way: There's much more going on and you have to remember your entrances, exits, blocking, and characterization in addition to your music. But there's a certain flexibility to it, as well, a sort of artistic emergency exit that exists because you can improvise. You're playing someone else—should anything go amiss, you can react, distract, escape. In short, you can move. Not so on a concert stage, where you are you, locked in place by the sheer density of population and furniture and, more important, by the unspeakable formality of the proceedings—the choristers rigid in their tight ranks, the players fixed in their chairs, every person with one eye pinned to the conductor and the other to their scores in apprehension of the exactitude required and of the gut-shriveling, hara kiri-inducing shame that is any tiny error in performance protocol. As if the hall were a throne room, or worse, an artistic iron maiden in which the unforgiving punish the already repressed by fatally crushing them onto the spikes of the conductor's autocratic displeasure.

If you do well, the combined effect of applause and the release from pressure at the end can be shocking and euphoric, like landing safely after flying through a thunderstorm. And if you don't, the rites of bowing and exiting and returning to bow again amid the dwindling spatter of handclaps just feels like the last sadistic push on the door of the torture device within which you already stand dead, rictus affixed.

Fortunately, the solo parts of the Eighth are relatively brief, and my main bit didn't come until the second half, so I was able to focus on my physical, rather than artistic, distress for some time. Usher was then a roundish hall of dark wood and cream walls, not as old as many, but redolent of an austere and down-at-heels dignity. The audience were arrayed in a semicircle round the stage in steeply raked rows, surrounding a large dark spot formed of child choristers in the upper-center seats, who would look and sound angelic while no doubt sniggering behind their folders about everyone facing them on stage. I tried not to look at them and instead concentrated on breathing calmly and evenly, despite the hard chair back that cut into my shoulder blades, the chorus basses thundering "Veni Creator" behind me, and a dangerous desire to lean forward and try to catch the eye of Donna, the soprano, seated on the other side of the podium.

As impulses go, this was stupider than most, but also nearly irresistible, and it kept me shifting in my seat and sneaking sidelong glances that revealed only the flailing arms and flapping hair of the newly knighted maestro, whose brainchild this whole overpopulated pageant apparently was. By turning my head slightly to the right and straining my peripheral vision, I found I could see past the tenor, the contralto, the alto, and the other two sopranos just enough to detect the smooth knot of shining dark hair on Donna's head, but nothing else. There were witticisms I wished to try on her, sardonic observations about the proceedings I was eager to make to see if they would twist that coolly elegant face sideways into the smile of amusement I had seen earlier. It was a smile that seemed to make some sort of pact with me, as if we shared something only we two were smart enough to appreciate—a smile both approving and, at the same time, shrewdly undeceived.

Hours yawned between the present and the moment when I could explore the complexities of that smile further; until then, my objective of not looking like an idiot became ever more imperative. We stood for the first septet, and before I came in, I heard Donna's voice spin out her *legato* notes like a line of calligraphy written in silver. I remember wishing all the others would sit down and be quiet so I could hear how Donna's voice blended with mine.

It went well, the first half, ending with a climax of blaring brass and tidal waves of choral sound that shook skeins of dust from the ornate ceiling. The soloists were guided back to our dressing rooms, but I didn't stay long in mine. Instead, I quietly stepped round the corner to Donna's and knocked. My hand and nerves wavered. She opened the door a tiny crack, saw who it was and, gratifyingly, opened it a bit wider. I said "hullo" and started to tell her that I thought her singing had been excellent but, without speaking, she pointed to her mouth and shook her head.

"Oh, um, I see. Vocal rest, good for you. I suppose I ought to do the same. Just wanted to ask you if you'd like to join me for a bite to eat, after, if, you know, you're not too tired or..."

This time, she held her finger up to her lips in a shushing way and I stopped, dismayed. She looked right up at me and nodded yes slowly, that twisted smile just beginning to form as she gently shut the door in my face.

I sang my rather histrionic, romantic solo that night with more sincerity than usual. "Schauemende Gotteslust!"—foaming, divine happiness, a feeling that meant more to me in terms of champagne than God, though neither mattered whatsoever as long as I could spend an hour or two with this electrifying woman.

The rest of the piece passed by like a series of thunderclaps in a rainstorm, the choruses singing in translucent sheets of sound shattered by Mahler's sobbing violins and grandiose blasts of brass. As Donna sang her final and quite celestial set of sustained high notes, giving me an attractive side glimpse of the effects of her lung capacity on her decolletage, the massed voices and instruments rose in the finale's great, long crescendo, a towering wave of choral sound cresting with a crash of trumpet, cymbal, and tympani that ebbed and built again in a last, lingering cataclysm of emotion.

Then the ceiling fell in.

It seemed to fall rather dreamily, perhaps because the initial bits didn't weigh much and fluttered as they dropped, or perhaps because I was confused by what I was seeing and didn't quite believe it. But in a split second, a large circle of decorative plaster pulled loose from the dome above us and plummeted like a gigantic saucer that had been stuck to the bottom of an uplifted teacup, crashing to pieces in the space between the stage and the first row of seats. The deafening ruckus that ensued left Mahler's lingering triple forte literally in the dust.

Everyone screamed except the conductor, who was facing the wrong way—like the deaf Beethoven at the premiere of his Ninth—and turned around, mouth silently agape, to see powder-coated patrons scrambling frantically over and around their seats to get out from under the dome's bomb bay. All of us near the edge of the stage had flinched away violently from the impact; music stands were toppled and the stupendously heavy contralto had managed to tip her chair over backward in her fright, depositing her elaborately coiffed head and boulderous upper storey in the concertmaster's lap. Masses of people poured up the aisles in spite of the stage manager, who had run onto the platform to urge everyone to remain calm and been roundly ignored. The ushers looked to be fighting for their lives, or at least their footing.

All this within seconds: I leaped up along with the other soloists to escape the danger; the tenor, bass, and I righted the contralto, to the extreme relief of the concertmaster, who had only just endeavored to yank his Stradivarius out of the way; and I found Donna pressed tightly against the stage-right wall with the other sopranos, hair as chalky-white as the Lord Chief Justice's wig. She was gripping a fistful of the stage manager's sleeve.

"Should we stay or leave?" she was asking him urgently.

"Go to your dressing rooms, quickly," he ordered, and hurried away toward the podium, dodging bodies and chairs while we soloists crowded toward the stage door. Before I went through, I glanced back and saw the maestro turn to his still-seated, rigorously obedient ensemble and lead them into the serene *Imple superna gratia* of the symphony they had just completed, to soothe everyone while the newly arrived police evacuated the public from the hall.

Remarkably, no one seemed to be injured, though the concertmaster clearly was going to need his tuxedo pressed. The other soloists kept up a hysterical babble of exclamations all the way down the corridor, with the tenor muttering, "My fucking God" over and over and the contralto simply whimpering as she swayed along on her tiny, overburdened feet.

The bass winked at me jovially. "Guess old Mahler should have included a warning in that score: Don crash helmet before playing."

Donna just kept her hand pressed to her mouth; I wondered if she felt ill. But when we reached my dressing room, she seized my hand and pulled me along to hers, slamming the door behind us. She collapsed on the couch and I realized that she was giggling uncontrollably.

"What, laughing at catastrophe, you heartless wench?"

I stood over her, arms folded, while she rolled from side to side, gasping.

"What *is* so hilarious?"

I couldn't help it, though I tried—she was so funny, trying to speak through completely incapacitating belly laughs and getting a fit of seismic hiccups that made her entire plaster-filled hairdo lurch sideways and fall. I began to laugh, too, finally doubling over in a way I never had before and tumbling onto the couch next to her. Time after time, we'd subside into a limp quietude marked only by harrumphing little aftershocks of mirth, only to erupt again in yelping convulsions. We were barking, both of us.

At last, I asked her one more time, with a dangerous remnant of chuckle bubbling up in my voice, what had set her off.

She gazed at me deeply and said, "I have no idea," which dissolved both of us all over again.

While we were falling about, I did something so unthinking that it still scares me. I pulled her in to me and kissed her.

My relationships with women up to that point had been numerous enough, but generally short and always the result of noticing someone good-looking and systematically seducing her. I liked to plan my approach carefully—it helped me to maintain a useful distance and lessened the chances of disappointment. So I had never impulsively grabbed a girl the way I grabbed Donna. It was as if I'd shot a firework through my own head. Parts of me seemed to be exploding and everything about her—her soft, wry lips, her slim body in its slippery brocade sheath, the strange smell of her, part rose garden, part construction site—etched permanent marks on my nerve endings and memory.

Most important, she kissed me back.

And then we were interrupted by someone knocking on the door, who turned out to be the hall operations director, apologizing profusely for the calamity and announcing that the cars were waiting to carry us all back to our hotel. He took in Donna's appearance with distress and asked if she had been hurt, needed a doctor, wished to call anyone. Mystified by his horror, she glanced in a mirror and burst out laughing for the zillionth time that night.

It is hard to remember now how freeing I once found her ability to find humor in anything.

I left for New York the next day, and Donna for Sydney, where she was engaged to sing the Queen of the Night in the opera house's *Magic Flute*. Our dinner hadn't lasted long—she was dreading the long flights and both of us had felt suddenly exhausted once we had got to our rooms and cleaned up—but we managed a comparatively sedate hour in a quiet alcove of the hotel bar over drinks and sandwiches before heading, rather uncertainly, to our respective beds.

I had watched her closely while she ate, still somehow amused even though neither of us was laughing. Her lips were the exact same shade as her fingernails.

She was from some middle part of North Carolina and had studied at Indiana before taking a year abroad and, essentially, never coming home. She had, she explained while working on a gourmet concoction of smoked salmon and capers on a croissant, fallen completely in love with Paris and, through school connections, gotten herself accepted as a pupil by the great coloratura, Madeleine Svorka. Madeleine, a formidable eighty and still genuflected at by music directors and hall managers the world round, had launched Donna's career.

I told her about Gunter and Juilliard.

She licked a tiny bit of dill mayonnaise from her pinky and settled back with her glass of wine, one eyebrow arched.

"Why do Juilliard graduates all talk as if they'd survived the Spanish Inquisition?"

"Oh—haughty, demanding, mercurial professors, insanely competitive students, extravagant emotions, punishing schedules. Are you saying Indiana wasn't like that?"

"Maybe for some people. We sure had our share of drama queens. But they were pretty easy to shrug off, maybe because Indiana is just this heartland-America school. Most everyone around us was so normal and laid back, it was hard for me to work myself up into some sort of hysteria about being a star. I just liked to sing. And my professors seemed to like how I did it, so I never felt like I had to claw my way past other people."

"Perhaps Indiana's not as…rigorous a program."

The other eyebrow went up, too.

"A program that's had the majority of every class debut at the Met within five years of leaving Bloomington, including Timothy Gillette, Mae McCandless, and Arthur Wu?" She grinned. "Maybe Juilliard's rigor is all mortis."

My instinct to flare at this subsided as I took in the glint in her eyes and the glowing skin that disappeared temptingly into the deep V of her blouse.

"Maybe it's easier for a beautiful woman to get ahead than for those of us whose gifts are merely musical."

"Is that a compliment or an insult?"

"Which do you prefer?"

"Whichever is the thing you really mean. I like to know what I'm dealing with."

"Alas, I am well-schooled in the arts of obscurity and personal mystery."

I think I was genuinely warning her. She narrowed her eyes, but didn't stop smiling.

She said, "Then I guess I'll have to decide whether or not your secrets are worth knowing."

IX

We exchanged addresses and phone numbers that night, but neither of us suggested anything as firm as a next date. Planning would have been difficult even if I had been inclined to risk asking her where we could meet next—after all, we lived on different continents and kept busy international schedules. I kissed her goodnight with only a slight regret that I hadn't tried harder to bed her.

And arrived in New York on the cusp of the new artistic year. Though it was still bakingly hot, especially after Edinburgh, all the musical organizations were already in a frenzy of preparations for the September events that would open their seasons in the next three or four weeks, and an exciting energy pervaded the island. I had ten days off before beginning rehearsals for *L'Ormindo* at the Bouwerij Baroque Opera in lower Manhattan, but also needed to begin learning Massenet's *Manon* in hopes that I would be offered the role of de Bretigny in a sort of postmodern production coming up at what was then called the Théâtre Musical de Paris. My agent and coach both thought venturing more deeply into French repertoire would be a good stretch for me and had started circulating my name to companies with appropriate programming.

But I had resolved not to sing at all for a couple of days, having developed a worrying rasp in my voice on the plane back from Scotland, probably resulting from a combination of jet travel, dry onboard air, vocal fatigue from the Mahler and my having gone to bed on a full stomach after my late night with Donna—always a bad idea and always a struggle to resist, because almost no one in a cast ever eats much before a performance and, consequently, nearly everyone is starving afterward and wants to go out and party, against better judgment. Even if the roof's fallen in on them.

I was actually looking forward to the enforced rest and the chance to be alone in my apartment, studying my scores and drinking a lot of therapeutic tea with honey and lemon. It works quite well, especially if you're froggy from a cold. Tea in America, by the way, is usually a contemptible experience of bags full of what tastes like dust from the bottom of a compost bin, dipped in a mug of fuzzy, not-quite-boiled water from the microwave, especially in restaurants. But by extreme good luck, I had discovered an excellent import shop not two blocks from my door and so stayed well stocked with tins of the loose Ceylon tea that I preferred, brewing it properly in a china pot.

At that time, I lived on the Upper West Side, which was just beginning to be gentrified, subletting an enormous, rent-controlled flat belonging to a friend of Gunter's who had joyfully taken a three-year post at Spoleto and understandably had no intention of leaving Italy again until he had to. The place came with a piano and a tiny sunroom that, I was relieved to discover, enjoyed a few rays of natural light only between noon and two on clear summer days and could be shielded with rattan blinds. No eye of God would penetrate my small cleft in the walls of the concrete canyon.

The radiator clanged as loudly and faithfully as church bells, though far less musically, and the whole place was furnished in that mid-century modern stuff with skinny teak legs and no comfortable cushions. The walls were covered with black-and-white head shots of jazz greats, all signed, with whom my landlord had apparently worked. I had no idea who most of them were. I believe all I ever added to the place, besides clothes in the closet, were my stacks of scores and a framed photograph of Gunter, Debbie and me at my graduation from Juilliard. But I was happy to let the flat leave its mark on me, rather than the other way round. I remember the furious rattle of Mandarin and Spanish that spattered through the windows on warm mornings from the just-opening restaurants and shops below like a bombardment of gravel. There was only one plug for four appliances in the kitchen, so I had to temporarily disconnect the refrigerator to use the coffeemaker, the toaster or the can opener. The spigot in the bathroom tub dripped incessantly. All the rooms smelled of bus exhaust and egg rolls.

It was marvelous.

I had taken to New York from the moment I became a student there. The city always gave me a sense of having been admitted to an exclusive club for rare talents who shared both a smug kind of solidarity—the kinship of insiders—and an absolute delight at not having to have much to do with one another. Living there made me feel that I arrived at the center and apex of all worthwhile people and endeavors and, paradoxically, that being alone there was the pinnacle of happiness.

Juilliard had been New York in microcosm. By the time I had completed my first year at the Chicago Conservatory, I knew that Juilliard was where I wanted to go. Even Debbie, concerned as she was about what the chilly atmosphere there might do to me—whom she had nicknamed "Robinson Caruso, the self-sufficient singer" one evening after Gunter commented that voice study had become another kind of island for me, where I liked to manage for myself—even Debbie had to admit that Juilliard was the best and that going to school in the same performing-arts complex as America's premier opera company would give me an edge as nothing else could.

And it did. I saw every single Met production staged in those four years, sitting in the balcony when student tickets were available or earning a standing-room spot at the back of the house by handing out programs, and eventually taking an occasional role onstage as a super in the more populous shows, always watching the best in the world do what I wanted to do. It took only one semester for me to abandon piano altogether, the way a slave would abandon his manacles; the sense of, not just release, but of being reunited with myself—of my desire to create music and the freedom to make my own voice the natural medium of that creation suddenly fitting together—gave me a short experience of pure euphoria that I've never felt the like of since.

I only gradually realized that the ecstasy had simply masked the presence of Mother in my head, not banished it.

She had not discovered my singing until she flew with me to New York, to deliver me to Juilliard after my final summer vacation at home. Gunter and Debbie had met us there, to help us cope with the logistics and, though they never said so, to provide a neutral diplomatic zone between Mother and me. We all stayed at the same hotel in the West Sixties for three days, Mother accompanying me to orientation meetings and helping me unpack while the Hellmans compiled shopping lists and went out foraging for dormitory furnishings and supplies to brighten my dull-green cubicle of concrete blocks. It was at our meeting with my advisor when the musical scales, so to speak, fell from Mother's eyes. If not her ears. This advisor, a round, rather jolly functionary of the music department, was carefully running down my list of courses, explaining why the required ones were required and suggesting paths my studies could take when the basics had been got out of the way, when we got to my voice and intro-to-vocal-performance classes. In that instant, the air in the room seemed to crystallize into a mist of particulate ice. Dr. Miller's own voice wavered and failed mid-word as he gazed at Mother, correctly identifying her as the source of this unnerving atmospheric phenomenon, but visibly bewildered as to its cause and alarmed at the contrasting blaze of rebellious fury on my face.

I had known this moment was coming, of course—had known I couldn't hide it from her any longer and didn't want to—but bracing for it hadn't made my fear and resentment any less. I abruptly stood and walked to the window, while Mother pretended not to have heard the professor correctly.

"Choice? Choice class? You mean he must choose an elective?"

Each word landed with a cold bang, like an ice cube dropped on the floor.

"N-o-o-o-o-o…" Miller stalled, taking a moment to knock the dottle from his pipe into the metal dustbin by his desk.

Apparently, it had gone out in the sudden subzero temperature. Out of the corner of my eye, I could see Mother staring at him. He stared at me. I stared at the traffic on Broadway.

"Voice. Voice is what I said," he enunciated loudly and slowly, turning to Mother. "Your son will be studying with Borrelli, one of our best—a baritone himself and an opera artist of the first rank."

Mother stood and faced me, though she didn't seem to see that I was there, her gaze stopping at some middle point between us. She said, "I wish he had been born mute, if he had to be born at all," and left the room.

I didn't see her again for years.

She evidently went straight to the hotel to pack, leaving a one-line note before taking a cab to the airport. She didn't even tell Gunter and Debbie she was going. I went searching for them after the horrified Dr. Miller first tried to follow her, then jogged back to me nearly incoherent with distress, apologizing and offering to call her and help me, muttering with every second breath, "I'm sure she didn't mean it," and running his hand through his hair. He insisted on walking me to the hotel and, when Mother couldn't be found, stayed with me while I knocked on the Hellmans' door two floors up. They didn't answer, but emerged from the elevator just as Miller was urging me to come back to school with him and wait. He told them what had happened without repeating Mother's words; Gunter's lips got thinner and thinner, while Debbie put one hand on my arm and the other over her mouth.

I don't remember saying a syllable. Eventually, Miller left after assuring Debbie and Gunter that I could call on him for anything, and we went back down to the lobby to get a key to my and Mother's suite. She had clearly decamped. The note said, "I've paid for the hotel and for my sins and your life is your own now to ruin as you wish."

She didn't sign it.

Gunter and Debbie got me moved into the dorm, took me to dinner, made sure I had cash and my new bankbook and phone numbers and my schedule. They wanted to stay on an extra couple of days, but I didn't see the point—I'd be busy getting used to my whereabouts and roommate and they had students to prepare for back in Chicago.

I knew they blamed themselves, regretted not insisting that I tell Mother about the singing when I first started. They didn't see that the timing wouldn't have made any difference to Mother—I knew all along that she would react badly and irrevocably to my desire to sing, no matter when she found out. But it would have made a terrible difference to me. If she had found out earlier, she would have tried to stop me. But she hadn't got that chance. And now I was a promising talent, about to study my art at the best school in America and likely to succeed at something I loved, maybe all the more passionately because she hated it so strangely. My way was paid through my own ability. I didn't care that she hadn't wanted me. I didn't care.

"Do not take those words to heart," Gunter said before he and Debbie got in the cab to LaGuardia. "They were meant to wound and I know they did. But I promise you they are not true. Your mother is deeply afraid for you, I think. I wish I knew why."

They hugged and kissed me and left.

I was on my own in New York. And as I said, I took to it.

X

Six months after the Mahler Eighth, I got the role in *Manon*. I'd actually put rather a lot of effort into it, for me: endless language study with a French expert that David found for me over my, I think justifiable, protests that all those high-school courses plus language diction at Juilliard ought to be sufficient; daily score study and practice at home; and two sessions per week with David instead of one, until I could sing my entire part perfectly from memory and practically *a cappella*. My agent said his contact at the Théâtre Musical told him that the music director assumed I *was* French after hearing my tape. I've always had rather a gift for languages, especially German, which I prefer. It has backbone.

Still, I was excited about the *Manon*, which was scheduled for the following year and which I would never have got at all if the baritone they'd originally cast months earlier hadn't been made a better offer by La Scala. *Traviata*, I think. Not only was *Manon* quite different in period and style from most of what I'd been singing, but it would also be my Paris debut. Also, though I wasn't admitting it to myself then, the faint possibility of seeing Donna again was sending disproportionately powerful shocks through my nervous system.

I certainly hadn't been going out of my way to think about her. In fact, ever since the Edinburgh trip, I'd been distracting myself nicely with two other girls: one a fellow student of David's who'd just graduated from Yale and moved to the city, an alluring but aloof alto who tepidly agreed to go to dinner with me once in a while when I could break her ferocious focus on career development; and the other an enthusiastic little girl with mouse-brown hair, who was from Queens and worked in the Lincoln Center music library. Her astonishingly copious and undulant breasts—like twin bowls of fine custard, they were—

counted as her only above-average quality, but she made up for this in valuable ways. However, knowing I was going to be in Paris revived the memory of Donna's effect on me and she began to present herself in my thoughts at unexpected moments.

I'd heard from her only once in all this time and only in response to something I'd sent her a short time after we left Scotland. It was an item from the *Times* noting that Usher Hall was to be closed for the remainder of the year, the trustees regarding the disintegrating ceiling as the signal for a thorough renovation and redesign of the entire facility. I'd circled the area in the accompanying photo where we had been standing when the plaster fell and labeled it "The damned spot in our Scottish play. Hope your 'Hölle' didn't bring down the house—in that way, at least—in Sydney. Cheers, etc." A month later, she sent a postcard from Atlanta—a picture of the football stadium, with the note, "Back in the South again, singing for my supper: the Schubert Mass in E FL and "The Star Spangled Banner" in NFL. Happy holidays, Donna."

Witty, blithe, unrevealing; except for the fact that she'd sent it at all, no indication of interest whatsoever.

I was tempted to write again to tell her I'd be in Paris next winter, but kept being stopped by the feeling that next winter was both too far in the future to capture her attention and not far enough to prevent her from planning to be somewhere else should she wish to elude me. So I capped my pen, as it were, and let spring flow by in a steady current of professional preparations, minor engagements stateside, and as much diversion as I could coax from my available hours and companions. Among the appearances I was looking forward to was a weekend at Tanglewood that would allow me to meet up with Rob, who had stayed in Massachusetts after graduating from Berklee and was dividing his time between the band he was in and a small recording studio he had launched somewhere out near Framingham. He was planning to drive out to hear me sing *Carmina Burana* with the BSO and then take me back with him to the Boston area for a couple of days.

It had been nearly two years since I'd seen him last, on a visit to Chicago, and he'd been somewhat scarce at the time because he was painfully involved with a girl who ended up jilting him for her forty-year-old literature professor at Wellesley. I have to say I wasn't surprised—Rob couldn't see through women any better than he could see through that prodigious mop of hair I assumed he still had.

We seldom called or wrote each other, but Rob would occasionally drop a tape in the mail to me so I could hear what he was working on, which had gone, over the years, from intricate, improvisatory stuff that sounded almost like electronic Bach cadenzas to a much simpler, rattly and raucous sound, like football fans chanting while banging away on dustbin lids. Rob referred to this as "The New Wave." In spite of his taste for electrified bashings, though, he was quite enthusiastic about hearing *Carmina*, which even musical ignoramuses had become enthralled by in recent years because some filmmaker had scored his horror movie with it. Rob, of course, was not an ignoramus, but he did tend to respond to the more colorful and thrilling works in the classical canon, rather than, say, your Schoenbergs and Pendereckis. And I had to agree with him about Penderecki, at least, who always made me feel as if I'd been marooned on a desolate asteroid with a toddler and a drawerful of silverware.

I was expecting to enjoy *Carmina*—we singers have limited opportunity for giving the audience that kind of rollicking good scare—but in the event, it turned out rather better for the musicians than for the crowd: A thunderstorm broke just as we began "O Fortuna," which heightened the piece's powers of darkness to hair-raising levels, but most of the lawn-sitters had to flee because there wasn't room in the Shed for all the extra bodies. Luckily, I had got Rob a proper seat, so he was able to hear the entire performance, which he labeled "medieval and macabre, man."

"Like *The Name of the Rose* meets the *Monster Mash*!" he marveled, leaning against the wall of my dressing room with his hands in the pockets of his carpenter pants as I changed out of my tux and into some jeans for the car trip to Boston. "That guy's real first name oughta be Boris, you know? Then it would have been written by Boris Carl Orff. How appropriate is that?"

"What's *The Name of the Rose*?"

"You still don't read, do you? It just came out—kind of a demonic murder mystery set in the Dark Ages. Lots of evil, hooded monks, like the emperor in *Star Wars*. And don't say, 'What's *Star Wars*?'"

"Yes, even I know what *Star Wars* is."

"Anyway, great concert. Thanks for getting me in."

"I'm glad I got you all the way in, or you'd have been soaked." I pulled a plastic bag over the tux and picked up my overnight case. "I'm starved. Let's stop somewhere to eat before we get on the highway, shall we?"

"We shall, man, as long as you promise not to use the archaic conditional auxiliary when you're ordering fast food, okay?"

We wolfed down cheeseburgers and fries at a diner outside Lenox and hopped on the turnpike around midnight, driving through a Western Massachusetts night made black as a locked closet by looming hills, huge trees, and remaining storm clouds. Rob had a giant box of tapes in the car and sang along scratchily with Squeeze and Sting and abandon while I rested my own voice and dozed a little, vaguely seeing the momentary aureoles of light that were signs for Westfield and Springfield and Worcester fizz through my eyelashes. Eventually, my sleepiness wore off and I sat up, trying to determine how far from Rob's place we might be.

"All right, Rob? Want me to drive for a while?"

"No thanks, man, I'm okay. Besides, when was the last time you were behind the wheel of a car? Senior prom?"

"As I'm sure you remember, I didn't go anywhere near senior prom. And it hasn't been *that* long ago—I drove Gunter's car around Winnetka last visit."

"So, what, a couple years? Anyway, no point now—we're almost there."

He indicated an upcoming exit sign for Northborough and Framingham and changed lanes. There was almost no one on the road but us, and yet Rob carefully checked the mirrors and signaled before steering to the right.

"You drive cautiously for a hippie rock musician."

"Anybody who had to ride with my brother when he had his learner's permit would end up driving like a librarian in a funeral procession. I'm still amazed to be alive after that time he tried to turn into the mall and missed and ended up doing a full doughnut on Lake Cook Road at rush hour."

"I think I remember you telling me about that. The car was completely unscathed, wasn't it?"

"Unlike my psyche. After we got home, it took my mom about a half an hour to pry my hands off the armrest. I had upholstery fibers in my braces. Look, there's my studio!"

Rob was aiming the car up a crowded commercial strip of garish franchise restaurants and gas stations, all closed at nearly three a.m. He slowed the car and I followed his finger to a non-descript block of masonry lighted a dull pink by the neon sign of a hair salon next door. There didn't appear to be any windows on the first floor; on the second, the shabby stucco-looking walls were broken by long slits, like gun emplacements, skirted at the bottom by semi-circles of wrought-iron bars. Above the heavy wooden front door were the words Sancho Studios.

"Did you choose the building because it suited the name, or the other way round?"

"Actually, I picked the name Quixote first, but pretty much nobody in the music business could pronounce it right and I knew if the name Quicks-oat stuck, I'd spend my life explaining that we were not a cereal company. So when I found this perfect building, I decided on Sancho, instead. Suits me better, anyway."

"Why, because you're always getting your ass kicked?"

"My ahss? Yeah, it happens on a daily basis. Sometimes I even kick it myself. And how would you know about Sancho and his ahss anyway, you British book-o-phobe?"

"It's an *opera*. But how would you know, when you think all music began with Little Richard?"

"It *did* begin with him. He's a reincarnation of whatever Greek guy invented that phriggin' mode."

"That's pronounced FRIH-jee-an."

"I know, you ahsshole."

Thus we stayed alert for another couple of miles; Rob lived in a flat in a rather charming old Victorian house on a street of enormous and even older maple trees several blocks from the thoroughfare we'd been on. He hadn't lived there long, I found—he'd camped at Sancho during most of the remodeling process, sleeping on a mattress in the upstairs office of what had recently been a bar and dance club called Seville—and so most of his stuff was still in boxes that were currently serving as tables and footstools. But he did have a proper bed in the bedroom and a fold-out couch in the sitting room, and so we got to sleep just as the sky was graying.

It must not have been long after that I found myself struggling to wake up. Even though I somehow knew I was still asleep and dreaming, I could see the light coming and felt a growing desperation to get out of bed. The sky outside the window got brighter and brighter, soundlessly turning from blue to violet to pink, and I tried over and over to rise, frightened that orange-yellow would follow and I'd glimpse the edge of the disc, too late to move, too late to hide from God's eye. It would catch me, and I'd be exposed, trapped. My arms and legs were cast iron, immovable; my chest strained upward against the blanket. It was coming—a blazing silence—it saw me! And at that instant, a great shadow moved between me and the window like a cloak spreading out to shield me, a cloak that swayed and whispered, not as in a breeze, but as if alive. And I thought it had saved me, but it grew darker, blotting out everything, and in terror I saw a thin ray of light pierce the cloak, burning through it and through me like a fiery stake. And this pinpoint flame, this fierce iris in the eye of God, was Mother's eye, and the cloak was Mother, and she rose up to wrap me in her darkness and I couldn't breathe or move or make a sound. She had become the thing she feared and fought against and I was pulled down into it as if the sun had become a black hole.

I woke hearing my name and when I opened my eyes, Rob was standing next to me with his hand on my shoulder and a disconcerted half-smile on his face. Rain poured outside.

"You okay? That must have been some nightmare."

"I didn't…" I coughed and sat up. "I was…it was like drowning in my sleep and knowing I had to wake up to save myself and not being able to."

I wiped my face with the damp sheet.

"Well, you were putting up a good fight. You were yelling and thrashing around so loud, I thought Mrs. Emmett was going to come bang on the door."

"Yelling?"

"Well…actually, more like sobbing." Rob shrugged in a careless way contradicted by the worry in his eyes.

I didn't answer. The terror was still with me, a terror that was of something like death, and yet worse: an imprisonment in silence and solitude. I felt I had been struggling against being buried alive, trapped where no one would ever hear or find me.

Rob sat on a corner of the fold-out while I pressed my hands to my eyes and tried to breathe slowly, as if holding a long note, but without vocalizing it. The familiar exercise calmed me a bit and, at length, I got up to get a drink of water.

"Better?" Rob asked when I came back from the bathroom.

"Somewhat, yes. Thanks."

"It's only nine—you wanna go back to sleep?"

"No. But I can find something to occupy me if you do."

"No, I think I'm up. And even if I weren't, I'm too ravenous to go back to bed without breakfast first. Feel like food?"

My stomach instantly felt cavernous and echoing. "*Yes*. Let's go out. I'll buy. Where is there?"

"Great diner half a mile away. They'll make you anything you want."

I forced a smile. "Will they make me a star?"

XI

After heaps of eggs and bacon, as well as several cups of muddy-tasting, but therapeutically strong hot tea that fully brought me round at last, we drove about for a while, Rob serving as tour guide, and finally ended up at the studio. I wasn't expecting much and was, apparently, visibly surprised when we walked in, because Rob laughed at my expression.

The downstairs had held a kitchen, bar, and dance floor when the place was Seville, with a private party room, rest rooms and offices on the second floor. Rob had created a small lobby out of the entranceway and coatroom: It held a semicircular, wood-and-steel reception desk and an enormous black-leather couch, above which glowed an abstract piece of artwork made from neon tubes. A short, gray-carpeted ramp with wrought-iron railings rose from the floor at the back to a black inner door. Behind that, the refinished dance floor had been encircled by sound-proof walls painted a dark, smooth red to make the main recording studio; the bar area had been turned into a glass-fronted control booth. The ramp and the interior walls all curved like the reception desk, giving the whole space a sinuous kind of flow that Rob said was his attempt to give physical shape to music.

I'm afraid I stared.

"That's astonishingly...conceptual." I squinted at him. "Did you give me any clues in our youth that you were capable of intellectual depth?"

He grabbed a capo that was lying on a nearby amp and pretended to whip me with it.

"My blacklight poster of Bullwinkle was a dead giveaway, nimrod. Don't tell me you weren't impressed even then."

"Well, I'm impressed now. Ouch."

"Whoops. Got away from me. But you deserved it."

"So what about the second floor?"

"Not done yet. It's still a mess, but you can take a look if you want. Just watch out for the ladders 'n shit."

We climbed the stairs and picked our way among paint cans and stacks of ceiling tiles while Rob told me how the business was set up—how his dad and a band promoter Rob knew had each put up a fourth of the cost of the building renovations and furnishings, and Rob had got a bank loan for the other half using his tons of musical instruments as collateral. A cousin in Braintree was helping with the books, five other bands he knew from college had signed to do their next albums there and his own bandmates and former classmates and professors were promoting the studio to all the musicians they knew around the Northeast.

I only half-listened after that. I felt weary and strangely discouraged: My spirits seemed to be falling like the barometric pressure, giving me a sensation of distance and disorientation, as if everything around me were small and far away. I didn't want to hear anymore how supportive Rob's family and friends were of his ambitions. The shadow from my dream suddenly reappeared in my head and I shuddered.

"Hey, what's up with you, anyway?"

Rob was standing at the top of the stairs with his car keys in his hand. "I've asked you three times if you want to go now and you haven't heard me at all. You look like you don't feel too good, either."

"Sorry. Tired mostly, I think."

"Wanna go get a beer or something?"

"Sure, I... Why do you still have *that*?"

I had looked past him into the office, at a framed photo propped up on the windowsill. A young woman with long blond hair and denim overalls was laughing as she pointed a water pistol at the camera—the girl who'd jilted Rob two years ago.

Rob shrugged. "Why not?"

"Why not?" I flung my arms wide. "Where do I begin?"

He started down the stairs. Halfway to the bottom, he turned around and said, "I like the picture."

I caught up to him. "Still like *her* is more like it. And after what she did to you, the bi—"

"Don't call her that."

Even though he'd flicked off the lights, I could tell he was frowning; Rob never frowned.

"Yes, I still like her, okay? In spite of what she did. Maybe she never really loved me, or maybe it went to her head, landing a famous Pulitzer winner, or maybe she just honestly fell for him, I don't know. But she meant a lot to me and that was two good years that I'm not gonna just pretend didn't happen."

He locked the front door behind us as if locking a lid on the subject, but I wasn't finished yet.

"And you're going to keep her picture right there so you can see her mock you every day and never forget the pain and rejection, I assume. That's just pure masochism, Rob. If I were you, I'd burn the damned thing."

"But you're *not* me. You're absolutely nothing *like* me." He stopped dead in the parking lot as if fully registering the idea for the first time. "You know, I've always tried to cut you some slack about the way you react to girls—women—because it's clear that you have a problem with your mom and it spills over onto your world view of females, okay? But I've never seen you give *them* a break. Eh-ver. They're just people, not some conspiracy of demons sent here to fuck you over. They're as insecure and confused as we are."

"Speak for yourself."

"I *am* speaking for myself, but I have to speak for you, too, because you never admit to any weaknesses, even when they're practically stamped on your face like 'fragile' on a shipping box."

"Oh, bullshit. Whatever problems I've had have forced me to wise up and be tough, not sit around mooning like a sap over some mercenary bit of tail who turned me down."

Rob took a deep breath.

"Tough is not the same thing as offensive. Have a nice walk to the train station, dickhead."

He got in the car.

"Sorry. Rob, I'm—"

He drove away. Actually left me standing on the pavement with my mouth agape. And bloody stupid I was to have opened it in the first place, I realized. It took a lot to make Rob mad, whereas my own anger lay very close to the surface, and I seldom made any effort to suppress it, most people being the provoking idiots they are. But Rob wasn't an idiot; I was genuinely fond of him and I didn't want him to punish himself with mocking reminders of this collegiate she-Judas. He *was* being a sap, but I supposed I shouldn't have said so in quite that way.

I had turned around to start the trudge back to Rob's place in hopes of finding him there, when his car bounced back into the parking lot and pulled up beside me. He gave me a grim little smile.

"Just because *you* fly off the handle doesn't mean I should, too. C'mon, get in. You're gonna buy me that beer and we'll talk."

I climbed in and he wrenched the wheel, steering from the thoroughfare onto a two-lane road that quickly left suburbia behind and wound through fields and thick stands of trees, interspersed with dilapidated bungalows, gaunt farmhouses and the occasional, rusty-looking old gas station or shabby market. He eventually pulled into one of the last, which had been extended with a boxy addition of rough planks painted dark brown. A lighted beer sign hung in its single dirty window. I followed Rob into this smoky hole; he hailed the man behind the bar like an old friend, raised two fingers and nudged me toward a rickety table in the back room. Except for us, the barman and a seedy figure in greasy pants working the lone pinball machine near the door, the place was empty. Rob plopped down on a metal chair with a torn vinyl seat. I sat gingerly on its twin; the barman brought over a pair of brown bottles, opened them, and returned to the bar without a word.

Rob took a long pull on his beer, and while his mouth was occupied, I said, "I apologize for what I said. I didn't mean it. It was…I was…wrong."

He gave me a look. "That's the first time I've ever heard you say that. How hard was it?"

"Pretty hard."

He grinned. "Should be easier next time, then. But you're wrong twice: You did mean it, no matter how sorry you are for pissing me off."

I didn't answer—what could I say?—and he took another swig in the silence.

"I think," he said, putting his bottle down and reflectively peeling bits of label away, "that what you're *not* wrong about is the masochism. I suppose it is kind of dumb to want to keep reminding yourself about somebody who ripped your heart out, but it isn't the pain I want to hang onto: it's, like, the euphoria—every moment with her was special, everything I saw and felt happened in this kind of DayGlo color, like I'd never been really awake before and now I was, and life felt *electric*, like a charge was running through me all the time. Just because she was in the world. And life is so gray without her that the jolt I get from looking at her picture is the only way I can tell I'm not unconscious."

He drained his bottle. "Hasn't anyone ever made you feel like that?"

"I'd never *let* anyone make me feel like that," I said, but stopped abruptly. My automatic sarcasm felt unexpectedly dishonest; Donna's face had appeared in my head and I knew suddenly—or maybe *admitted* is a more accurate term—that she had, in fact, made me feel exactly that way for a little while. And I had liked it.

"What are you scowling about?" Rob's gaze was curious.

"Oh, nothing."

"Be-e-ep! You just set off my lie detector."

"I'm not lying—it really is nothing."

I brought my beer to my mouth and discovered that I had already finished it. Rob's eyes stayed fixed on me, unblinking.

"I was just thinking about this soprano I met in Scotland," I finally muttered.

"Aha. And *what* were you thinking about her?"

"Only that she was rather more interesting than most females I know."

"In what way? Humungous boobs? Gymnastic skills?"

"No, no, nothing like that."

"*Nothing* like that? So what's the attraction?"

"I just think getting her into bed would be an intriguing test of my abilities."

"So she's either insatiable or a member of a strict religious order."

"No, you smug pain in the ass. She's very bright. Witty. Funny. An amazing singer."

"Jesus." Rob threw himself back in his chair. "Why is it so damned hard to get you to admit that you like a girl because she's a great human being and not just a great lay?"

"I don't know if she's a great lay. That's what I want to find out."

"Yeah, but the point is, if she does turn out to be a great lay, it'll be at least partly because you like her. Admire her, even. Right?"

"Possibly."

"I give up." Rob twisted around to catch the bartender's eye.

"Let me ask you this," he said as the second pair of bottles arrived. "Do you think there are any good women?"

"Well, of course. Debbie. Your mother."

"Two, huh? Well, okay: If you can recognize that even one woman on earth is a good person, why do you always assume that every girl you date or sleep with is a criminal bitch plotting to control and torture you?"

"It's easier to appreciate a woman who has no power over you."

"But you're still assuming that any power a woman would have over you would be evil. Why couldn't it be good power? The power to make you feel happy, loved, safe?"

"I'm about as likely to find a girl who makes me feel happy and safe as I am to marry Debbie."

"You're saying a kind, caring, trustworthy woman isn't sexy?"

"Well, not if she's thirty years older than I am. But that's not the point. The point is, no sexy woman is trustworthy because, one, a sexy woman knows she can get you to do whatever she tells you, and two, there's a long line of other guys waiting to take your place if you *don't* do whatever she tells you."

I knew a second beer would irritate my throat, but I started drinking it, anyway.

Rob smirked at me annoyingly. "Wow. Wow. So all sexy women are manipulative and fickle."

"Wasn't yours?"

He seemed to darken and diminish, like a match flickering out.

"I don't know," he said quietly. "But I don't think being jerked around by one means you're doomed to being jerked around by all of them. Unless you expect to be. I think if you expect to be hurt, you'll find a way to make it happen. You'll never be able to believe in a girl enough for her to believe in you."

I said, "Problem is, who goes first?"

XII

I had just trudged about twenty blocks in a filthy downpour that was as much ice as rain—rush hour, not a cab available on the entire island—and dripped up four flights to my apartment, slamming the door on an altogether abysmal day. Everything I had on was splattered with dark-brown spots from the traffic plowing through puddles; David had pestered me all afternoon about visualizing my head voice as a stovepipe, of all wretched things, in the pathetically mistaken belief that focusing my tone toward the top of my skull would miraculously open up the high Gs that he'd decided should be within my grasp. And the topper: That stupid little cow at the library had said she'd put aside one of the scores for Sessions's *Montezuma* for me, but forgot, and so they'd all been checked out before I got there and I had to go clear over to the Juilliard store and buy one. I was through with her as of that moment, and she knew it, going all weepy and clingy as a wet slice of bread, big tits heaving. I practically had to scrape her off me.

It wasn't until I'd showered and made my tea that I noticed the light blinking on the answering machine. It was a message from my manager. "More cast changes for *Manon*," he had said. "Delaurier is out—ruptured a cord practicing eight hours a day. Jesus, she needs her head examined along with her throat. So they got Donna Salter—from your Mahler Eight, remember? Seems she lives right there in Paris. That's your new Manon, assuming she doesn't bail, too. See you Tuesday."

My new Manon. I was going to be singing with Donna, singing *to* her, for four weeks in Paris. Even in that first shock of excitement—so much like what I always felt at the very second of realizing that the girl I was trying to make love to was going to let me—even in the midst of the hot hormonal rush of anticipation that the thought of seeing Donna sent through me,

I also felt a peculiar gut sensation of momentousness about our being brought together in this way, as if I were about to step off a cliff: somehow powerless in a way that was part flying, part plummeting.

I had my tea with no recollection of it, finding myself an hour later at the piano, with my hands running through the *Manon* score on muscle memory alone and my head full of wild scenarios. I was coldly glad all over again to have got rid of Ms. Custard Cups that afternoon, despite the anger she had cost me; now there need be no further scenes or dreary sobbing over the phone or let's-just-be-friends hypocrisies to endure should things heat up with Donna. There would be no need to call the alto at all—I could hold her in reserve, I supposed, and she'd never even miss me in the meantime, the ambitious cunt. I said the word in my head deliberately, to shock myself, and found that I was not awfully shocked after all, though a dark little bolt of shame at my own unfairness briefly shot through my conscience. It soon faded.

The holidays passed quickly, with several Christmas parties and a weekend spent in the company of Gunter and Debbie, who came through New York on their way home from a Hanukkah visit with their eldest son and grandchildren in Rhode Island. No word from Mother, of course, nor did I send any. I imagined her, hair graying, exchanging tiny remembrances with a tubby Brownlea in the glow of an artificial tree that they'd decorated with false cheer and Mother's ancient, disintegrating trove of glass angels. The usual tinned figgy pudding baking in the oven while the house baked in the sun. Brownlea pounding out "Good King Wenceslaus" and "Adeste Fidelis" on the piano that only he ever touched now. Mother pulling open her Christmas cracker and playing the old record of Strauss favorites without me.

I had gone to St. Patrick's on Christmas Eve to hear my old professor, Borrelli, perform *Messiah* with the Juilliard orchestra. The sanctuary had been packed with a brilliant crowd that reduced the godliness of the event to a bearable minimum of solemnity, and I'd joined Borrelli and his family and some of his students for a noisy dinner of lobster and champagne afterward in a private dining room at the Plaza, walking—on purpose this time—back across town alone after midnight, admiring the glow of the Christmas lights through a thin accumulation of flurrying snow that made each bulb resemble a frosted jelly candy. When I got home, no one made me wait until next morning to open my cards and gifts from the Hellmans or unwrap the Sancho T-shirt from Rob or say my prayers before being allowed to get into bed. No one forced me up at dawn to dress and play my piece at church before being permitted even to light the tree and see what was under it. No one prevented me from eating toffees and cake before I'd forked down some leaden holiday meal of ham and beef and sprouts.

For my Christmas dinner, I followed the toffees with takeout Chinese food and watched old movies on what I had long ago learned to call TV, until I fell asleep on the sofa. I lived by no one's leave now, abused by no one's love.

Eight weeks later, on a clear and frigid day, I reclined in a chair 30,000 feet over the Atlantic, wondering why on—or above—earth I was dizzily anticipating this encounter with Donna when I so entirely exulted in a life unbound by emotional obligations. Probably the moment after I got her into bed—*if* I did—she'd assume I was hers and start planning for me to do everything with her and for her from then on. Why do women always believe that the plugging of one set of genitals into another amounts to snapping shut a padlock that irrevocably bonds two lives, forever sharing some mysterious system of unseen plumbing through which whole hearts and souls are exchanged on the instant? As if two lodgers became one for eternity just because they shared a loo on the same hallway for a night?

Why couldn't it just feel good without feeling fatal?

And yet, some things might feel so good that you're willing to ignore the fact that you're risking your life to get them. Had my parents risked their lives for each other? One was dead, the other—what?—deranged, possibly, or perhaps just severely disappointed. Would it have been better for them if they had resisted their attraction instead of attempting to create a family? It seemed to me that it could hardly have been worse.

Outside the window, daylight was passing us going in the opposite direction; the sun setting behind us tinged the rough wool of clouds below with electric orange on one side, deepening the shadows on the other to a gray-purple that looked like puddles left by the misty, darkening sky ahead. For a moment, the vivid colors and the endless expanses of vaporous space looked so like sundown on our cove at home that I felt actual pain, as if I were trying to inhale with a great weight on my chest. Far below me, unseen, was the ocean, a body that held me, never entirely separate and never wholly joined, the two of us sharing a border the way uneasy neighbors share a property line after many years: with outward indifference and secret alertness to incursions. On all three of my islands—the England of my birth, the tropical outpost of my childhood, and the New York of my choosing and ambition—the ocean remained on its side and I on mine, both of us watchful, never friends, but momentary allies of circumstance each day when water swallowed sun.

It had been noon when my father was found, tangled in shoal grass and half-submerged off a windward beach a mile or two from our own. I had been at lessons all morning, distracted by arithmetic and William the Conqueror from the niggle of fear infecting me since my breakfast alone with a strained and exhausted-looking Mother, who said only that she had slept badly and that Father had—as he hadn't ever before, to my knowledge—left early for school. She didn't say why, and when I got to school myself, Father wasn't there. I knew something was seriously wrong, in the way children and animals do, viscerally, from a change in atmosphere and routine, a strange quality of light and silence made all the scarier by the density of unvoiced secrets in the air.

The grave-faced headmaster had come into my classroom

just before lunch and whispered something to my teacher, who looked at me with an expression that magicked the niggle into monstrous terror, freezing me to my chair when he told me to go with Professor Kemble to his office. The two of them coaxed me out from behind my desk with a gentleness more unnerving than anger. I walked wordlessly with Kemble to his study, my eyes fixed on the smudged paint and scuffed baseboards of a corridor I seemed never to have seen before.

"I'm very sorry to have to tell you," the headmaster said softly when he had closed the door and we had sat down on a pair of old leather chairs by a window overlooking the always-green cricket field, "that your father has had an accident. A… bad accident. You will need to go home, but your mother is quite upset, naturally, and cannot come for you, so I have asked Mrs. Embry to drive you there, and stay with you a while if she is needed."

Mrs. Embry was the school nurse. I thought Kemble meant that she was going to stay to help Father get better, and I didn't want her. I didn't like her and her short, mannish gray hair and thick fingers and I thought Father should have our doctor instead.

"Thank you," I remember saying very properly, "but I'm sure Father will want Mother to call Dr. Russell to take care of him."

Kemble rubbed his eyes. "Mrs. Embry is not for your father. She is for you and your mother."

He walked me to the infirmary and Mrs. Embry put me in her rusty old Midget, a disgraceful automobile that I was embarrassed to be seen in, and I cringed under the curious gapes of the PE class running sprints on the track by the car park. It was the dry season—a high blue sky with a few unthreatening cumulus clouds piled near the horizon, hardly visible as Mrs. Embry steered through the palmy residential streets between school and my home. She seemed to know exactly where I lived—at least, she asked no questions, didn't talk at all, actually, for which I was grateful. I don't think I could have spoken;

there was at once too much and nothing in my head, and I simply gazed at the window as if something out there mattered, when all I saw behind my eyes was black dread and all I felt was the downward pull of the great sickening stone that Kemble's words had stitched into my gut.

Mrs. Embry pulled the Midget over in front of our house, behind a police car—why were the police here?—and walked round as if to help me out, but I wasn't a baby and got out by myself before she could touch the door handle. She smiled at me in what I suppose she intended to be a kindly, heartening way, but there was a dark pity in her eyes that made me want to smash the look off her face and I ran up the steps and through the door without waiting for her.

Mother was standing in the middle of the sitting room with a policeman who was holding a clipboard. I don't know why I remember the clipboard; I don't remember anything else about either of them except that when Mother looked at me, all I could see in her eyes was horror. Not love or grief—just the stark, blank, bottomless stare of someone about to be executed. She didn't embrace me; the policeman must have wondered about that. But he just excused himself and stepped into the kitchen so that we could be alone.

I said, "Mother, where's Father? What's happened to Father?" and she crouched down until our heads were about level and grasped my shoulders, more as if to steady herself than me, looking at my face with that stare that didn't seem to see me at all. She said slowly, as if testing the words, "He drowned. He's…dead."

I shouted at her, "He's not dead! Father's not dead!" and burst into tears.

She let go my arms and sank to her knees and didn't say another word. I cried and called for my father until Mrs. Embry and the policeman both came into the room to comfort me. Mrs. Embry hugged me and I let her. The policeman cleared his throat and laid his hand on my back for a moment. "Your dad was taken to hospital, son. We hoped the doctors could do summat for him, but they could na'. By the time he turned up on the beach, it was too late. I'm sorry. Everyone's sorry."

Keeping hold of me with one meaty arm, Mrs. Embry patted Mother.

"Madam? Madam? Would you like me to call anyone?"

Mother made no sound. Mrs. Embry pulled a clean handkerchief out of her uniform pocket and wiped my face with it.

"Do you have any other family here?" she asked me. "No? Any friends we could call on to help?" I shook and shook my head. No close friends. *Not* the priest. At last, I gasped out the doctor's name and she telephoned him after sitting me down in the kitchen with a glass of milk and a biscuit I didn't want. Dr. Russell arrived just as the policeman had given up trying to get any more information from Mother.

"She's in shock," I heard the doctor say. I didn't know what that meant and deduced she must be ill, because I saw him give her an injection and I began to cry again because I thought Mother was going to die, too. The kitchen was warm—it was February and brightly sunny out—but I couldn't stop shivering and soon Dr. Russell asked Mrs. Embry to make me a cup of tea or cocoa and see that I drank it.

I awoke hours later, in the dark. My brain felt murky and strange, like the room itself, as if my thoughts were trying to rise from the bottom of a well full of treacle, but my stomach understood that some profound disaster had taken place and I was sick all over my sheets in the nightmare blackness of this alien space. Feet came running and the opening door poured light into the room, but the silhouette bending over me was not Mother—it was Mrs. Embry, and though I was glad to recognize something, my memory of the afternoon burst in along with her and I screamed and screamed until I thought I would suffocate, while she held me to her, sick and all, and rocked.

I don't recall anymore how much time elapsed between that first night and the funeral, just the hallucinatory flicker of hours and people as they passed, bringing light and shadows, leaving things and taking things away, accompanied by a continuo of low murmurs. I stayed in my room a great deal, I think, lying on my bed amid a pile of storybooks and sporting magazines that Mrs. Embry had given me along with sandwiches and glasses of lemonade on trays. She seemed to have adopted us.

On the day of the funeral, she came to my room and said she had made me some porridge, and that after I ate it, she would draw me a bath so I could get dressed in my Sunday clothes. We would be going to the church.

I saw Mother awake, sitting on the edge of her bed while Mrs. Embry tried to persuade her to drink some tea, finally leaving the cup on the nightstand and asking Mother which dress she should pull from the closet for her to wear. I lingered in the doorway, hair wet and combed, my good shirt and trousers on, and Mother saw me without changing expression—simply held out her hand until I took it and stroked the back of my neck absently when I began to cry, face buried in the blue nylon sleeve of her wrapper.

Someone drove us to the service. We sat in the front pew, facing a huge, closed box. They said my father was inside it. In a box, as if he were a pair of shoes or a shop cake. A dead thing that couldn't feel or speak or move. I told myself that he would never walk home from school with me again or pick me up under his arm and swing me round until I laughed myself limp. That I'd never hear his voice anymore.

And it felt like lies. A frightening, made-up tale the adults had conspired to tell me so I'd believe it and never ask questions, letting them keep their secrets to themselves. Mother's first great lie. How could he be dead when he was just here, when I could still feel his goodnight kiss on the top of my head, when I still remembered his warm, cotton-shirt smell? I could *see* him—how could he be gone? And if he were gone, how could he be in a box? And if he were in the box, how could he be in heaven, as the priest said? The stories didn't match up, there was something they didn't want me to know.

The sun had moved round until a beam fell squarely on Mother and me, and I felt her shrink from it, covering her face with her hands as everyone intoned the prayers and the choir sang under the direction of someone who was not my father. God has taken him, the priest said. The God whose eye is everywhere. Had that eye seen Father? Had mother left the shutters open by mistake that last day? Was dying what happened when God looked straight at you? Had Father tried to hide from God in the water?

At the cemetery, they lowered the box into the ground the way the dockworkers lowered cargo into the holds of ships, so it could be taken somewhere far away. Those left behind could find comfort in God and in his blessings, the priest said, but mother shook, dry-eyed, when he said it and people threw dirt on the box. And I knew God had murdered my father and that Mother had let him.

I stared out the porthole of the plane until the last trace of light had drowned in the somber layer of stratus that partitioned sky and sea, until the passengers around me had clicked on their reading lights, leaving me nothing to see in the glass but my own reflection.

XIII

The director's assistant was leading me to a costume fitting when I saw her. We had descended a stairway to a floor below stage level, gone down a narrow corridor unglamorously outfitted with fluorescent bulbs and rubberized floor mats over the slick tile and were nearing an open doorway in which several people had collected, chatting. I glanced at them—two men and a woman with her back to me—and noticed that one of the men had his arm tightly round the woman's waist in the same instant that I realized the woman was Donna.

She turned slightly at my approach and our eyes met. Without the slightest change of expression, she raised and lowered her chin fractionally, as if pointing at me with it, and resumed her conversation. I had hesitated in mid-step, but as she looked away, I renewed my pace, striding after the assistant as if ferocity of purpose could mask my staggered pride.

In the costume shop at the end of the hallway, the assistant turned to introduce me to the designer and they both took a step back at the sight of my face. I didn't care.

My thoughts, so often formed in words, had become nothing but a soundless wail of loss and fury and bewilderment, mental stormwater surging between the sure, eviscerating knowledge that she didn't want me after all and the desperate, excuse-making hope that I'd got it wrong, that there was an explanation. Round and round in my head, my ego rode these peaks and troughs while the designer and wardrobe assistant nervously questioned and hurriedly pinned.

I relished their discomfort. I wanted to punish someone; they would do nicely.

"Something has angered you?" the designer ventured once, in Polish-accented French, and I shouted, "I don't feel like talking!"

so loudly that heads peeped from behind sewing machines and racks of clothes throughout the room.

She stared at me. "Then it is silence you will have."

She pulled off my back the leather blazer she had been adjusting and propelled me by the elbow out of the room and into the corridor.

"Au revoir," she said, and slammed the door behind me.

I had never been so angry. I stared at that door and the ugly beige walls and I wanted to pull down the theater brick by brick and bury that woman under the rubble. This was the end of her career. I'd see to it. She and Donna. We were through.

"What was all that about?" said Donna's voice.

I whirled on her and the smile that had started puckering the corner of her mouth vanished.

"Hardly *your* business," I snarled, and tore away toward the stairs, brain boiling with rage.

"Yikes," I heard her say. "Fun seeing you."

I knew I was supposed to go from the fitting to a cast meeting, but I didn't want to be anywhere near anyone, and headed toward the hotel across the Place du Chatelet. Pigeons scuttled out of my way or flew up briefly, blending with the overcast sky and gunmetal Seine. When I went back to the meeting, I'd complain to the director about that costume bitch.

By the time I got to my room, I'd gone from maddened to grim, but was still too discomposed to concentrate on anything, so I opened the narrow French doors that led to a tiny balcony and stepped out.

It was surprisingly quiet for a weekday morning. Leafless trees lined the street below. A few people walked unhurriedly along the row of graceful buildings, cream and gray as the sky, that stood opposite my perch. Shops were open; customers entered doorways empty-handed and emerged again with bags and boxes. In a cove of my mind isolated from all the turmoil, I noted and filed away the location of a pâtisserie that would make a good place to eat breakfast should the hotel's roomful of hard-boiled eggs and muesli prove unappetizing in the morning.

So life and breakfast would go on in spite of Donna, this objective bit of me admitted. I would sing my role. I would just be alone, as I preferred to be anyway. I was in Paris. If I did want company, there were other women. I would not be jumping off the balcony today.

My lips twisted in a bitter little echo of Donna's sardonic smile: I was still going to have to figure out how to get from wounded to impassive while working with her over the next few weeks.

An odd sort of long-distance calm was taking over. I saw myself and my position with weird clarity, like a musical performance I was watching from the far back of the house. I realized that in my months of fantasies and in my immediate assumptions about Donna's behavior—right though they might be—I had rushed the tempo of our connection instead of letting it develop at its own pace. Her gaze at me had been so cool and unrevealing; I had seen secrets in it, and desertion. Treachery. I was sure I had. I was sure. But I needed to look again.

I walked swiftly back across the Place to the meeting I was now ten minutes late for and slipped into the last empty chair round the rehearsal-room table, murmuring my apologies to the stage director and making no eye contact with anyone. The table held a scale model of the set. Around it lay sketches of costumes for each character. Donna was four seats away, examining a drawing while the director explained his reasons for changing the setting of the opera from the late nineteenth century to the current, money-obsessed, self-indulgent decade, and I carefully avoided looking in her direction. The costume harridan unsmilingly half-stood and shoved the de Bretigny designs at me: There were three, all variations on drug-dealer and underworld looks, including the leather coat she had abruptly peeled off me earlier.

The point, the director concluded, was to highlight the thin gray line that has always existed between the upper classes and the demimonde and that was becoming slimmer and slimmer in our own time as establishment power and criminal influence together used the seductions of money to corrupt the vulnerable, whether individuals, businesses, or entire peoples.

"So I'm staging a sort of hostile takeover of the publicly held Manon company, is that it?" I piped up, daring to glance sidelong at Donna. She did not look at me; her eyebrow, however, arched sharply.

The director tossed his head of artfully shaggy hair and lightly clapped his hands. "*Exactement.* You can read all the relationships as both personal and societal, literal and metaphorical. In our modern times, the world of *Manon* is repeating itself."

Standard updating, I thought, although the set looked interesting: a series of panels curved in two open lobes, like the top half of a lopsided heart, that created a small, semicircular space for interior scenes and a somewhat separate but adjacent large one for the outdoor scenes. All the details—wainscoting, draperied windows, trees, railings—were painted on the flats in a hard, artificial, contemporary style, like color illustrations from a slick magazine, all shiny surface and no depth, glitz exuding an air of money and risk.

All the interiors, with appropriate changes of lighting, furniture and props, would occur in the same spot, because these scenes—the love nest, the casino, the church—were all about gambling of some kind, the set designer explained. And the exteriors, from the coachyard and the street festival to the prison grounds, were literally courts, public places where Manon and others were judged by society and approved or persecuted. The painted trees, with their arrow-straight trunks and crosspiece branches, even looked like gallows.

Before I could say so, Donna joked, "How many of us will be hanging up there by the end of the show?"

As if she had been inside my head. Without thinking, I jerked round to stare at her and she was looking right at me—through me—with the daredevil light of complicity in her eyes.

The costume bitch was looking at me, too, with a lot less amusement.

Donna left after the meeting before I could speak with her—

fled, I'm tempted to say. On any ordinary day, I probably would have tracked her to the hotel and invited her out or myself in, but my peculiar out-of-body calm had persisted throughout the afternoon and I knew I should just go to dinner by myself. It didn't matter where—I assumed that any restaurant in Paris was likely to be excellent and so, failing to accurately translate the word Bavardien on a sign, I walked into the nearest one I saw on the Place and ended up dining my first night in Paris on Wienerschnitzel.

The next day brought our first rehearsal—not on the set, which a battalion of carpenters and painters was rushing to complete—but in a large, bare room behind, and two floors above, the stage. It was mostly a walk-through of the blocking, so we could begin getting used to where we were to stand on stage and how we were to act and move while singing; as usual, the locations of flats and furniture were demarcated on the ugly gray-lino floor with bits of tape.

Donna and I—and a lot of other people, irritatingly—had a scene together in the first act, though mostly on opposite sides of the space, she as a naïve, rural girl just disembarked from a motor coach at a city hotel, I as a member of a boisterous party dining on the hotel terrace. Amid all the contradictory stage directions and confused shifting of positions, as if we were all chess pieces deployed by tipsy opponents, I had no opportunity to speak directly to her, and so stood about a great deal with studied nonchalance, trying to catch her looking at me. She was wearing a loose cardigan over a leotard top and tight jeans; the jeans were tucked into tall boots that she'd covered with enormously thick, bunched-up socks of the sort ballerinas wear to keep their leg muscles warm. The exaggerated size of her calves made her thighs and waist appear especially slender. In fact, the strategic cling and billow of her clothes created a tantalizing distraction, as if I were watching a nude figure at a window, her shape clearly revealed only in tiny, shifting glimpses by a windblown curtain.

And I was, apparently, not the only one fascinated by the view. Our porcine Guillot, taking his lecherous mobster character to heart, stuck to her like a ball of suet, laying a hand on her arm or back at every opportunity and chuckling suggestively after everything anyone said, while the Lescaut and the des Grieux winked and smirked at her so relentlessly that they seemed to be suffering from twin neurological disorders.

I realized that it had been the des Grieux who'd had his tentacle snaked around Donna's waist the day before. He was quite famous, both for his voice and for his backstage conquests. Clearly, Donna's was to be the next scalp on his belt. And perhaps she wanted it to be.

At long last, the director reached the part of Act I where Guillot, a kind of crime-world kingpin, catches sight of lovely, innocent Manon standing near the street and comes to the edge of the terrace above to proposition her, and my de Bretigny—a shady but not heartless government official—notices her for the first time. I was instructed to emerge onto the terrace, ask Guillot what he's doing, peer over his meaty back at Donna/Manon, who is laughing at Guillot's advances, and be impressed by the girl's beauty. We walked through it at first without singing at all, pulled this way and that by M. Le Directeur, who repeatedly got up from his chair to adjust us, turning our shoulders and chins with moist, finicking fingers that I wanted to pour salt on, like leeches.

Looking up at me was part of Donna's job at the moment and she held my gaze blankly while Clammy Hands tilted her head farther back, forcing her mouth to open a little in an expression of what the audience was to feel was guileless amusement. Then we went through the scene again, singing very gently—what we call marking—with an accompanist playing the piano score. I leaned over the hillock of flesh to stare at her appreciatively and softly sing, "This time, the fool has, through sheer luck, discovered a treasure. Never has a sweeter expression lighted a more graceful face," and was rewarded by another raised eyebrow, which prompted an outburst of, "*Non, non, non, trop sceptique, mademoiselle!*" and cranky hair-tossings from the head annelid.

A not unsatisfactory morning.

At the lunch break, I slipped out of the theater to walk along the Seine, crossing the Boul'Mich and wandering round Notre Dame like a tourist, though a gingerly one, as my liking for the buttresses and gargoyles and stained glass did not dispel my sense of being in the enemy's camp. Ironic that the place should be so dark within, as if the very people perpetuating the notion of God had wanted protection from his eye, too—a fearful monument of sinister beauty, where God and Satan truly seemed one.

As a place to celebrate life and hope, I'd take an opera house anytime.

I had never associated God with buildings much, in any event. I remember quite clearly once when I was tiny, perhaps three or four, asking my father why we had to go to church every Sunday. He said that we went each week and on special days to pay our respects to God at his house, to visit with him and get to know him better. And I said that I didn't think God lived in his house, that he was like Blackie, the neighbor's huge, staring Great Dane, who had a wooden kennel in the garden next to ours, but was hardly ever in it, preferring to prowl. Father asked why I thought God was like Blackie and I said, because he follows Mother about all day.

I saw the smile on my father's face die when I said it.

A few steps from the cathedral, I found a rather charming bistro that served up braised lamb chops aux flageolets and ripe figs in raspberry sauce so delicious they made me a little giddy, and more than compensated for my inadvertent Deutschification of the night before. I returned to the Théâtre humming.

The next few days went forward like a game of tag as Donna and I circled each other, metaphorically speaking, until one of us scored a hit in word or action and then retreated, leaving the other one to watch, as the designated "it," for an opportunity to retaliate. It was obviously a duel and the blades had edges. Yet the combat created, not injury, but excitement. Her omnipresent retinue of male toadies looked on uncomprehending or in self-satisfaction, apparently mistaking the tension between Donna and me for actual hostility and oozing to her defense with smug blandishments. Me they treated with a dim pity bordering on scorn, until I opened my mouth to sing.

I found the Guillot's stupefaction on the first occasion quite rewarding. It was at dress rehearsal, the day we stopped marking and sang full voice. I even thought I saw the des Grieux widen his eyes a bit as he stood in the wings, though not being baritones, neither could have cared that much. The Lescaut did, but he affected not to, pushing me about with a rough nonchalance during our struggle with des Grieux at the top of Act II and trying to drown me out vocally. But he couldn't top me for power. Or for pitch. He went an entire quarter tone flat during his blessing-of-the-lovers recitative. Donna openly winced.

We still had spent no time together aside from work. Every time I managed to get her by herself and within two feet of me, she'd elude me somehow, all sly comments and sideways motion. After nearly two weeks, I'd resigned myself to the likelihood that banter was all I would ever get from her. A tease, that's all she was—probably having it off with the irresistible des Grieux, whose pull with opera managements would no doubt help her land leading parts for a year or so until he dumped her for a new and sweeter bit of tail. I could see this, calmly still, when I was alone. When she was in view, my anger grew.

The house was overflowing on opening night. The French-language opera and the sparkle of our des Grieux's name seemed to draw the whole of Paris. Even the president of France was there, as was confirmed excitedly over the intercom by an assistant stage manager who had a full view of the orchestra-level seats from his post in the control booth above the balcony.

Our des Grieux straightened the collar of his open-necked shirt under the Italian silk sport coat that was his costume. "*Tant pis*," he said, "I didn't vote for him," and looked at all of us in the green room with an expectant smirk that got even smirkier when Donna laughed.

"*Tant pis*," she answered. "I live here, but I can't vote." They locked eyes for a second with a glow about them as unctuous as corn oil. My gorge rose and so did I, quitting the room and wandering the backstage area until I found a door to a loading dock and stepped outside, deep-breathing the air of Paris, with its signature mix of car exhaust and garlic fumes, until I stopped feeling sick over Donna and began to worry that the stench was corroding my throat.

I went inside just as the stage manager called places and I brushed past Donna and the others without so much as a "good luck," taking my station behind the flats of the terrace set. The prelude started; I hummed along with it, a trick of mine that I'd got in the habit of to reassure myself that my voice was functioning and to ease my nerves a bit. My lungs felt rigid; pressure was growing inside my head. As I hummed, I tried to take slow, relaxed breaths, but the area around my solar plexus continued to feel tightly knitted up.

The rest of the cast playing the partying lowlifes in the first scene collected near me in the darkness, all of us huddling just millimeters from the paint- and glue-smelling flats in a space already cramped and hot. Increasingly odoriferous, too—our Rosette, Pousette, and Javotte, whom Donna and I called "the Tarts of Hearts," and their piggy Knave, Guillot, all reeked of makeup, nylon wig hair and sweat, as I supposed I did, as well. It was enough to make one swoon, and I held on to one of the rough wooden supports holding up the flats to steady myself. Without really looking, I could tell the others were mouthing words and mugging at one another in the silent hilarity that often served to ease pre-curtain tension. In my head, I pictured them with their lips retracted from huge yellow teeth and their eyes rolling in circles of white, like a team of panicked horses. I seldom suffered much stage fright anymore, but perspiration was trickling down my back under the ridiculous black leather that squeaked when I moved, and the notes of the prelude were ticking by inexorably toward the moment when I would have to move and sing in front of several thousand people who would judge and remember me on the basis of my initial moments onstage, and I suddenly couldn't remember my words, couldn't remember at what measure I was to enter, couldn't remember anything. My mind became a reeling void; I felt unmoored, at once far away and microscopically focused on the approach of doom. I desperately listened to the orchestra, trying to get oriented in the score as I mentally saw myself humiliated in front of a sneering Donna and her conceited star lover, in front of all Europe. I couldn't feel my legs, couldn't breathe, couldn't think. I bent under the blackness and terror, suffocating.

And then the prelude ended, the Act I music began, the lights came up and I somehow found myself onstage, ambling sociably with the others from hotel lounge to terrace, and exuberantly singing, "We're thirsty!" in agreement with Guillot's first statement, "Hey, where are you, Monsieur L'Hotelier? How long must we shout before you condescend to listen?" And the sound I made, strong and clear, reminded me why I was there, filling my head and heart with something that had both caused the fear and was driving it out.

Performing on piano had never affected me so. I had controlled the piano. I had made it speak or fall silent. It had been something outside of me, something I mastered and wielded, a weapon. But when I sang, I was the thing I played, and I stood stripped of all anger and contempt, unprotected, wanting only to hear my own voice and know that others heard and were moved.

The conductor was taking the music at far too slow a tempo—I wanted all of us to race, to blow the roof off the theater with our power. We were, abruptly, a team, from little fireplug-shaped Rosette, spilling out of her hot-pink disco dress, to des Grieux, rapturously swanning about with his hand ever pressed to his temple or chest, all watching out for each other, urging each other on, working together to create an unequalled glory of sound and emotion.

At least until the Guillot upstaged me, the fat wretch.

I had just moved to the coach park from the terrace with the Tarts—to mock-sympathize with Guillot over Manon's disappearance with des Grieux in Guillot's own limo—when, halfway through my line, the bastard gathered his twenty-five stone and hip-checked me out of his way. As I staggered back, with the audience roaring and the singers staring, he planted himself in front of me at center stage as if he were a huge egg that had just been laid, and delivered his final vow of revenge against the escaped lovers before the curtain came down.

The instant it hit the floor, I pitched into him.

"How dare you! How dare you interfere with me like that! You all saw it," I shouted, turning to the others, who looked variously shocked and amused. None of them replied.

The Guillot gave me an indifferent glance through tiny eyes and shrugged. "You are a little snot," he said, and lumbered into the wings.

The stage manager hurried over, muttered, "I'll speak to him," and hurried away again.

The others gazed at me for another second or two; Pousette squeaked, "We have to change for Act II," and they all seemed to awaken, striding away to their dressing rooms.

I met Donna on the stairs. She reached out to stop me.

"What happened? Everybody came down shrieking about you and the Knave. I've never heard the word 'shit' used in so many languages at once before."

I told her the story, staring furiously at the scarred walls. "I'm going to speak to the director about him," I said, finally looking at her. I felt defiant. "I won't share the stage with such an unprofessional...*lout.*"

Donna absently tugged the red satin of her costume down more tightly over her chest, taking my gaze with it.

"I've seen worse than him," she replied—coolly, I thought. I started down the stairs.

"You know," she murmured as I passed her, "in this business, it works better to get even than to tattle."

Tattle! I slammed the door of my dressing room shut. I supposed she thought I was a little snot, too. Well, I'd rather be that than the slutty opportunist she was turning out to be.

I threw off the damp leather blazer and sped into the security-guard uniform that de Bretigny wore in Act II to bluff his way into Manon's and des Grieux's love nest. Donna was probably to blame for this whole situation—why else would that huge pathetic lump try to humiliate me, if not out of jealousy? You'd think the idiot would be more upset at the des Grieux than at me, considering his better luck with her. Perhaps he sensed that Donna and I secretly made fun of him. That would be surprisingly perspicacious of him, thus unlikely. So it must be jealousy. Well, if he were annoyed now, imagine how purple he'd turn if it actually were me that Donna loved.

My hands smelled of her perfume, for some reason. I ran back up the stairs just as the last call for places came over the loudspeaker, feeling strangely elated. I suddenly couldn't have cared less about the malicious Guillot, who wasn't in this act anyway, and had probably retired to the green room with a dozen cupcakes—did the French make cupcakes?—and a magnum of wine. I was searching for a glimpse of red satin.

Donna was standing just offstage, waiting for the curtain to go up so she could make her entrance. I stepped behind her and put my hands on her waist, startling her; she twisted round to see who it was and leaned away when she recognized me, her eyes wide and wary. I didn't let go, feeling her tiny, silent gasp as I bent down and whispered, "Bonne chance" in her ear.

The curtain rose. She broke free and immediately walked onstage. By no glance or expression did she reveal any feeling unrelated to her performance. And yet, I wasn't dismayed.

Some intensity was growing around me, like heat or a cloud of oppositely charged particles. An irresistible current of change. Her shining voice rose in my ears like mercury and I soundlessly sang with her, "Avez-vous peur que mon visage frôle votre visage? …Vous avez peur?"

My entrance was coming up—I needed to get to the other

side of the stage. I rushed down the corridor behind the stage wall, reentered the backstage area and found our Lescaut pacing in the wings. He sagged against a prop roulette table at the sight of me.

"Where the hell have you been?" he hissed. "I was just about to tell the stage manager that you were a no-show. What were you doin'—tying Erik's shoelaces together?"

Erik was the Guillot and our Lescaut was an American who had evidently learned his vengeance techniques at summer camp.

"Hardly." I checked to make sure I'd threaded my belt through all the loops in back. I felt flushed. "Just paying a social call."

He squinted at me suspiciously, but let the remark go. "You goin' to the after-party? Food's supposed to be *outstanding*. Working in France is dangerous, you know? I've gained five pounds this week alone."

"*Erik* must come here all the time," I muttered just as the stage manager cued us.

We entered noisily, the Lescaut punching his fist into his palm and snarling random words of aggression in a portrayal of fury over Manon's and des Grieux's offense to family honor, I remonstrating with him in a show of common sense as we approached the smaller portion of the set—now an apartment parlor—through the larger part, which had been changed from terrace to flower garden. Lescaut pounded on the door in between, shouting, as a servant looked out its tiny window to see who we were and went away again; I tugged at Lescaut's arm, pretending to urge calm, and then, at the correct moment, we burst through the door.

Donna/Manon ran to her hero, des Grieux, to clutch his arm and peep round him at us in fear of Lescaut's wrath, but it was at me she stared, and in that second—a single image I can still see of her, all huge eyes and long, dark hair and clingy scarlet dressing gown—something passed between us that seemed to pull me out of my own body, as if she had shot a glowing hook into my solar plexus that evaporated everything but my voice, my vision of her and the sensation of tugging on the breathless, irradiated knot that had been my gut.

The lights gleamed gold from the black around us and this elation that was all that was left of me hovered above the stage, buzzing with the ferocious focus of sound in the air, watching from a strange distance a being that resembled me as it sang and moved and acted with a power that came from some outside source. And yet I never took my gaze off Donna; I was the one tugging now, and the sheer intensity of my excitement pulled her concentration back to me over and over even as she sang of her terror to des Grieux. I drew her and was drawn, closer as Lescaut moved des Grieux aside for a conference—closer than we had ever rehearsed—for de Bretigny to warn Manon of des Grieux's impending abduction by his own father, to whisper of de Bretigny's own desire for her and his offer of riches.

I sang, "Manon! Manon!... The hour is come for you to be free!"

Donna riveted me with her frightened, pleading look, answering back, "Oh, what torture for my troubled heart, what torture!" in a voice with point on it like a dagger's. "Leave now!" she sang, and I knew she meant it, but it was too late: I was standing over her and neither of us could look away.

"Listen to me!" I burst out.

"Leave, oh leave," she keened again.

And then I kissed her.

It was a hard kiss, hard and quick and totally unplanned, and as Lescaut began his next section—"It's perfect"—both of us broke away, shaken and alarmed.

Lescaut was gaping at us; I gasped out my next line to him, "I follow you!" a little behind the beat and saw an uncontrollable smile light up Donna's face, a face supposed to be anguished with Manon's grief and indecision.

I have no recollection of my last minute in that act, or how Lescaut and I got off the stage.

XIV

We ended up back in the States. It was a struggle, but I prevailed: Donna had wanted us to live in Paris because of the proximity to so many of Europe's opera houses and concert halls, and because she loved it, but the idea of giving up New York and burying myself outside the center of everything in some soft Old-World enclave, no matter how charming and elegant...well, it was insupportable. So Donna sublet her place to a friend in the Paris Opera Orchestra and we found a small, unfurnished flat just off Central Park West at Sixty-Third that we thought we could afford on two growing incomes. We moved in right after the wedding.

It was a good wedding, as these things go. Small, but handsome, and fairly painless, considering what went before: a not-unexpected row with her family, who believed Donna's duty was to be married in her childhood church in Statesville, with a punch-and-cookie reception immediately after in the community room, followed by a backyard barbecue at home. Donna and I were actually united in our opposition to that—she went ashen at the very suggestion—and, at length, we persuaded Pa and Ma Salter to brave the seething menace of Manhattan for an evening ceremony and sit-down dinner up in the Kaplan Penthouse at Lincoln Center, after which Donna and I would spend two nights at the Plaza before we had to begin moving our few belongings from my sublet to our new home.

It was quite a magnificent setting, the penthouse. We rattled around in it a bit, our party being so few—just Rob and Donna's younger sister as attendants, the whole Hellman family, a range of Salter grandparents, aunties and cousins, and a handful of our school friends and colleagues. But we enjoyed the luck of fine fall weather and carried things off well, I think, seasoned performers that we were.

And we didn't—or I didn't, anyway—mind the lack of a wedding trip, as we had essentially taken the real honeymoon before the engagement.

Everything had moved very quickly after that opening night of *Manon*. Donna had fallen into my arms and I into her bed almost the second the curtain came down, and we scarcely emerged for the rest of the run but for performances and very late forays into restaurants for dinner and breakfast. She was a composition of contrasts—sharp mind and shimmering voice, hard strength and tender, silken surfaces—woven together in endless variations that demanded to be explored, and yet eluded definition. For a long time, she was all I wanted to think and feel and sense.

She had turned to me that first morning, eyes half open and lips dry and cracked from kissing, and murmured with a hint of a drawl I'd never detected before, "'F'you hadn' grabbed me last night, I don' think I woulda given you a second chance."

"Mmmm." I peeled the sheet down to her waist and began methodically nipping at everything in view. "And what does that mean?"

She propped herself up on her elbow and scraped a tangle of dark hair away from her face. "I mean, I was scared. You're not 'zactly an easy person."

Her eyes and speech seemed to clear abruptly as she gazed at me critically. "That's actually one of the reasons I've been attracted to you, but it doesn't promise a peaceful existence."

"Is that why you were hanging about with Pepe LePew instead?"

"Pepe...? Oh, our star. I suppose you could say that. I sort of made him my cover. He gave me a reason to avoid you and he's so in love with himself, he never even noticed."

"So you *were* trying to get me to give up? It certainly seemed like it."

"Yes. I knew you were trouble. You *are* trouble, a regular porcupine in a paw paw patch, like my mother always says."

She bit me.

"Your mother sounds like a colorful character."

"Not as colorful as you. You turn inhuman shades of violet when you're angry. And you're angry a lot."

She sat up suddenly, pulling the sheet up to her chin.

"Seriously. I hate arguments. Do you think it's something you'll grow out of?"

I felt a flash of annoyance. "Trying to change me already?"

The eyebrow twitched and she tilted her head slightly, warily, then plunged her hand under the sheet and ran it lightly up the length of my leg. She smiled wickedly.

"Why, I think part of you is growing out of it already."

A half-hour later, I woke from a momentary doze and found her staring at me, green eyes unreadable.

When the production closed, we decided to go to Wales. Both of us had a few unscheduled days; I'd always wanted to see it—the homeland of my father—and Donna had never been, either, so outwardly, the trip was an impulsive lark. The idea of going off on an adventure with her, unencumbered by fools and obligations, was glorious: everything we saw or talked about in those days was a discovery, not only of what was around us, but also of the ways in which we were alike or different, what we thought. She wanted to know everything about me, and though there was much I did not wish to reveal, I willingly answered all questions that did not seem like prying. I found I enjoyed describing my island and its hybrid culture to her, as well as my life with Gunter and my experiences in New York. I was amused that a girl who had summarily dumped her Southern hometown and nested in Paris as if born to it could marvel so sincerely about the staid Anglo-exoticism of my colonial childhood; in turn, she laughed at the incredulity with which I absorbed her tales of pig pickings and Sunday youth group and nights spent watching the jets take off and land at the county airport, all related in deadpan renditions of the indigenous accents.

There were different accents and dialects on the island, too, but I wasn't about to imitate them.

We huddled together on the chilly train to Calais, staring far more at each other than at the rain-lashed countryside passing by outside the fogged windows, sex-stunned and borderline delirious with the good fortune of reciprocal lust. At the ferry, afraid of seasickness, Donna took anti-nausea pills and slept the whole way across the Channel, head lolling against my shoulder and mouth slackly open in a way that would have revolted me in a stranger but was, in her, vaguely charming. With her eyes closed, I could see the flaws of her face: a faint scar over her left eyebrow whose story I had not yet heard; the nose rather too long and sharp; a mist of pale brown hair on her cheeks near her ears; lips that came together slightly off center. I was aware of her imperfections, had at times found myself wishing her legs were a bit longer and her laugh less unrestrained, and yet every time she looked at me, I found her completely beautiful, uniquely irresistible. It was not unlike having been gassed at the dentist's.

By the time we got to Cardiff, it was dark and still pouring, so we stayed in, had genuine Welsh rarebit in the hotel dining room—neither of us having to care what liquid cheese would do to our voices—and tucked up in a big bed under a thick quilt for the rest of the night. Some of which we actually spent sleeping.

The morning was gorgeous and mild and Donna literally dragged me out of bed as soon as it was light. "Come on, damn it! I'm not going to let you snore till lunchtime on our first day here. Get up! Get. Up."

"Ooooooh, grab me again like that. Oh, I think I *am* up."

"Don't be lewd. No being lewd before breakfast, or we'll end up right back where we started from."

"Paris?"

"In *bed*. No, don't…don't…Augggh!"

She yelled as I pulled her down on top of me.

"So just me being awake isn't good enough, eh? You have to wake the whole hotel? Ow, watch the knee. Oh, now see what you've done. I may never get up ever again."

"I'm sure I can fix that later," she smirked, struggling to her feet. "Right now, I'm getting in the shower and you can either join me or lie there in a dirty heap all day while I tour your ancestral nation and all its unpronounceable landmarks by myself."

We finally got through the shower, in spite of certain delays, filled up on tea and buns and embarked on sightseeing. Both of us were keen to see the new concert hall, St. David's, but it wasn't open until later in the morning, so we strolled about the castle, wandered into shops and sampled a wide variety of biscuits and cakes and, somewhat later, beer. St. David's, when we at last got in, turned out to be a giant bowl lined with mismatched shelves, but handsome in a modernistic way. The shelves, cantilevered slabs that were sections of seating, each jutting out at slightly different angle from the others, gave a kind of primitive monumentality to the whole space that was very impressive, like a curving mountainside of rock ledges. The hall was rumored to have marvelous acoustics and Donna and I decided we would try to get ourselves invited to sing there.

By lunchtime, we were ready to move on to Caerphilly and bought fish and chips in paper pokes for the bus trip. Donna tried to encourage me to look up family members there, but I made it clear I didn't want to, and she eventually let it go, glancing over at me now and then from behind her magazine while I pretended not to see her assessing gaze. She was somewhat less easygoing than I had first thought, though her humor always bubbled up again, as it did when Caerphilly Castle came into view and she could not resist pointing at the creatures on the grass and exclaiming, "Look! Welsh rabbits!" I made the expected gagging sounds and we both laughed and were all right again for a while.

I didn't want her to know that the thought of inviting myself into the homes of completely unfamiliar cousins and making chitchat about Mother and my dead father chilled me to the marrow, no matter how curious I was about his parents and early life. Their questions—I knew I could not bring myself to answer them, any more than I would be able to force myself to keep up the acquaintances with annual Christmas cards or obligatory visits every time I performed in Britain. I hadn't had a real family when I wanted and needed one, and now I could summon no desire for any at all. They were pains, nothing more. Donna would have to do without the standard clan introductions from me.

But I didn't need the bonds of blood kin in order to be claimed by Caerphilly. It sang to me instantly—the humble and unapologetic shops, the self-containment of its atmosphere, the stark silhouette of its looming, islanded fortress against a sky turned moody with the gray light of scudding clouds. I could sense my origins there, as if it and I had been written in the same key.

Donna felt it, too—we made a little tour of the lake, looked round the public buildings and sat for a time in the garden of a pub on a hill overlooking the castle, and all she said was, "It's beautiful," but I could see that it had worked some ancient, shadowy spell on her, as on me.

She took my hand as we walked back to the bus. "We should come back someday," she said, with a smile that was at once grave and elated, and I surprised both of us by kissing her deeply—in public, for the second time in three weeks—right in front of the ticket queue. I heard my voice say, out of nowhere, "I think we should get married."

My own expression must have been as shocked as hers; her eyes stared at me with the mixed glint of apprehension and skittish excitement I had seen during our encounters at *Manon* rehearsals. Foreboding fluttered at the edges of my brain like batwings, but I did not want to take my statement back. I said, "Think about it, would you?" and we rode back to Cardiff in silence, still holding hands.

XV

One thing is true about classical singers who marry: they care too much about their voices to scream at each other.

Some people might mistake the silence for satisfaction.

On our second night at the Plaza, I had got an excited call from my manager, who told me that Van Dam had had to drop out of Maazel's Beethoven Nine at the Staatsoper at the last second because of some injury and they were desperate to find someone familiar with the piece who could get there in twenty-four hours.

I wasn't pleased at the sound of "desperate," especially as I'd sung the part in Chicago three years earlier to good notices. I was also lying in bed next to my naked bride, whose tousled head was converting the one-sided trickle of information filling her ears to pools of dismay in her eyes.

I asked him to hold and covered the mouthpiece.

"You have to go," Donna said grimly.

"I haven't even told you—"

"I could hear Sam clearly. You can't turn this down, it's too good."

"But we just got married! And we have to start moving tomorrow."

"Are you saying you don't *want* to go?"

"Well…no, not exactly. I mean, I'd like to sing at the Staatsoper, it'd be my Vienna debut, but you can't want me to just leave all of a sudden, it's too—"

"Well, I don't want you to leave, but I don't see what else you can do. This is an amazing chance and you have no conflict to prevent it—"

"*You* are my conflict."

She sat up vigorously. "I am *not* your conflict, and you're not mine. We've known right along that we're going to have to be away from each other a lot. We do the same thing for a living, we know what the business demands. It won't be fun, but we'll manage. And conveniently for you, I have nothing going on until the 15th, so I'll just stay here and do the moving."

"Ah. Well, clearly, you can do without me quite nicely."

"I didn't say that!" she whispered fiercely, automatically avoiding strain on her cords. "You ought to go and I need to stay, that's all. Go enjoy your glorious debut and I'll have the sheets and silverware all arranged by the time you get back." She grimaced at me. "I'm trying to be generous here."

"And I can see that it pains you. Well, as it happens, I agree that I ought to go, and as you so graciously volunteer to be a proper housewife, I accept."

"Why are you being such a—"

"I beg your pardon." The phone was emitting a series of muffled squawks. "Sam. Sam. Yes, sorry to keep you waiting. I'll do it. Yes. Yes. Good. Try to book an overnight flight for me, would you? Less jet lag. I'll get brushed up on the part in the morning. Right-o. Thanks."

Donna had left the room. I half-wanted to go after her, half-didn't. It really was awful to leave her now, but why didn't she make up her mind? Urging me out the door with one breath and pouting with the next. Jerking me around, she was.

I felt my face flush in anger. My own fault, no doubt, expecting her to be above womanly tricks. Probably had the whole manipulation planned out: playing the martyr, guilting me to get what she wanted. I didn't know what that was, but assumed it would be at my expense. Tears would likely be the next ploy.

I rolled over and turned out the light, my ears sharply tuned to any hint of snuffling from the sitting room, but detecting none. A point of stony cold, like a tiny icicle, had developed in my gut, a wish that this hadn't happened, a wish at war with my excitement over the chance to impress Vienna—Vienna, the grail of classical musicians. I was a bit worried about my voice after a wedding week of stress, little sleep, and endless talking. I would have nothing in the morning but tea with lemon and honey, and warm up very gently—just a few vocalises—and then mark through the Ninth's last movement a couple of times to make sure I remembered it well. No full-throttle singing until the afternoon of the concert, just to make sure the notes were there, and then complete vocal rest until my pre-concert warm-up. I was determined to be brilliant.

But Donna wouldn't be there to hear me. The icicle stabbed me and I buried my head in the pillow, suddenly feeling apprehensive and miserable. Why didn't she come back? She wouldn't have been able to come along; even if we hadn't quarreled, it was too expensive and we did have to get our things out of the sublet, but I didn't want our wedding weekend to end like this. I wanted her with me, in the circle of my arm, and yet wasn't that just what she was after? To have me come crawling to her, begging for reconciliation, so she'd win? Only one day married and already her puppet?

No, thanks. I wasn't having any.

I must have begun to drift off, because I thought I saw Mother in the glow of city nightlight surrounding the curtained window, Mother as I had seen her on that last day at Juilliard, with a hard white face like a marble statue, unforgiving and remote. She sat on the far edge of the bed without looking at me, near enough to touch, but untouchable, and I called to her. I said, "Mother, why did you leave me?" She didn't answer, she didn't even turn my way, and I knew that no one would ever love me, that I would always be alone, shut out—that her work was done and I was trapped by her and her God in a soundless prison whose bars were beams of pitiless light that would separate me from affection and solace and security forever. I struggled to get to her and sat up, abruptly realizing that it wasn't Mother but Donna sitting pale-faced beside me, watching me sleep with sad eyes.

I reached out for her and she came to me.

"I thought you had gone," I muttered into her hair. "Where did you go?"

She pulled away to look directly at me. "I was only in the next room, you know. Why didn't you come talk to me?"

"I...I was annoyed, I suppose. Angry. You seemed to be telling me one thing, but expecting another."

"I was torn, that's all. I want you to be wildly successful, but I don't want to be sidelined in the process. And you seemed to want to punish me for that. Insult me. Demean me. You treat me as if you think my love is an act I'm putting on to take advantage of you somehow."

I wrapped my arms around her again, held her, but there was a distance between us that had not been there before.

I said, "Please don't leave me."

She pulled back to look at me again, and this time I saw fear in her eyes. She kissed me cautiously.

"Please don't drive me away," she said.

The Ninth was an incomparable experience, a triumph. To sing that piece, in that place, with that ensemble of artists—the audience were moved to tears and screams of rapture and I knew that I had never sung as well in my life. People recognized me on the street the next day, and at the airport, and Maazel personally thanked me before I departed the hall after the performance, saying he looked forward to having me back and mentioning that the Staatsoper was planning a *Don Giovanni* in three years to celebrate the opera's 200th anniversary. His words had the tone of an invitation.

I tried to sleep on the way home, but was too keyed up. I couldn't wait to tell Donna everything, to call my manager, to read the notices that had yet to be published. This performance felt like the transformative moment that every artist longs for, the moment that would cause my career to begin its rise to the summit of my hopes. I would be what my father had lost the chance to become, a version of what Mother had always envisioned for me. Would it please her to know that singing was taking me so far, or would she always revile me for abandoning the path that she and God, my unelected pilots, had planned for me to follow?

I suddenly wanted to know.

We had exchanged no word for ten years. My only news of her came from Brownlea's annual Christmas and birthday cards, in which he was careful not to say too much. She was alive, I knew that much. Still deaf to my desires and qualms.

But she was aware that I had married—I'd sent Brownlea a wedding invitation, which he had graciously declined, sending us two full place settings of our china from the old Royal Doulton shop on Gloucester Street. It had crossed my mind that the gift mightn't be entirely from him.

And yet, what did that change? She hadn't come to me. I couldn't—wouldn't—go to her. And no other means of direct contact would serve. A phone call was entirely too intimate, quite out of the question; a letter or telegram, too easily ignored. Brownlea offered the only possibility. But I had no idea how to begin, nor was I certain that I truly cared to.

Upon landing, I took a cab from Kennedy to my sublet, thinking Donna might be there, packing still. But I found no sign of her or her belongings and only a few of my own, in a box by the door. She didn't answer the phone at the new place, either, so I got my bag and the box into another cab and went round to see if someone in the rental office would let me into the apartment. The agent gave me a key and I went up, but it was many minutes before I could bring myself to try the door. When I did, I found a white envelope on a small table, just like the one I'd discovered a decade ago. As silent and final as the marker on a grave.

I was sitting on a packing case staring at it when Donna came in and threw her arms around me.

"Just like you to show up during the only three minutes all day that I haven't been here," she exclaimed, brisk and breezy as the October wind outside. "I went to the corner to get a sandwich. Didn't you read it?" she added, indicating the note.

I shook my head, still too incapacitated with relief to speak.

"I've had some good news," she continued brightly, with a kind of hardening of her gaze. "I'm going to England for a three-month residency."

XVI

So in February, Donna went off to Aldeburgh on her prestigious residency, while I came and went on a number of well-paying, but not terribly glamorous, gigs in Philadelphia and Atlanta and St. Louis, returning home for a week or two at a time to mope around the apartment, pretending to study *Don Giovanni*—an exercise in wishful thinking, if ever there were one—and putting our household things to rights in desultory fashion, hanging a photo here, organizing my music in a bookcase there. I wanted to be having a thrilling time that Donna would envy, that would convince us both of my utter self-sufficiency and blithe good spirits in her absence, but circumstances did not oblige and I found myself, far more often than I liked, sitting at home listening to records or writing Donna letters that I tried to make humorous, but that ended up sounding sarcastic and accusatory, even to me.

I knew I had stung her into this, I knew it—probably if I had not allowed myself to believe that she was glad to be rid of me so soon after our wedding, if I had been willing to admit that she was trying to be fair, she might have turned the residency down. After all, she had applied for it before she and I were together and her priorities might well have changed. But I had provoked her to retaliatory action and now I had to live every day for twelve long weeks with the proof that she had not submitted to being patronized and had done the opposite of placating me. Worst of all, I had discovered that life was dull and lonely without her. I felt dependent and resented it at the very same time that I wanted more than anything to hold her and talk with her. The whole situation was quite unbearable and at last I wrote her what I hoped was a lighthearted note, announcing that I was planning to visit her for a short, joyful time in the salt marshes of Suffolk. She phoned me a few days

later and even over a bad transatlantic connection sounded genuinely enthusiastic about the idea—called me "darling," which
she never had before, something I attributed to a slight case of
going native in Britain—and chattering about everything she
wanted to show me and all the people she thought I'd like. I felt
considerably better afterward.

But it occurred to me on the plane over that it had been more
than a year since I had flown to Paris, nervously anticipating a
meeting with Donna just as I was now, and that in some ways,
nothing had changed. We had courted, if you want to call it
that, confessed our love for each other, married; I was her husband now, not just a lover, and yet I felt no surer of her com-
mitment to me than I had in the rehearsal rooms of the Théâtre
Musical. I didn't even know who she was half the time. We
had spent our first Christmas together at her parents' house in
North Carolina—a debt we owed them for having married off
the reservation, as it were—and as soon as we walked through
the door, Donna turned into a Southern teenager, talking at a
speed that typists only dream of and literally squealing over her
mother and sister and the successive waves of old friends who
showed up to welcome us. Her vowels melted and stretched
into singsong *portamenti* of five diphthongs each. My wife, the
woman with the aloof cosmopolitan sophistication and ironic
wit, seemed to vanish, leaving me with a giddy, romping girl
who rolled on the floor with the dog, ate too many cookies and
didn't appear to have a tense muscle or an ounce of restraint in
her entire body.

I caught her friends looking from me to her in wonderment
and I rather suspect I echoed their expressions in reverse. How
could she have come from these loud, simple-minded people,
I marveled, while their eyes asked what she could possibly be
doing with an acid, alien stiff like me. Donna, on the other
hand, seemed determinedly unconcerned with what any of us
thought and got more uninhibited and funny by the moment.
At one point, she came downstairs in an old tutu and a huge

pair of rubber boots she'd apparently found in the back of her
closet and proceeded to flap and caper about like a stoned Sugar
Plum Fairy, giving us a radiant smile at the end that revealed her
two front teeth to be blacked out with licorice chewing gum.
Her family roared; I gaped, dumbfounded, half amused, and
half painfully embarrassed.

The private wink she gave me was my only clue that the
adult I loved still lurked within this appalling apparition.

And yet, when we were alone, walking through the pine
woods that bordered her street or snugged up together in the
small, white-quilted bed in her childhood room, her dignity
returned; she would become almost detached, as if noting from
a slight distance the effects of some experiment she had under-
taken with herself as subject. At times, I noticed her watching
me with the same analytical gaze.

So I felt unsure whether the Donna I knew best or some
other, surprising version would greet me at Aldeburgh. Assuming I got there at all: after flying into Gatwick, I had to take a
train to Ipswich and then hire a car to take me on the endless
drive out to what I imagined to be a large-ish sandbar on which
the village of Aldeburgh stood, waiting for one good wave to
wash it out to sea. It was nearly nightfall by the time I arrived,
famished and jet-lagged, on the doorstep of a sprawling old
beachfront place called the White Lion. I thought I would
phone Donna and then shower while she was coming over
from the music center, but when I opened the door of the
room she had booked for me, she was in it. Somewhat later, we
had dinner sent up.

We talked a long time that night, in spite of my fatigue. She
confessed to feeling sorry that she had thrown down the residency like a gauntlet at my feet, although she was quite excited
about the work in which she was collaborating—a cycle of
little-known Finzi songs that she was recording to be used in a
multimedia art installation about Christian symbolism, involv-
ing film loops and electronic feedback—and I told her that I

had missed her. A silence hung in the air for a moment that I knew she expected me to fill with my own apology, but I didn't feel that I should have to ask forgiveness for taking her advice and going to Vienna, even if she had really wished I would not. And as for calling her a housewife, well, she of all people ought to be able to take a joke. So I told her about Philadelphia, instead, which had been a debut, though it was only *Carmina Burana* again, and she didn't utter another word until I got up to shower, at last, and brush my teeth.

And then, rather out of the blue, she said, "I've noticed since being here that British people almost never explain themselves. They seem to expect everyone else to cope with whatever they do by just keeping quiet and carrying on, as if reasons don't matter."

"That's a bit of a generalization, surely," I replied, digging for pajamas in my bag.

"Isn't that what you expect of me?"

I straightened up and smirked at her. "Why, is keeping quiet too hard for you?"

She didn't smile back. "Yes, I think it's much harder to be kept in the dark than to be shown the truth under a strong light. I like to know *why*. At least then you know what you're dealing with."

"Some people find too much light invasive," I said, and snapped the suitcase shut.

"Is that," she said, suddenly watching me closely, "why you close the blinds all the time?"

I could see she was half joking, but also truly curious. I had never told her much about Mother, other than a little basic information about the tensions resulting in our rift. She knew more or less how I felt about religion, had accepted with no alarm the fact that I did not care to go into churches unless I had been engaged to sing in them, and somewhere along the way, she'd obviously recognized that I disliked my rooms being violated by direct sunlight. But she had not connected the first two to the last, and I wanted to keep it that way. It was a personal matter, off limits even to wives.

So I simply said, "I suppose I'm a casualty of too much time in the tropics," and changed the subject.

Next morning, we breakfasted in the hotel dining room at eight o'clock, and by eleven I had seen what I'm quite sure was every leaf, timber, and reed of the Aldeburgh Music campus and fully half its people, from the executive director to the spotty tea boy. These included Donna's collaborating artists, a rather glum, ferrety filmmaker from Toronto and a hearty Glaswegian of a composer-cum-electronics engineer who looked as if he could carry his enormous synthesizers and mixing desks around on his shoulders, possibly snacking on them.

All of whom gazed at Donna like beagles at a biscuit.

She happily pretended to be unaware of this, sweeping me along in rhapsodies of enthusiasm over each person we encountered, charming the men one by one into states of helpless, fawning want and observed with narrowed eyes by each politely smiling female.

And yet, on occasions when there were no other men in the room to contend for, the ladies seemed to like Donna well, to share—or at least to appreciate—her humorous outlook and to find her companionable. It was as if men were strategically advantageous territories or valuable natural resources for otherwise friendly women-states to war over, like individual-sized Frances and Germanies and Englands, who maintained their peculiar balance of power until America, in the form of my wife, joined the conflict and excited both envy and resentment with her unfair wealth of beauty and brains.

There was nothing childish or extreme about Donna here, just an aura of alert, irresistible purpose that she used to ingratiate herself with absolutely everyone, establishing acquaintances and sleuthing out intersections of taste and interest that I could see would provide her with opportunities in future. It was a gift, I supposed, perhaps nearly as useful as her magnificent voice, this ability to be tactical and seem genuine at the same time.

But after two days of riding about on her arm, so to speak, and being the dutiful spectator at her show of chummy cordiality, I'd had enough of Donna's desire to put herself forward and her unguessed-at willingness to endure imbeciles.

The evening before I was to leave, we were chatting with some people about buildings, probably because we were standing at the entrance to Snape Maltings, the old malt house that had been converted into the music center's concert hall, where we were to witness the presentation of some work-in-progress by a few of the other resident artists. One of these, a weedy, frowsy-looking blond fellow with a tiny ponytail and a face full of stubble, began extolling the virtues of postmodernism, which frankly made my eyes glaze over instantly, but I couldn't prevent myself from hearing him as he asserted, in tones of the most fatuous pomposity, that the new telephone-company tower in New York had changed, not just architecture, but also the entire world of design forever by returning ornament to preeminence and bringing the Bauhaus to its knees.

"Rubbish," I blurted, and immediately got The Eyebrow from Donna, which I ignored. "I've seen that building dozens of times, starting from when it was a hole surrounded by a fence, and it is nothing but another enormous office box with a silly part in its hair that makes it look like F. Scott Fitzgerald."

The others laughed and the blond weed turned from his normal greenish pallor to red.

"You've missed the point," he insisted. "That part, as you call it, isn't silly at all. It's a brilliant stroke, brilliant, and it will teach the public to expect the unexpected in other buildings. Soon they'll be demanding visionary design from the new generation of architects like myself."

"I see the point quite clearly. Actually, two of them and they're right there on the telephone company building's head. Really, how very daring, topping an overused skyscraper style from the past with an overused bookcase style from an even older past. You may call it vision all you want, but anyone with sense would call it hindsight."

"I'd call it quits," Donna purred almost inaudibly, taking my arm with a gentle pressure that I would come to know irritatingly well. "Trevor," she said, turning to the skinny fool with a dazzling smile, "I think I understand what you're getting at: What matters most about this building is not necessarily whether it's great architecture in and of itself, it's the fact that it will spur other, maybe greater, innovations. You see it as a catalyst."

"Exactly! Exactly!" breathed Trevor, looking as if he would fall at Donna's feet from either adoration or weak ankles.

The lights flickered. "Oh, we should take our seats, darling," she observed and, waving a gracious farewell to the others, steered me into the auditorium.

"What a despicable equivocation, *darling*," I hissed, finally freeing my arm from her fingers. "All you did was repeat his own statement back to him in fancier translation." I sneered at her. "You've turned into quite the lickspittle here, haven't you? So eager to insinuate yourself with everyone that you side in public with that dim dandelion against your own husband."

She looked at me steadily. "Once again, you're twisting the truth to present it from the worst possible angle. You were tactless; I was trying to smooth things over because I have to associate with that guy. There's nothing suck-uppy about getting along with people, you know? Although clearly, you don't."

"I think it's contemptible and dishonest to nod and smile and encourage the twaddle of self-serious twits. That particular twit was only mouthing the nonsense he's heard other, more important twits say, and such nonsense ends up becoming accepted wisdom because people like you think it's impolitic to challenge the bleating ninnies who repeat it. All your supposed social skills accomplish is the breeding of more idiots."

We had reached our aisle and were about to edge past a number of already-seated people who were watching us with alarmed attention. Donna leaned her head close to mine.

"And all your ringing self-righteousness is just a lame excuse to be rude and cause a scene," she said in withering *sotto voce*, and moved unhurriedly down the row, smiling and apologizing to everyone she disarranged.

I turned and walked out.

The night, already humid with a strong sea breeze, had become drizzly, as well. I didn't want to return to the hotel, but I also didn't want to go walking, and there weren't many other choices. For the first time, I wondered if I had made a mistake in marrying Donna. Not whether marriage in general was the right thing for me—I had been worried about that from the moment I proposed to her. But I'd never had a second's doubt before now that Donna was who I wanted, whether I married her or not. I had wanted her in my bed, I had wanted to know what she thought, what she'd say and do, how she would respond to me. And her responses had always been intriguing, challenging; even when I didn't actually like them, I had felt that we were playing an exciting match of some kind and that winning meant I could get her to admit that I was special to her as no one else was. And I had.

But this cozying up to everyone, the blandishments I heard her utter, the unctuous, pandering chitchat to which she sank to get in good with the kind of people whom she would have mercilessly ridiculed six months ago... Had she always been like this and I simply hadn't seen it? It was nauseating and infuriating—sickly sweet to everyone else and turning that sharp tongue only on me.

Her calculated charm seemed manipulative, slick and fake, a subterfuge. She was hiding something, some agenda, she must be. What was I, just a stepping stone to someone better? The shifty bitch, playing up to these prats she thought could do something for her and cutting me down for seeing through them and her.

I found I was pacing round and round the barnlike Maltings like a trapped beast, sodden and wildly angry, ill with fear that Donna didn't really love me and yet determined to break with her. I couldn't live with this, I couldn't. I would just leave.

I struck out across the grounds, skidding down slopes in the wet grass, nearly racing toward the distant lights of the village. I was sorry I had come—this place had revealed Donna to be a performer, indeed, an actor who had taken me in with a show of love and truthfulness as fraudulent as her flattery of Trevor. I'd be moved out of the apartment by the time she got back to New York.

I was having trouble breathing. I leaned against a tree, trying to inhale slowly, fighting the pounding of my heart, but my lungs wouldn't expand. I began gasping and bent over double, dizzy, then sat suddenly as my knees gave out. I didn't know what was happening; I feared I was having a heart attack, but I had no pain, just the tightness encasing my lungs. I couldn't focus my eyes. Flashes of light spun in front of me. I realized I might faint and lay flat on the wet turf as if someone had fished me out of the nearby pond like a perch and left me there to suffocate. I was too far from the Maltings to call for help, probably couldn't have managed a shout anyway. So I lay in the cold April grass in the dark in my good coat, listened to the wind in the reeds, and tried to stay conscious.

I had never had such an episode before. What if I had a weak heart? No doctor had ever mentioned such a condition to me, and I wasn't even twenty-nine yet. But my young father had somehow drowned—what if it had been his heart that failed him? I tried not to think about that, keeping very still and concentrating on feeling my stomach rise and fall, rise and fall, for many minutes, until I felt the tension in my muscles relent a bit. I listened: my heart was beating more calmly and evenly, and I found I was able to take a couple of deep, quivering breaths that made me cough a little, but seemed otherwise normal. What had gone wrong with me?

The spitting rain had stopped and a shred of moon shone through the leaves on the tree I had sagged against. I slowly sat up and then stood—all seemed well enough, except for my clothes, so I carefully walked the remaining distance to Snape and found a pub where I could clean up a bit in the loo and find out where to catch a bus back to Aldeburgh.

Donna had not left my mind once, though I felt as if we had both left our marriage. She lurked at the edges of the pictures in my head like someone you try to see in a dream but can't, a faceless shadow who is always just out of view. Instead, I saw myself—in the pub mirror, in the dark windows of the bus—a solitary figure in a black coat, whose grim eyes and austere line of mouth invited no greeting. A man alone. And I wondered if that was what I chose to be, or if others had made me so.

When the bus stopped at Aldeburgh, I got out and walked down to the sea. The surf was strong with the wind behind it, and the rhythmic crunch of waves on the beach nearly drowned out the sound of my shoes on the shingle as I wandered, as wholly inside myself as if I were invisible. Did I need her? Did I need anyone? Did the death of love make life unlivable? If I were shaped or sentenced to be alone all my life, could I survive it? Swaying there in the roar of air and water, as bleak inside as it was out, I knew I could. I'd never had love in the first place, had I? Not since Father. And I could sing, and music was a partner that had never let me down. I would trust in that and no other.

I strode back up the beach, comfortable in the concealing dark and the fading cloak of whispers spun for me by the complicit waves.

Donna was waiting at the hotel. She rose from a chair when she saw me and we went to our room together without speaking. As soon as the door was shut, she confronted me, face very white and still.

"Why did you leave? What's happened to you?" she asked me in a voice as thin and taut as a violin string.

"Why did you insult me?" I answered coolly. I had already accepted how this discussion would turn out.

"You were obnoxious to Trevor. *You* called *me* a lickspittle— *and* contemptible *and* a liar for trying to make him feel better. You implied that I was disloyal for not letting you get away with acting like a jerk, as if I should just shut up and let you make me an accomplice to your bad behavior. Is that really your idea of what a marriage is?"

"Well, evidently, your idea of marriage is one in which you call the tune and I dance to it—and a very typical little female tune it is, too. Why don't you marry Trevor? I think the two of you are a much better match than we are. A perfect match between manipulation and ignorance."

"Oh, that is so you—I have to bend and compromise and tolerate all your strange little rules, but if I expect you to do the same in return, oh no, that's *castrating* and I'm an evil, controlling witch. So I must never take anyone else's side against yours in public, but you can embarrass me in front of my colleagues, huh? And you can say any horrible thing you want about me and you expect me to stay put and take it, but the minute I fight back, you run away. How can you be so talented and be such an idiotic asshole?"

"Who on earth would want to stay with you and be humiliated?"

"You're confusing humiliation with being told the truth. That's what you can't take."

"The truth is I'm rude? I suppose you'd think any man with a backbone was rude."

"Sometimes you *are* rude! Not all the time, but you do make scenes. You're a legend in Paris—that costume designer probably sticks pins in your headshot every night, and everyone in the theater heard you squawking about the Knave shoving you out of the spotlight. That's not professional! I'm trying hard to be professional so people will want to work with me, but you don't seem to give a damn who you vent your spleen on, or how much you're going to make them loathe you. It's as if you *expect* them to dislike you and reject you and you're determined to make sure of it. Why do you do that?" Her focus on me seemed to sharpen. "And why are you all dirty?"

"No reason that would interest you. In fact, my reasons are none of your business at all."

"But of course they are." She gaped at me. "I love you. If you have reasons, why won't you tell me what they are, so I'll understand? Why won't you talk to me?"

I turned away. "Isn't that what we were doing?"

"Oh, bullshit!" She half-laughed in apparent exasperation. "We're not talking, and you know it. We're fighting. And I *told* you I hate fighting. And you're still not telling me what I need to know about you. And as for marrying *Trevor*..."

She doubled over with great silent guffaws from which she couldn't seem to recover long enough to inhale at all, reminding me oddly of my own attack earlier in the evening.

"Hooooh, my God," she finally gasped, "he really does look exactly like a dandelion," and fell back on the bed, her flat stomach bouncing with laughter as if something inside were trying to box its way out.

"With the brains of a milkweed," I added sourly.

But my resolve to be done with her had evaporated at the sight of her lying there, and I climbed on top of her, a muddy gabardine knee on either side of her slim, skirted hips.

She smiled that wry, shrewd smile. "That won't silence me," she said.

"Just as long as it doesn't make you laugh."

I was spent and half-asleep with her in my arms when she spoke my name, searching my bleary eyes with a deep, urgent gaze.

"I hope this is a good moment," she said, with a hesitance that signaled my attention. "I didn't want you to leave without knowing and I wasn't sure myself until yesterday morning."

I raised my head, apprehensive. Behind Donna, the sun was rising, sending a beam through a window whose curtains I had forgotten to close. I looked from it to her.

"I'm pregnant," she said.

"Oh, my God." I stared at her. "But we agreed—"

"I didn't plan this any more than you did. It must have happened the morning I left, remember? We made love that night and you woke up really early and wanted to do it again and I was too sleepy to put in more spermicide? I thought just leaving the diaphragm in as it was would be enough. Obviously, it wasn't."

She sounded a bit bleak. I was still so shocked, I didn't know what to say.

"What do you want to do?" I finally asked.

"I've been thinking about it—about nothing else, to be honest. I'm not going to stop working, so I don't know how we'll manage, but I think we should keep it."

A baby. Nothing had been further from my mind. Nothing I wanted less. Cancer, maybe.

I forced myself to look at Donna and her smile was only a grimace.

"So now you really want to leave," she said flatly.

"No, of course not"—though I had been furious enough to plan on it last night, even before I knew she was pregnant—"of course not, I just can't take it all in yet. When…?"

"I'm not sure, maybe November. I haven't even seen a doctor yet, you know—just bought a pregnancy test at the drugstore. I'll have to go to someone here to start, and then go to my own ob-gyn when I get home."

"Do you feel ill?" It was easier to talk about medical details than about the prospect of parenthood.

"Not really. A little weird when I first wake up."

I laid my hand on her smooth abdomen that still curved down into a warm, silky plain between her hip bones. No sign of anything. The whole idea was hard to believe in, except for the dark dismay in Donna's eyes. I didn't want to believe it.

"Are you sure you want to go ahead with this?" Desperate for her to say no.

"Don't you?"

I was being forced back into what I had escaped. I could see it surrounding me, the silent, shadowy prison of an unhappy child, a new prison, one of my own making, and child or parent, I didn't want be there. I knew I'd never get away again. I had to say no, I had to. No!

Her eyes waited, hurt brimming.

"We're grown-ups," I heard myself say. "We're married. We have a pretty good income."

I found something like a smile, screaming inside myself at my hypocrisy. "I think we could carry it off."

"Such rapture." She smiled faintly too.

I got back to New York just in time for rush hour and a gray, chilly evening with no hint of green on any tree. I'd left the apartment in some disarray and, with my last atoms of energy, was putting things away when the phone rang.

It was Brownlea. Mother was dying.

XVII

I woke up in a chair.

It was a large one, all right angles and heavy wood, with a padded back and seat, but highly uncomfortable, nonetheless. I had somehow curled myself into it sideways and my first semiconscious thought was that I needed to call for help: I was clearly trapped or injured or both, and I couldn't feel my legs.

My second thought was that Brownlea looked old. He was asleep opposite me in a matching chair, bolt upright but for his head, which lolled forward under a curtain of straight gray hair not quite long enough to hide the deep creases in his neck.

I had imagined him all these years as perpetually fortyish and mousy, with a growing paunch, and was shocked to discover that he had dried, and smartened, up instead—a silvery twig in a good-label cotton polo and pressed khakis. Only his perpetually slipping glasses and the hair falling over them recalled the man I had known.

Rather, the man I had hardly known. Why had he so devoted himself to her, a woman who would never marry him? I had always assumed, when I thought about it at all, that it was because he had so little to offer anyone else.

And yet, as always, he had met my plane on the afternoon I arrived in the islands, following a frenzy of phone calls to Donna, Gunter, Sam, and the airlines, and a fast repacking for a flight out the next morning. He never seemed to doubt that I would come any more than I doubted he would be there to pick me up. We'd given each other a long look and then he'd shaken my hand as if my last visit had been six months ago and not ten years, and silently insisted on carrying my bag to the car.

"She's been in hospital for a week now," he said, pushing his glasses up on his nose and carefully backing what I'd been amused to note was an elderly but exquisitely well-cared-for

Aston Martin out of the airport car park. At long last, a racing car in a size he could drive. A DB5, no less. "I've been urging her to ring you, or to let me, ever since she was admitted, but she's kept on refusing and finally I just called you anyway. She doesn't know you're here."

His eyes flicked toward me and then back to the road; it was leading us to an impressive, multi-laned bridge that had been built between the main island and ours, and he seemed to want to pay close attention to navigating across it.

"I'm a bit surprised I'm here," I blurted without meaning to, and he nodded slowly without answering.

He'd explained over the phone that Mother had obviously felt unwell for months, but wouldn't tell him what was wrong or go to the doctor. She'd gotten very thin—it had worried him—but it wasn't until he came to take her to dinner the previous Sunday and found her lying in the hallway, unable to get up, that she would admit she was seriously ill. He had driven her to the emergency room. The doctors had discovered within minutes that she had an advanced-stage melanoma. They'd blamed the tropical light; the English should stay out of the sun, they'd said somberly.

God knows she'd tried.

Neither of us spoke. Brownlea gripped the highly polished wheel with a determination that always startled me to see in him, as if I'd cut into a pudding and struck steel. The water of the channel flickered by in dazzling turquoise mosaic squares made by the gaps in the row of concrete stanchions we were passing at seventy kilometers an hour, under the burning sun that had killed my mother at last. I think she had always been sure it would.

Water, light, and silence—my unholy trinity.

Donna had offered to cut short her residency and come along—it's a family crisis, I should be with you, she kept saying—but she didn't belong to any of this, I didn't want her to. She was part of another life that Mother had rejected altogether, and what would the two of them do with each other but loathe on sight or, worse, unite in some unknowable she-fashion against me? No, the very idea made me shudder. I had been right not to give in.

I scarcely knew how I would speak to Mother myself. I couldn't tolerate having to mediate a first meeting between my new wife and my terminally ill mother who wished I'd never been born.

If anyone could have come, I wished it had been Gunter. He would have known what to say to everyone. He would have stood between me and Mother like this bridge. But he had just created a spring piano competition in Chicago and, as director, he could scarcely leave town on the eve of its debut, even for this.

"I want so much to go with you, my boy," he had rumbled over the phone. "In spite of all the heartache she has caused you, I know it will be a hard thing for you to say goodbye to your mother. But I'm glad you are making the journey and I hope you and she can say things that will bring you peace. Call Debbie and me anytime you need us, night or day, and remember we love you."

I rubbed my eyes and Brownlea glanced sideways at me again.

"We don't have to go straight there," he said, deliberately diffident. "I did book you a room at the Pink Palace"—what everyone on the island called the grand bayside Royal Palm Hotel—"but perhaps you'd care to stop at the house first?"

"No," I answered, a little too loudly. "Thank you. Let's just go to see her and get the suspense over with."

We had reached the end of the span, which turned into the newly widened Queen's Way. The gleam of refurbishment and expansion was everywhere: we cruised past sparkling hotels and shops in town before pulling up beside the great white wedding cake that was Princess Mary Hospital. I didn't want to go in. My father had been brought here, and now my mother—the first event such a deep, terrifying, scarring loss and this next perhaps nothing more than an unpleasant afternoon whose effect on me I could not predict. Whatever it would be, I wanted to avoid it and couldn't.

Brownlea led the way through the old-fashioned, high-ceilinged entrance hall with its indolent paddle fans and down modernized corridors of brilliant fluorescent light, shiny lino, and air-conditioning. It didn't seem possible that Mother had been incorporated by this brisk scientific institution, where all was relentlessly probed and exposed. I imagined her shriveled like a vampire bat under the glare.

We reached her room. Apologetically, Brownlea suggested, "Perhaps I should look in first," and disappeared behind the door. I heard voices briefly, and then he returned.

"I told her only that she has another visitor," he said quietly, and stepped aside to let me in.

I could barely force myself to enter. The air smelled cold and faintly chemical, but underneath that was a distressing trace of human odor. A pale blue curtain had been pulled halfway round the bed to shield it a bit from the doorway, and as I pushed it aside, I felt a flash of that panic that had struck me at Aldeburgh. Why had I come? I didn't want to see her. I couldn't look at her.

She was staring at me through half-open eyes as weary as they were watchful. They didn't blink, nor did her expression change; I wondered if she really saw me. Her face was sallow, sunken beneath the lank cascade of salt-and-pepper hair spread out in a tangle on the pillow. I had expected wires, bags, IV trees, blinking monitors, but nothing seemed to be attached to her except a clear plastic nosepiece and its trailing oxygen tube.

All this in a single second and then, against my every inclination, I stepped toward the head of the bed.

"Hello, Mother." I spoke loudly out of habit that I'd forgotten I had.

She turned her eyes up to look at me and her deliberate taking-in of everything about me left no doubt that she knew who I was. Under her scrutiny, I became conscious of myself, my appearance—the tight jeans and loose cotton jacket that I'd chosen for their high fashion and sophistication felt suddenly pretentious, a costume worn by an awkward boy for whom they hadn't been made.

She said, "Simon should have told me you were coming."

"Why? Would you have arranged to be out?"

She closed her eyes for a moment. "No. I would have brushed my hair."

She gestured weakly at the nearby chair. "Why don't you sit down? If I raise the bed a bit, I'll be able to see you well enough."

So I sat. I noticed several bunches of flowers in vases along the windowsill; she followed my glance and, in her toneless way, said, "The roses are from Simon. The others were sent by people at church."

"Why on earth have you continued to go to church all this time?"

This was not the line of questioning I had intended to pursue. Her face seemed to close up.

"Everyone goes to church."

"Not if they feel enslaved and tortured by it."

These things were popping from my mouth like sand crabs from their burrows. I hadn't realized until I said it that I had always known there was something wrong about Mother and the church. Something quite wrong.

"Is that why you came? To pass judgment on my faith?" The hauteur on her thin face accentuated the medieval severity of her cheekbones and lips.

"Yes." Another sand crab. "Partly." I changed the subject. "You must have known long before you fell that you were ill. Why didn't you get help?"

The starch seemed to flow out of her, leaving her limp and flat as the sheets on which she lay. "For whom would I have reason to live?" she muttered, and closed her eyes again.

There was a tap on the door and Brownlea's head poked round it, cautiously.

"All right, then?" he whispered.

"I'm very tired," Mother spoke up sharply, her disease having evidently improved her hearing. She fixed her heavy-lidded gaze on him. "I would like to rest now, Simon. Perhaps tomorrow around lunch, if you can leave the school."

And she turned away.

Brownlea beckoned, and I walked out behind him. Neither of us said a word.

"Would you care to join me for dinner?" he finally ventured as we quick-marched through the searing car park and began airing out the Aston Martin. "There's a rather good new place on the wharf—palm-thatched hut and conch shells and all that, of course, but top-notch fritters and stone crab legs, if you've a taste for them."

I shrugged. "All right, why not?" And then remembered I wasn't fourteen any longer and added, "Thank you for inviting me."

"She tires very quickly, you know." He was driving now, not looking at me. "Rather more quickly when there's something she wants to avoid discussing." A tiny, collusive smile tightened a corner of his wistful mouth and disappeared again. "But I don't see any reason any longer not to tell you that she finds excuses to mention you no matter what the conversation is about and she follows your career closely. Secretly."

"As she's done everything else." I wedged myself into the triangle formed by seat and door and crossed my arms. "See here, Mr. Brownlea—"

"Please call me Simon," he said mildly, with a measuring glance at me. "High time you did, really."

"As you wish." There was a pause while I weighed using the name, but could not. "I'm well past caring, but I suppose I should know what has happened over the last decade. To her. Did she ever tell you that she abandoned me in New York? Did she ever express even the merest atom of regret?"

"Not directly. She almost never admits anything directly, even now." He sighed. "The only reason I knew that she had come back early from New York is that I happened to see her in town, at a distance, the day before she'd been due to return. Posting some letters, it looked like. I tried to catch up with her, but she got into her car and drove off before she saw me. I'd planned to fetch her from the airport, so I was quite curious as to why she hadn't called me to say her plans had changed."

We were at the crab shack by now, and were shown a table overlooking the water and, mercifully, facing a cool breeze. We ordered pints and fritters to start and Brownlea downed a generous amount from his glass, gazing out at a pair of scraggly pelicans plunging and bobbing some yards out.

"So, to get to the point," he said abruptly, "she phoned me the next morning to say she'd heard a hurricane was brewing round Bermuda, which was true enough, and because you were so well settled in, she'd decided to come home early and avoid getting diverted and stranded somewhere by bad weather. She also said she hadn't called for me to pick her up from the earlier flight to spare me inconvenience.

"I never asked her specifically about you or Juilliard, other than polite queries regarding your health and how she found the city and such. And she never, ever hinted that anything disastrous had occurred. But something about her had changed. It's hard to explain what it was."

He chose a fritter from the basket, laying it aside on his plate. "When I first met her, nineteen—twenty?—years ago, I saw what looked like a civil war going on behind her eyes. She was so tough, so self-reliant, this young widow with a small boy— *prickly* she was, but I could sense somehow that the thorns were bravado. That deep inside, she was frightened and the fright made her angry—rather like you, when you were my student, if I may say so—and it was her anger, her sheer anger at her own fear and whatever was causing it, that kept her battling with herself all the time, that gave her the strength to live. As if her fear were a weakness that offended her pride and so she had to crush it. Quite a ferocious woman"—he looked at me, eyes amused behind the glasses—"as we know.

"But after New York, it was as if the war were over and she

had lost. She was no less prickly, no less unyielding, but it was a display to convince others, not herself. As if she'd decided that she and her life were lost causes."

Brownlea's voice seemed to be getting hoarse, and he paused to finish his pint and take an indifferent bite of his now-cold fritter. He swallowed hard.

"She subscribed to the Sunday *New York Times*, you know, after she got back. Flown in every Tuesday, it was. But eventually, from the lack of phone calls or any other first-hand information she had to report on your progress at school, it became obvious that you and she had fallen out. And then I asked if something was amiss and could I help. You can imagine the reception *that* got.

"One evening before Christmas, I came over and found an article she'd clipped from the *Times*—a notice on a Juilliard performance of *Amahl and the Night Visitors*. And you were mentioned in it. For singing."

"Ah yes. King Melchior."

"*Singing.* I was shocked, but not terribly surprised, as I'd got an inkling even before you left for Chicago, and I realized what must have happened, at least in part. I've always thought it odd that your mother dislikes singing so much, although"—and his voice grew tentative—"I imagined that it reminded her painfully of your father."

When I didn't seem irate at his mention of Father, he took a deep breath and added, "She did tell me seriously once, a few years ago and quite out of nowhere, that singing was dangerous. I suppose I was taken off guard, it was a funny sort of thing to say, certainly, but I made a little joke—trying to lighten her mood, you know—and said that if that's true, then she must believe the church choir is even closer to fatal than the Reverend Bainbridge's sermons. She looked at me with a horror I've never seen before or since on any face. Locked herself in her room. It took two weeks of apologies and explanations to convince her I hadn't meant any offense. I never did learn what had upset her so."

The waiter brought two more pints and our plates of crab legs. Brownlea picked up his fork and put it down again.

"I guess I honestly don't know many facts about her after twenty years. I've gotten hints, formed theories. I suppose I don't have what you'd call a whole relationship with her, any more than I've had a whole career. I'm going to say too much now and tell you that I love her, but it's a love based on what I sense about her rather than what she's shared with me. She needs me, in her way, but"—a little bitterly—"I know my place."

He fell to cracking crab shells. I sat watching him, not hungry, mind adrift. For the first time, I felt a bond with him. He was a decent fellow, probably could have had a nice wife and family. But he had chosen Mother and Mother made him suffer. Mother made everyone suffer, including herself. Not for much longer, of course—Brownlea'd said the doctors had given her a mere three weeks, maybe less, and had warned that she'd stop being able to communicate sometime before that. A combination of metastases, breathing problems, and not eating would sap her body and brain until she lapsed into apparent unconsciousness. Though most people could still hear at that stage, they said, with Mother's hearing being already pretty much gone, she would be truly cut off from everyone until she died.

And how would that be different from the way things had always been?

XVIII

I pressed my hands to my temples, startling Brownlea. "You feel ill?" he asked. "Headache?"

"No, I'm okay, thanks. But I want to go back to the hospital tonight. Would you mind taking me?"

In the end, he would not be dissuaded from taking me to the hotel first, waiting in the lobby while I went up and quickly showered and changed. It was already 8:30 by then and I wasn't sure whether or not I would be allowed to visit Mother so late, but I convinced Brownlea that I would be all right if he left me on the hospital doorstep and went home and, as it happened, no one stopped me going into Mother's room.

A nightlight afforded the only illumination round her bed; she was asleep, mouth half open, snoring in a way I'd never heard before, a few quick, hard breaths followed by a silence in which she seemed not to breathe at all. The silences bothered me; I felt the urge to wake her, to make sure she still lived. Her face looked strangely young in sleep, so thin and sharp, like that of a woman in her twenties, frown lines smoothed away. Yet she was not peaceful—she fidgeted irritably, shifting position as if unable to get comfortable and aimlessly worrying the blanket with limp fingers. She was shrunken in all ways. Her toes, showing where they had pushed away the covers, looked bloodless, a row of crusted bones. Her arm, protruding from the hospital gown she wore, was only a stick hung with trembling folds of pale gelatin.

I knew I should feel grief: my mother was dying; she would be gone soon and I would never see her again. Instead, I felt only appalled, revulsed that a human being could shrivel to this...this yellowed rind, this flaccid translucence drying up and decomposing before my eyes.

She was only fifty-two.

I sat in the twilight with her, the rasp of her erratic breathing and the hiss of the oxygen filling the room with the tension of unspoken struggle—like an alien music, made by the blowing and fretting and beating of a one-woman orchestra as she unconsciously played the same unresolved chord over and over. Could she hear herself? Or dream, with all the painkillers in her system? And if she could, of what did she dream?

The door opened unexpectedly, admitting a slice of light along with a plump nurse, who didn't seem put out to see me there, but said a cheery hello and asked if I were the son from America. I said I was.

"She been hoping you'd come," she declared, checking Mother's pulse.

I must have looked skeptical, because she added, "Oh, you musn't think she always like this, though she will be more and more, I'm afraid. She often quite chatty…"

Mother's eyelids fluttered open and, in a seamless transition, the nurse refocused her attention.

"Good evening, dear, sorry to wake you, but I must take your temperature," she said loudly. "And let's check to see if you need a change. No! Still dry. All right, hold this under your tongue, please."

Mother didn't notice me at first. She obediently faced the thermometer and closed her lips around it, watching the nurse watch the electronic gadget that registered degrees Celsius.

"Hmmm, you got a bit of fever tonight. Not unusual," Nurse sing-songed soothingly, turning to me. "At this stage, she getting what is called tumor fever, dear, it come from the tumors shedding cells, spreading. Often happens this time of night. They get the sweats with it."

If Mother registered that the nurse was talking to someone else, she gave no sign of it. Instead, she suddenly flung herself on her side, fumbled for the railing and began to pull up into a sitting position while rocking herself toward the end of the bed.

"Missy, what you trying to do?"

Mother's legs dangled over the edge and the rest of her looked to be sliding after them. The nurse grabbed her by the elbow. "Where you think you going, dear?"

"The toilet, I must, I must…" Mother repeated doggedly. She clung to the nurse and resisted her at the same time.

"You going to have trouble walking that far, dear, and you don't need to get up. You have your nappy, you can just lie right here an' go."

I looked at the floor, embarrassed, appalled again.

"Oh." Mother frowned. "Oh, I…but I need to make lunch, Simon is coming, I want to make something nice, we're so tired of the dull food at this hotel. I must telephone him to bring some good crab. Yes, crab and a ripe pineapple, we'll have salad, that will taste so fresh after all that, that tinned bouillon. And we'll need some…some…wine…"

"You hungry, missy? I can bring you some little salad, maybe some ice cream? That taste good?"

"Yes, yes, a big seafood salad with crisp lettuce and half a cored pineapple… Just go down to the wharf…"

With the nurse assuring and placating, Mother lay back down to await her feast, but began struggling to rise again only moments later. I stood next to the bed to block her, as the nurse had gone to order the food; she confronted my belt buckle and slowly lifted her gaze to my face, astonishment all over hers.

"Who…?" she began suspiciously, but was interrupted by the nurse, who came in with a tray. The tiny garden salad and fruit cup and bread and butter looked appetizing enough for hospital fare but, in the end, Mother wouldn't take anything after the first bite of lettuce.

"Everything tastes of metal," she fussed and began looking about the room distractedly. "My checkbook, where is it? I haven't seen it in days, where is it?" she shrilled, fully alarmed. "I have bills to pay, the rent…"

The nurse took Mother by the hands and looked her in the face, calmly commanding her attention. "You didn't bring a checkbook, dear. You visiting us here at hospital. All your important things safe at home. You ask Mr. Simon next time he come—he tell you everything safe."

"Home? It's at home? When can I go there? I want to go home…"

"Not quite yet, dear. You rest now. I be back just as soon as I find the doctor and see if he want you to have something to bring your fever down."

She bustled out.

Mother fixed her clouded gaze on me with a glimmer of recognition. "Are you still here?" she queried, with faint asperity.

"Not still. Again. Are you surprised?"

"Yes, I thought you'd gone back to…to…Chicago."

"Surely you mean New York."

"Yes, all right, New York. It's been so many years since I've seen you, I can't keep track of where you're living."

It occurred to me that, between the cancer and the fever and the medications, her mind might not be just temporarily addled. It might be going, and permanently. How much had she already forgotten? Another stab of panic shot through me. I took deep breaths.

"Well," I said after a moment. "I do live in New York and have ever since you took me there to go to Juilliard. Do you remember taking me there?"

She looked away and shut her eyes. "A sip of water," she said, eyes still closed.

I looked round and saw a plastic cup with a straw in it on the tray table. The cup was about half full of water and ice, so I handed it to her, but she seemed unable to guide the straw into her mouth. I took the cup and did it for her, but I could feel something shutting down inside me—nerve endings, thoughts—as if my brain were retreating behind a security door in hopes of not having to see something horrible. I knew my eyes were wide and as blank as my face.

She took several sips and let go the straw.

"Mother, do you remember leaving me at Juilliard?"

She would not look at me. "I remember opening your bank account and meeting your roommate and feeling that you were quite ready to begin school by the time I left."

I wanted to shout at her, had wanted to all day, wanted to call her the liar she was and the coward—my Joan of Arc, a coward in the end—but I didn't. I didn't. I sat back down on the hard chair and breathed, deep intakes and long, exhaled *diminuendos* of air, watching her and waiting for her to go on. I had more time than she did.

"Is that what you mean?" she asked at last, pettishly. "Or are you driving at something else?"

"You know the answer to that, Mother," I replied quietly. "Why won't you admit what you did?"

I pulled the chair closer to the bed. She curled away from me into the pillow.

"You walked out on me, Mother. You made it clear that you wished I had never existed and then you left me standing there in my advisor's office. You went away and you haven't tried to see or speak to me in ten years. I know you remember," I said.

I stood up and leaned over her, my face close to her half-hidden one. "Not even cancer has made you forget, has it? You told me once that you had to love God first in order to help me. Is that what your God demanded, that you abandon me at eighteen? That all through my childhood you never love me properly or make me feel wanted and safe? That you hurt me with your coldness and keep me lonely and scared? Did that put you right with him?"

I was nearly whispering. Whispering and watching her trying not hear. But she heard.

"What kind of God would want that and what kind of woman would believe in him? What terrible harm have you caused because of him? Or was he just an excuse for your own failings? What's the real reason you couldn't love me, Mother? What's the real reason?"

My hands were shaking, but I remained tightly in control.

"If you truly believe in this cruel, frightening God of yours, Mother, you must believe that you're going to see him soon. How are you going to face him if you can't even face me?"

I sat down again.

Mother didn't move. The night light, shining up from the fixture above her bed, cast a sickly, greenish glow over the plain white wall and bedcovers, making deep shadows of every slat in the blinds, every hollow of Mother's face and form. Noises—footsteps, the brisk chatter of nurses, the clatter of gurneys and bedrails—seemed to jostle each other to get through the barely open doorway, colliding dully against the metal and wood. The oxygen and air-conditioning whirred.

"I fought...against...loving you." Mother's voice was foggy, halting, scarcely audible. She didn't turn to me. "Fought it. I was...horrified...to be pregnant. Not even married yet."

"What do you mean?" I reached across the bed to tug at her arm, try to see her face. "Not married? Your anniversary is in September. My birthday is in June."

She shook me off, weakly. "We told you it was September, but it wasn't. It was December 8th."

I was stunned. "Are you saying you *had* to get married? That you wouldn't have if I—"

"No. No," she muttered, quite crossly. "We were already engaged. Married was what we wanted to be, married and together. The...*two* of us. We hadn't planned for a baby at all."

"Just like..." I caught myself.

"Just...like what?" Mother asked with feeble annoyance at the interruption.

"Never mind," I said.

"I thought my having a child so soon would hurt your father's career, stop him wanting to marry me. But he was so happy that he was going to be a father, so sure we could manage. So sure. I let myself be glad as well. I thought we were blessed in our love and our work. Our great work."

She groaned and flung the covers off, then almost immediately shivered and tried to pull them back up. I dragged just the sheet up to her chin and asked if she wanted the blanket too. She ignored me and resumed with labored breath

"I wanted to help your father become a great...conductor. He could have been. Travel the world. Your father was...my mission. He was everything. I sang for him in choir. For *him*. The sound he made from our voices raised me up...as if it were a wind for me to fly on. It came from God. I'd been asking God to give me my task. Father said I would have one, that men were given gifts and it was the task of women to help those gifts to flower. Mother's task was to help Father heal the sick. Sit up with them at night at the clinic, nurse them. She checked his cultures every day, typed his research papers. His success was her success. Her duty to obey, he said."

Mother's forehead was covered in tiny droplets. She was scarcely pausing for breath now, gasping and gabbling more and more incoherently.

"Sin to waste his genius, sin against God. Work and pray for his success. We had to pray on our knees she and I, first light, last light, he saw to it. Earning her bread. Genius demands sacrifice. He forced...he said..." Her voice deepened. "We sacrifice so I may...save lives as God saves souls! Serve me and serve God! Bible says, my helpmeet. She died. Helping. He going to London, big award, she pregnant. Exhausted. So tired, need to... Patients to tend, her duty. He made her promise, he made her, she, I...saw...sitting, resting. Up! Get up! Your work's not... Get out of that...or... Only eleven, pulling, pulling... Mother, try! Mother... He shouted, shoved...into the wall, I was crying...she...he... o! ...punched her, her stomach, the baby...she fell down. Never sit when I say! ...sick, he just stepped...over...gone. Shhhshhh. Shhh...hand up, never...all right, family...family secret. Family secret."

The droplets had collected into tiny streams coursing into her hair. I wiped them away with a tissue. She shook her head wildly and tried to get up again, fumbling at the rail and throwing her feet over the edge of the mattress. I got hold of her arm with one hand and rang for the nurse with the other.

"Late!" she muttered frantically. "Late! ...Do rounds or... don't...worse...rounds 'n round 'n round 'n round like her belly in her gown... all fall gown. Dizzy fall, can't...baby. Baby. Baby, no, no. Unnnnh!"

She pulled and slapped at my hand, sobbing. "Baby, soon... too sss...it par...par-ty, nnnn, no not... Parch. Parch. Parcher... parcher-ishun. Father's...word, no, Father, just...blood, blood, I...couldn't stop, she...she..."

Mother went limp, face crumpled. "Baby so...still. Mother! Mother!"

The nurse ran in, going round the bed and got a strong arm circled around Mother's shoulders. "It all right, dear, it all right, you safe."

Mother looked at her, bewildered, and then at me. The nurse said to me, "I was hearing her all the way down the corridor, but I had to finish with another patient before I could come," and turned back to Mother. "Now, missy, you don't need to get up, you need to lie down. Your legs not strong enough to hold you. Remember how you fell down the day you had to come here to hospital? You still have the bruises. Come now, lie back."

Nurse rearranged Mother in the bed, took her temperature again, persuaded her to swallow some acetaminophen and then reached for a small bottle with a dropper, gently but swiftly tilting Mother's chin and squeezing the tiny bulb. "This a kind of morphine," she said as she worked. "Doctor say she to have two drops every two hours if she have pain or become agitated. It help calm them down. She probably sleep now."

"Who are you?" Mother wailed at her, still a little wild-eyed. "Where's the nice nurse? She'll help me. She brought me juice."

The nurse smiled. "I am that nice nurse. Same one. Pauline. I be here every night this week. You want some juice now? Maybe a little something to eat?"

"Juice. Yes, pine...apple. Pineapple. Cold."

"All right. We have that here on the floor, in our icebox. I get you some. Maybe a little serving of porridge, too? Soup?"

Mother sat up a little and peered at me vaguely, face flushed.

"Died serving. For God so loved her…he said. Her duty, mine. Serve fathers on earth in heaven. Revere…us, fear us. Reverus fearus, fearus…servus."

Her eyes closed, then popped opened again immediately, round and searching. "Did I tell you I was in Switzerland?"

Nurse Pauline patted her hand and left. I followed her out to the corridor.

"Is she delirious?" I asked in an undertone.

She nodded. "That happen often. Could be the fever, could be the cancer, maybe both—they thoughts wander or they can have hallucinations. Sometimes they make no sense because they can't remember the right words for what they want to say. I suspect there may be disease in her brain, now. Has she talked about seeing anyone she knows, anyone who's already passed on?"

"N-no. No." I was taken aback. "You mean, as if they were in the room with her?"

She nodded again.

I shuddered without meaning to. "No. That *would* be disturbing."

The nurse smiled gently. "Sometimes it comforting. For the patient. I'll get her juice now."

When the nurse returned, Mother greedily sipped half of the cup of bright yellow juice, but accepted only one spoonful of porridge before turning away. The nurse changed the soaking sheets and left again.

Mother was restless, still burning. I touched her fingers to stop their twitching and they closed around mine, hard. I looked at her face and she was staring at me with dark eyes as hot as her hands.

"My…father," she rasped. Her grip tightened. "Hated. H-h-h-h-hated. Worked for him. Always. No friends. Work and church. Work and church. Wanted to s-sing."

I started back from her, unable to believe I had heard this, but she didn't let go.

"Choir. Extra hour every…week, he disapproved. My time

his, I was his. God expected. But I went. I went. My one defiance."

She smiled, a tiny half-smile, ghastly in its dying echo of teen rebellion.

"Your father." She tugged at my hand urgently, looking back and forth at each of my eyes in turn, as if to make sure one didn't drift off while she had the other commandeered. "Your father. Beautiful...singer. Pianist. Artist. Wanted to leave with him. Never see England again. My life would be his. Not Father's. Raise his gift high as God expected. That. *That,* my duty. That was...God's task for me."

She suddenly released me, covering her face with both hands. "So happy. I thought God was happy, too. Thought I could have what I wanted so much. To give your father...everything. And then I got pregnant."

The fever must have been going down, her speech was becoming more normal. "Your father was...ecstatic. But I had to tell my father. About the baby. We had to move up the wedding date, we couldn't wait until spring. I didn't want to tell him. He always...frightened me. And he was angry at me, very angry. For singing. For getting engaged. He thought I should be his... his servant. That God meant me for this, to take my mother's place." For the first time, Mother's expression had a glint of acid humor to it. She said, "He and God thought a great deal alike.

"He hadn't wanted to pay for the wedding at all. I think he did it only for appearances, thought people would talk about him if I didn't have a...a decent ceremony. So he went into a rage when he heard about the baby. You. He...pushed me down on the floor."

Her voice caught and she awkwardly pressed her fingers to her lips. "He...he grabbed my hair so I couldn't look away and told me I'd sinned in the worst way a woman could. That my soul and my body...disloyal. Corrupt. I would never be any good to anyone, not even my worthless husband. Said he would see me married, but never after, not me or my bastard. He put his face so near to mine, I could see nothing but his eyes. Said he ought to beat me, but that he didn't have to: God saw what I was and God would give me what I deserved.

"When he finally let me up, I ran from him. Locked myself in my room. I couldn't even pray, just played records on the phonograph until late, trying to calm down. *Bohème. Butterfly.* I loved music so much, the voices."

The fumbling hands covered her eyes. "When I woke in the morning, I couldn't hear."

She fell silent; her small frame seemed crushed by exhaustion. I watched her, as unmoving as she. I suddenly understood what she must have believed: that God had punished her for the love and the liberty she had enjoyed by taking away the source of her connection to my father, her ability to appreciate music. Overnight, she'd been sentenced to a life of dim whispers and vibrations where there had been vivid beauty and passion. She must have felt marooned, left in a kind of isolation that tortured her with faint echoes of the joy she used to cherish and the daily sight—as if they lived in separate glass chambers—of the man she adored still inhabiting a world of music she could no longer fully share with him.

I tried to imagine how it would be if I could no longer hear my own singing, or the sound of the orchestra. Or Donna's voice.

"Mother?" I patted her knee gently, the way I knew my father had. "Would you like to sleep? I'll come back in the morning."

"No." She wiped her eyes with her hands. Her face was gray, dreadful. "No. You haven't heard everything I have to say, and now that I've been forced to start, I will finish it if it kills me. As I expect it will."

She gestured toward the cup of water, but it was nearly empty, so I left to find the nurse and ask for a fresh one. When I returned, Mother had drifted off and her breathing was rougher than before. What flesh she had left seemed to be evaporating before my eyes. For the first time in my memory, I felt a sad sort of affection for her. If only she had told me before, I might have understood why she behaved as she did—this sensitive, traumatized girl who was sure she'd been cursed by the God she'd tried so hard to please. Who'd lost nearly all her hearing, and then her husband. I might have helped her overthrow her superstition.

"What are you looking at so sentimentally?" Her eyes were open, their irises as dull and hard as shale.

"I…it made me sorry, that you suffered all that, that you're suffering now."

"You can keep your pity, and give me the water instead."

We confronted each other wordlessly for an instant. My momentary compassion gone, I grimly shoved the straw at her and she drained the cup in long, ravenous sips. I went out for more.

"Should we keep trying to get her to eat?" I asked the nurse.

"We offer her plenty of food and she could have more if she want it, but I expect she don't," the nurse answered regretfully. "She came to us at such a late stage that she's already lost her appetite. We urge her to take at least a few bites, so her system work and keep her more comfortable, 'specially fluids. But her body no longer really need any nourishment, dear. It shutting down. You'll know the end near when she say no even to water. I'm sorry."

I wasn't sure I was. I took the full cup and returned to Mother's room. It was nearly midnight and she appeared to have dozed off again. But when I sat down, she began talking with her eyes shut.

"We went to doctors, of course, your father and I. No one could say what had happened to my hearing, though they all had theories and treatments to offer. For a while, I imagined I was getting better, especially on our wedding day. But in fact, nothing worked. I thought my life was ruined and that I'd ruined your father's too. How could a deaf woman help a gifted musician? A few weeks after the wedding, I had a breakdown."

Her eyes opened fully and focused on me, detached observers gauging the effect of her words.

"I tried to kill myself. And you."

I stared back at her.

"You wanted to know," she said. "You've always wanted to know."

And she coughed until I gave her some more water.

"Your father stopped me. He loved me and he wanted you, you see." Her tone was bitter. "He turned down important engagements because they would have forced him to be away. He wasted his great talent on little jobs near to home so that he could tend to both of us, and then he took this dreadful position in the islands so that I could finally leave England. He said that all he wanted was a happy family. He didn't seem to care about his gifts, but I did. I did not forgive myself for what I'd done, and God did not forgive me either. Deafness was my punishment for love and motherhood, the symbol of my failure of will and my disloyalty to God. And you and your father were temptations to love again too much. I had to watch myself as God watched me, relentlessly. I knew if I ever showed such love to you or him again that God would strike us down."

"So you trained yourself not to love."

"I tried to protect you and your father from the vengeance of God," she shot back, fiercely. "God, who thought my love was sinful and my service to him worthless. God, my other vain, sadistic father. I thought my love was nothing but poison to all of us. Something it was better not to have, and nothing either of you would miss if you concentrated on your art. And I am paying for that too."

My frown deepened. "What do you mean?"

"I mean that the more frightened I became that God would visit tortures upon us, and the more I tried to love him and not you and your father—to appease him—the more tortured you both became. I wouldn't touch your father, nor sleep with him. I couldn't bring myself to expose more children to God's eye, and I hoped our sacrifice would bring your father the artistic success he deserved. Instead, it made him miserable. I couldn't please him and God both, and I loved your father deeply, but

I feared God more. He tried to be understanding, your father tried to help, but all I could see were those eyes burning into mine and telling me that God would see me suffer. I had to be all ice, all self-control, to feel safe from them. Finally, your father couldn't take it anymore."

Her drained face turned to me, the bones showing beneath her concave, waxen cheeks as if her head were already nothing but a skull.

She said, "I don't think your father drowned by accident. I think he killed himself."

As she has herself, I thought. After all.

What did I feel at that moment? I waited to see, and so did she. Would it be horror? Agony? The devastation of acknowledging that, somewhere in me, I had guessed the truth long ago? Anger or sorrow that, together, my parents had made it impossible for themselves and me to have anything like happiness?

I didn't know. I looked at her, trying to triage the effects of this collision on my heart and brain, and all that I sensed was a tiny irony, like the disembodied grin of the Cheshire Cat floating in the cold void of space, that told me her God's will had been done. In her terrible determination to avoid it, she had carried out his vengeance herself.

The last thing she said before she fell unconscious was that she hadn't meant she wished I'd never been born, just wished I had not been born in that way. It was the singing, she said—she and Father had been seduced by singing as by an apple, and from the lovely exhilaration and desire and ambition and joy it brought them had come the love and the sin that doomed us all. My passion for singing had been God's vicious little punchline to the whole story. She said this with a wry smile, and then ceased to speak at all.

I called Brownlea at two a.m., school or no school, and asked him to come. We spent the rest of the night sleeping uneasily in our chairs at Mother's bedside. In those hours, and in my disturbed state, I thought I heard the small voice that was

joining Donna's and my own, like a tiny alarum, a harbinger
of something inescapable that would be as dire to us as I had
been to my family, growing stronger as Mother faded. For ill or
good, it would come. And would it end the silence I had always
known, or deepen it?

XIX

Such enormous dark eyes. They just watched and watched, uncomprehending and yet intelligent, taking everything in. As if she were filing it all away for the moment when she could triumphantly pull a bit of it back out again, to perfectly match it with some words she'd just understood. Like a missing puzzle piece or a suddenly recognized face.

She spoke in gibberish, though she believed she talked: lips pressed or pursed in humming, smacking sounds broken by bursts of wide-open mouth and vowels, gauging her efforts by the expressions of her listeners. She didn't know what was hers, what "hers" could possibly mean; it was a concept beyond her. On some shadowy, instinctive level, she'd realized her fingers were her friends, her feet excellent neighbors, familiar in the unquestioned way of things ever present. She accepted as good the feel of a soft blanket, the touch of those who cared for her, the warm smell of food approaching. Her bedroom was her world, strong arms her transportation for the small journeys from bed to bath or chair and back again.

When she looked at me, what did she see? A mass of unexplained contours. Two eyes staring back at hers, equally enormous, in whose changeable light she could already read approval or discontent. A mouth of fluid shape and sound and infinite, mysterious meanings, communicating in a code she somehow knew she must crack and so studied it, rapt, as if it were a movie, to see what would happen next.

Unaware, she saw white wooden slats and a pink knitted sheet. The slow twirl of tiny pastel bears above her head. Lamps and windows that glowed or didn't. Why? Cream-yellow walls and a doorway in which people—what were people?— appeared and disappeared bewilderingly, each identifiable to her by a particular scent, though only Donna's prompted an instantaneous response.

She was emerging from a nothingness as profound as death, taking shape at the same quickening pace with which she apprehended what already was, starting with the flavor of her own thumb.

We called her the Pitch Pipe because, we joked, she set the tone for the whole household. But the truth was just the opposite: she reflected forces that played on her like a violin string sensitive to every nuance of atmosphere and tension.

Donna had returned in May and her pregnancy immediately dominated both our schedules. Though she had been assured by the London obstetrician whom she'd made several trips to see that she'd feel quite well enough to sing during her second trimester and at least the early part of her third, she dreaded the many far-flung appearances she'd agreed to ages ago and yet worried that canceling any of them for less than a true emergency would hurt her reputation. I, on the other hand, eagerly anticipated my summer months of back-to-back dates, especially my debut at the American Spoleto in a performance of mixed songs and solo piano pieces with Gunter at the keyboard. It was something we had long talked of doing and, over several beers each and a large, stuffed pie at Edwardo's, Gunter had been able to persuade the director—who had come to Chicago to attend Gunter's new piano competition during my stay in the islands—to let us do an evening of Vaughan Williams, Barber/Rilke and Rorem works.

So I was feeling a bit hemmed in by Donna's needs and my own guilt over wanting to be off pursuing my career when she clearly was hoping I'd be home with her more often. And I did want to help her and watch the baby grow and take care of them both. Just not every single moment.

Thus, we were snappish with each other rather a lot and a furious, hushed row became the normal conclusion to any discussion of our plans, punctuated, as was every few hours of our lives in those days, by Donna running for the toilet. I always felt torn by a dutiful urge to run after her to make sure she was all right, and an equal but opposite one to flee the place for good while she was distracted.

Once, I actually did leave. I'd been planning to go out any-way—I had a session scheduled a bit later with David, and Donna knew it—but when she went into the loo, the thought of overhearing her being ill one more time brought such a wave of blank desperation with it that I simply grabbed my music and went out without telling her I was going. I would have arrived at David's a half-hour early if I'd taken the subway, so I walked, relief and guilt tumbling about me like a pair of big dogs freed from the leash.

I'd wanted a brilliant professional life and I'd married a bril-liant, sexy woman with whom I'd thought I would share ardor and sophistication and glamor and great artistry. A home, too, yes, but a home in which we would love and work intensely, a private corner of the large, glittering, passionate world that was ours. A world of adults. And now, because she hadn't fully prepped her damned diaphragm just once, our home had become a cell as full of dreary obligations as a closet is full of laundry and mops—a domestic laboratory of fluids and sounds and functions that could not be politely hidden or ignored, but required comment. Participation. Enthusiasm. And any flinch-ing, any failure to fully embrace the experience of gestation, no matter how mundane or distasteful, was regarded as criminal callousness and treason, punishable by days of sulks and weeps.

The big guilt dog took a leap even as I thought this. I knew it was far worse for Donna than for me. Hers was the body afflicted by all the changes and I knew that hormones were to blame for nine-tenths of her emotional plunges, not to men-tion all of her physical suffering and—she'd confessed—grief and dread over her swelling shape, exhaustion, and roughening voice. Vomiting three or four times a day is about as bad for your voice as drinking lye.

But the fact was, in spite of our determination to cope, and our being genuinely moved and fascinated by the baby, we were both scared all the time, scared and on edge from wondering what we'd got ourselves into. We weren't even used to being a couple yet, much less Mum and Dad. The careers we'd worked so hard for felt suddenly endangered. We weren't enjoying ourselves and each other; instead, we were creeping, terrified, along the narrow ledge of a tall building above a car park full of broken glass. Our apartment seemed too small to hold all the anxiety.

And it fell to me, as I suppose it did to all husbands, to comfort and cheerlead twenty-four hours a day. Apparently, it's somewhere in the job description that fathers, throughout all pregnancies, can never be tired or worried or in need of a break themselves, but must be on permanent call for reassurance, delivered—like the emergency milkshakes and massages and unofficial medical opinions—with a calm, competent, but never patronizing smile. Except that my performance seldom satisfied, as Donna routinely pointed out with tears and glares.

Behind my eyes, all the time, I could see my dying mother, saying with her thin, downturned lips, "We hadn't planned for a baby at all." I had been that baby, who became the product of my mother's terror and a defensive strategy so twisted it defeated even my father's deep attachment to us both. At least my father had wanted us to begin with. Through him, for a short time, we had known real love. My parents had truly wanted to be together. Would my child be able to say that?

I had thought I wanted Donna, but Donna as she used to be, without the nausea and painful breasts and bottles of horse pills, without the panic and constant air of accusation. If I were no longer sure I could live with my wife, or she with me, how could we hope to sanely raise a child neither of us had asked for?

I was coming down Broadway toward Forty-Fourth, still moving at the near run I'd broken into as soon as Donna shut the bathroom door, and had begun to feel a bit damp, so I went into a corner grocery to buy a soda and cool off in the air-conditioning. A few years earlier, you would have seen a wide variety of panhandlers and flophouses in the Times Square area, but the neighborhood had begun changing for the better and now the streets were full of families gawking at the new theaters and glitzy chain stores, while actors and business people elbowed past them with airs of weary superiority. The two-car-garage-sized grocery was wall-to-wall prams; I found the cold-drink case blocked by a cushy contraption that held a tiny boy busily sucking on the grubby yellow plastic duck he clutched in both miniature hands. None of the nearest mothers seemed to be his and I was reluctant to move him out of the way, so we gazed at each other, he with huge, inscrutable eyes the color of treacle. He seemed to mentally interrogate me, but without the slightest disruption of his serenity, as if I presented an intriguing diversion of no consequence whatsoever.

"What are you? Where did you come from?" he asked imperturbably. "And why do you keep standing there?"

Would my baby look at me like that? And how would I reply?

I suddenly realized, in the middle of this ordinary store full of everyday things, that I didn't know who I was, not the way this baby meant. He wasn't interested in finding out that I was a man, or a singer, or a British subject. "Are you a good thing or a bad thing?" is what he wanted to know, but only academically. It was all one to him. I wasn't his.

My child would want assurances that I was a good thing. And I knew that I couldn't say I was.

The boy's mother appeared from some other aisle, smiling but looking askance at me, and I smiled in return and murmured my apology for needing to get into the refrigerator case as she wheeled her infant away.

But the faint little voice stayed in my head, questioning everything I did, from the soda I chose to the notes I sang at David's—a soundless "why?" whose timbre of innocent curiosity masked a dark, implacable demand for answers I didn't possess. By the time I walked home, this time from the less punishing distance of the subway station, the voice had acquired a cherub's mop of curls and precocious, all-seeing eyes, ever turned on me, assessing.

"I'm home! Donna?" I called cautiously as soon as I'd unlocked the door.

There was no response. Quietly, I set my folder and keys on the couch and put my head round the bedroom door to see if she were napping. Again nothing, but the bathroom door was closed, so I tapped on it.

"Donna? Are you all right?"

I heard what sounded like a groan and, alarmed now, pushed the door wide to find her, fully dressed, curled up on the floor with her head on a wadded-up towel, apparently asleep.

"What's wrong? What in God's name are you doing on the floor?"

I crouched over her as she turned to me foggily and attempted to sit up. I wrapped an arm round her shoulders to help.

"What time is it?" she asked, pressing her hands to her forehead. Her dark hair was bent in odd tufts.

"Nearly four. I just got back from David's."

She pulled back and eyed me. "You left while I was throwing up."

"Yes, I'm sorry. I shouldn't have done."

"Why did you do that? What kind of guy walks out on his pregnant wife while she's sick in the bathroom?"

"I said I'm sorry, all right?" I could hear the irritation in my voice and fought to sound nicer. "I don't have an excuse; it was just a thoughtless reaction. I just couldn't bear being within earshot again. I know it was wrong." Still grudging. "I will never do that again, sweetheart." Better.

Her hard expression eased a bit. "I know it must be awful to be around, but it's pretty awful to go through, too. Everybody keeps saying I'll feel okay by four months, but it hasn't happened yet. I was so exhausted from heaving this time that I just had to lie down here and sleep."

She put her head down on her knees with such dejection

that I suddenly felt genuinely sorry for leaving her alone and hugged her tightly.

"What would make you feel better? Would you like me to run you a bath or get you a glass of ginger ale or something?"

She kissed me. "I'm actually starving again, believe it or not. Think you can make me some mac 'n' cheese while I take a quick shower?"

I guessed so and went about boiling elbow pasta and mixing it up with milk and the nuclear-orange cheese slices Donna always bought, while she wolfed some crackers to see her through, and then went to get cleaned up. She came out to the kitchen after half an hour, wrapped in a pink terry robe with little white socks on her feet and, for the first since she'd come home from England, looking clear-eyed and gorgeous.

We held each other for a long time, until I remembered the pasta. I seated her at the table like a gentleman, served her tea—supper, to her—and sat with her while she ate, talking of nothing important, but watching her as she chewed and wondering if she were naked under the robe and if we'd get an evening in bed together for the first time in two weeks. She finished, and I took her plate to the sink; when I turned around, she was fast asleep, with her head on the table.

So I tucked her in for the night. Before she closed her eyes, she held my hand to her abdomen and smiled at me when I vowed to her that I could tell it was bigger than the day before.

Inside, the cherub regarded me, unfooled.

I sat alone in the living room afterward, turning off the lamps and opening the drapes to look out the window at the glowing-in-the-dark of Manhattan.

"What was it you loved so much about her?" I heard the tiny voice ask.

"Love, not loved," I corrected it. "Her talent, her humor, her beauty. Her self-confidence. Her independence."

"Oh, be honest."

That irked me. "I thought I was."

Nothing.

"All right then, I loved that I could make her want me enough to give up her independence. But now that she has, now that she really needs me—"

"Because of me."

"Because of you. Now she resents her being dependent on me and so do I. I think she can't decide if she wants her life back or if she just wants me to lose my own in the same way, by fatal domestication. And I either want us as we were, or to be left in peace. Nothing else will do."

The cherub was silent. I tried to imagine its face—the face that my and Donna's baby would have—and could envision only the pictures of fetuses I'd seen in science books and photos of myself as an infant. Pale outside, shadowy within.

"Are you a boy or a girl?"

"What does it matter, if you don't want either?"

"Curious, that's all. I can't help being curious. You're entertaining as a supposition, I guess.

"But as a fact?"

"Horrifying. A danger. I'm sorry, I don't mean to hurt your feelings, and I feel guilty saying that, but you told me to be honest."

"What could be so dreadful about a baby?"

I didn't reply.

"Come on. Is it all the extra work and being tied down and life not seeming exciting anymore? I could understand that. It's a big change."

"Partly."

"You're sure you love her?"

"Of course."

"Well, we'll let that go for now. What else, then? You're not too young. You're not poor. I'm running out of ideas."

"You won't be able to understand. You think you're quite cute, don't you? Irresistible. You can't imagine a father not wanting his own pretty child. You've no experience of parents yet."

"It would be your job to teach me."

"I don't want to teach you. I don't want to."

"Lazy?"

"No, damn you! I don't want to have to relive everything for you. All that anguish. You have no idea, you little idiot, that anguish is all I have to teach. And if that's what I give you, my God, you'd be me all over again, and I'd be…I'd be…"

"Isn't that how it works?"

"Is that what you want? Look at me! Look at me, and pick someone else."

"Too late, you know. Without you, I'm nothing. Literally."

"I don't think you'd like the something I would make of you."

"You're not alone in this. Did you forget that, or have you already moved on?"

"I don't know what you're talking about."

"She has as much influence as you. Maybe more, at least at first. Does that help?"

"It depends on whether she loves me or not. You haven't asked about that."

"So you think she doesn't."

"I think there are moments when she believes she does. I also think there's a lot she doesn't tell me."

"Why?"

"You ask a great many questions. Is this a taste of how you'll be at two?"

"I'll be like this half the time. The other half, I'll say no to everything you tell me. Now: why don't you trust her?…Hello?"

"Very well. If you *must* know, I expect every moment for her to admit to herself that I'm not what she wants at all. I think she already knows it's pointless, but because of you, she feels obliged to deceive herself and me a while longer."

"You think she'll leave, then?"

"No one else has ever stayed. Why should she be any different?"

For a second, I clearly saw the cherub's eyes. They were nearly black, like Mother's. It said, "Maybe the question is, will you let her?"

"Leave?"

"No, be different."

I awoke at three to find myself still on the couch; Donna was snoring gently when I climbed into bed beside her, but flung her arm across my chest in her sleep. I pressed it close to me, trying to memorize its weight on my heart.

Five months later, the baby was born.

XX

What do you hear? What is that?"
She turned her face like a light, shining her eyes and glowing cheeks on the keys.
"See? Push."

My large hand picked up her tiny one and pressed it gently down, creating a soft ping deep within the instrument. She crowed and flailed, slapping the board over and over, eliciting a spotty jangle of tones worthy of Penderecki. I took her forefinger, curly and pink and damp as a baby shrimp, and tapped out the start of "Three Blind Mice" with it as I sang the words; from my lap, she twisted her neck, trying to look in my mouth, to seize my intriguingly mobile chin with her other hand.

I reached around her to play the entire song with chords. She simply stared, apparently waiting for an explanation or the next miracle, and I grabbed both her hands and clapped them together—"Hurrah for Daddy! Hurrah!"—making her laugh. I kissed her silky head, pretended to eat her ear, bounced her on my knees, and she gurgled uproariously. I was her largest toy, her pet, her human sedan chair.

I was going away again.

Only to San Francisco, but it would be my third out-of-town engagement in six weeks. My career had soared since Vienna—those were Sam's words, he'd been getting calls from all over, including Asia and South America. It had been hard to say no to any of them—well, to most of them, a few were clearly duds—as each venue sounded more exotic and exciting than the last. I had a solid three years of gigs lined up, some of them for significant pieces I'd never sung, which made me nervous, but Sam insisted I say yes to anything at a major opera house or with a major orchestra, as long as the composer fell within the general spectrum of my repertoire.

"What the hell you worried about?" he said. "You're a quick study and none of these are beyond your range or style. I'm making sure you have enough time off before the new ones to learn 'em, and I always leave you some free time, don't I? It's dumb to turn big stuff down when you're hot. You're gonna make a fortune. So relax. Go sing some scales or something. Enjoy your fame."

Just between late winter and next fall, I was doing the *Duruflé Requiem* with the London Phil, with a recording after, and *L'Enfant et les sortilèges* later at the Proms; *Eugene Onegin* in Buenos Aires; another Beethoven Nine, in Israel this time; Edinburgh again for a solo recital including Poulenc's *Tel jour telle nuit* song cycle at the festival; and my trophy, my seal of approval, Figaro in *Barber of Seville* to open the Met season.

A gold-medal schedule. And yet, not perfect. I hadn't heard from Vienna about the *Giovanni* and felt uneasy about it. I so wanted the part and Maazel made it sound as if he intended to give it to me, but time was getting short. Sam said he was doing what he could, which didn't feel like enough to me, and we'd had a bit of row about it—he thought the politics of Vienna would demand that an Austrian get such an iconic part in an anniversary production of this magnitude, and I thought he was making excuses for his own ineffective efforts to get it for me. I had tried to talk to Donna about it, but she had just rolled her eyes and said in her new, extra-cutting way that I should probably sing the part of the Stone Guest, instead, since I'd been getting so much practice being a guest in my own house.

Frankly, I preferred thinking about my engagements to thinking about my marriage. I had come home from working with David on the Duruflé the day after Donna made her bitter little jest and found her pacing up and down the length of the apartment with the baby in her arms, both of them red-eyed and wailing. She hadn't even said hello, just thrust the sweaty little baggage at me and walked out the door. Didn't come home for two hours and then said only, "We're getting a nanny," and,

"I'm going out for dinner," before stalking into the bedroom, changing clothes and stalking out again.

She's angry, isn't she, Daddy?

Yes, little girl, and I think I'd feel guiltier if I weren't angry too.

"Just what is it you're so angry at me about?" I had asked Donna. It was midnight—she had just climbed wordlessly into bed beside me in the dark, smelling of Chinese food and beer. I didn't even know whom she'd been out with.

There'd been more silence.

"Not even a hint? I think criminals in this city are required to be told what they're charged with *before* they're pilloried…?"

"Oh, shut up. Just SHUT UP." She bounced into a sitting position so aggressively, I strained to see if her fists were cocked. "You're so in love with your own cleverness all the time, all arch and haughty and ironic and all that…*crap*. Why don't you just ask me what's wrong? In plain words, without sneering or acting so superior. Just 'What's the matter, Donna?' as if you maybe actually cared."

I sat up too. "You're in a bad mood so much of the time now, it's hard to care what each episode is about. It seems like all one big snit to me."

"I'd have a lot less to be in a snit about if you simply did your share around here. You swore we'd split everything fifty-fifty—the baby chores, the housework—but you're never here! It's off to Europe or off to the West Coast or you have an interview or an urgent lesson or some bullshit to do and, once again, I'm staying home changing the diapers and vacuuming and cooking and struggling to get her to the doctor or having to haul her along on errands. It takes an hour just to get her clean and changed and ready and then she needs to eat again! I can't go anywhere I want to go! I haven't had any gigs for five months now and my career is turning to shit and you just keep leaving me here to cope with everything while you make a big name for yourself and hang around in luxury hotels! Why am I the one who has to give everything up?"

"Seems to me this set-up is your own choice. *You* wanted to nurse. *You* told me you wanted to be home with the baby at first."

"But not alone! I thought we'd be together! You said you wouldn't travel much until I was ready to go back on the circuit, but you keep saying yes to everything—except me and her!"

"That's ridiculous! I didn't go anywhere but to a few one-offs on the East Coast all during your last trimester and went *nowhere* for her first two weeks. One of us has to work *some*time or did you fancy living in a bus shelter?"

"Oh, as if your going on one less trip a month is going to bankrupt us. You're eating up the idea that you're some kind of star now, and you're not about to sacrifice a single second of being slobbered over in order to pay attention to the family you helped start!"

"I told you, Sam says I need to take as much of this work as I can, for exposure *and* money. For our future."

"Oh, very noble! Taking calls from Giulini and Levine and lunching with Te Kanawa!"

"That was one time, and it was the whole cast!"

"And I'm lunching on the baby's leftover applesauce, with rice cereal in my hair! I'm tired of being the only one stuck at home!"

"Well, it's not like you're getting a lot of offers right now, anyway!"

"I'd be getting a lot more offers if I could accept the ones I have! And you're the reason I can't!"

"Oh, I see. So it's not your fault for messing up and getting pregnant or deciding to play at being the stay-at-home mother—it's mine for having a more successful career than yours and wanting to make the most of it! You envious little hypocrite—you're determined to shape us into the model family, but only as long as you don't have to conform to your own role. Some wife you are—instead of complaining about my success, you should be doing everything you can to help it. That's a woman's proper job!"

She was very still. "Do you really believe that?"

"Yes!" Did I? "And where did you go tonight? And who with?"

My throat was hurting from the strain of my own whispered fury. The baby began to cry in the next room. Donna got up and put on her robe, turning to me just before she walked out, her face invisible in the shadow of the door.

"You'll never know, will you?" I could hear the laughter in her voice. "Sleep successfully."

Sometime later, she woke me with a silent push of my shoulder and stood there with our fretting daughter until I reluctantly got up and took the little monster out to the living room, where she cranked and I walked and rocked and bounced for an hour before I finally collapsed, unmoving, in a chair. She immediately fell asleep on my chest. I didn't even try to put her to bed, partly for fear I'd wake her up, but mostly because I didn't want to lie down next to Donna. I still felt a deep, stinging, unreasonable vindictiveness toward her that I wasn't ready to let go of. Of course she was entitled to her career, of course I admired and supported her talent, of course I wanted her—and thought she deserved—to enjoy the greatest renown and the choicest engagements in the business.

Theoretically.

I suppose that was the problem. I wanted success for her in every way, up to the point where the demands of her work made doing mine more difficult. I was *pissed off*—pissed off at the way things were turning out, at having a kid, at having a stormy and fragile marriage when I thought we'd have fun, at being made to feel guilty about throwing myself into my career, which was the only thing in my life that was going as hoped. And I didn't care at the moment about Donna and her sufferings. I was focused on me. I didn't blame the baby herself, exasperating as babies were. I patted her warm little back and wondered why that was. Perhaps because she hadn't asked to be born to two people who weren't sure they wanted each other, much less her. I hadn't asked to be born to my mother, either.

But the situation caused by the baby's arrival was unbearable. I resented it. And I resented it at the same time I resented being nagged by my awareness that my father had given up his own career for the sake of his wife and baby. Well, I had loved my father, but I wasn't about to do as he had done. *Did not want to.* Didn't think I should have to. Simply would not.

My success: the reincarnation of my mother's hopes for her husband and herself, the reason for all that they and I had suffered, the cold fire that consumed her. That must thrive, or what would be the point of my having survived them and their damned love?

I adjusted the baby slightly.

I wish you no harm, little girl, but I will never refuse a good job just so I can be on hand to boil you an egg in the morning.

What's an egg? I heard her ask.

We'll get a nanny, so your mother can resume singing. Lots of people grow up with nannies. You'll probably be the better for it. And if Mummy and I can concentrate on our careers, perhaps we'll be able to stay married.

So your being apart will keep you together?

You're too young yet for irony. And there's no guarantee that anything at all will keep us together. My mother was discontented with herself, to put it mildly, and that ruined her marriage even though she reportedly adored my father and he adored her. If two people's adoration of each other can't survive having a child, how well do you think we'll do, when your mother is mostly discontented with me?

Don't you want to love her?

Yes, I want to love her.

Do you think she knows?

She ought to.

Not the same thing at all. You sit in the dark a lot, you know. You go out by yourself. She might get the idea you love her a bit better if you did more with her. Or do you stick to yourself because you're afraid *she* doesn't want to be with *you?*

You're too young for irony *and* you're too young to be a

marriage counselor. You keep wanting it to be simple—that if we just *act* loving toward each other, we'll have a lasting love. If we just care for you, we'll have a happy family. If we just take turns working and staying home, we'll both have brilliant careers. It should work like that, but it doesn't.

Why?

Because people aren't logical.

Does that mean I'm not logical, either? I cry when I'm hungry or wet or cold or scared. Isn't that logical?

You also cry when your tummy's full and your bottom's dry and I'm holding you tight in my arms, rocking you. That's how we got here in this chair, remember? And I don't know why I can't make you happy any more than you know what to do to help me. Plus, you're only a baby.

But I see you. I saw you yesterday. You paused in the doorway and smiled at her and me and looked as if you wanted to talk to us, but when she looked up, you walked away. You told Sam on the phone a few weeks ago that you didn't want to take the Berlin engagement because it would mean being away from us for three weeks, but later, when she asked you not to go, you told her the Berlin job was essential. You call this not simple, not logical, but it is.

Why?

Now *you* sound like the baby.

And you're just being cryptic. That's a ridiculous quality in a four-month-old.

She squirmed in my arms and settled back into her quick-march rhythm of heartbeat and breath. What did she really see? So much that must be meaningless to her. And what could be the actual thoughts of a being both pre-verbal and uncomprehending? Emotions and sensations, that's all—nothing conscious. Just primitive, base-of-the-skull responses that somehow, someday, would grow into a complex understanding of cause and effect, of symbol and sound. She would look into my eyes and recognize something there. That color—Daddy. That particular smell (of what?), that shape and funny feel of earlobe—Daddy. The large, pale hands that would swing her around in circles until she was breathless with giggles—Daddy.

The quick frown. The biting remark. The refusal to bend. Daddy, I see you. Can you see me?

XXI

Coming or going. Always coming or going.

The scratchy, dark-wool overcoat with big buttons like tiddlywinks, and the black bag with the train-track zipper up the middle. Or a loose cotton shirt—gray-striped or green with squiggles—hanging floppy over jeans. Black folder; skinny, black, lace-up shoes. The blast of hot or cold air from the corridor, stale, metallic, faintly foody.

Hi! Bye-bye. Kiss-kiss (why are you wiping it off?). Lifting up and pressing tight, soft, plump armlets around creased neck. Short, smooth hair, humid-smelling skin.

"Your ear feels like a toad."

"Thanks a lot, tadpole. Down you go."

"No!"

"Don't brush her off like that, she hardly ever sees you."

"She sees me quite as much as she sees you."

Frowns. Whispers.

Hate this. Hate myself, hate you more. Scared. Miserable.

Mrs. Willis's eyes look tired, her face droops like that dog's on TV. She takes the little hand, a gravitational force, pulling out of the room.

"No! Don't want to! Don't like you!"

"Don't say that! How very rude! You will apologize."

For the truth? "No!"

A little sponge, soaking up the bitter poison. Can we get through a meal, through a single conversation, without this seismic tension, the scalding overflow of irritation, hurt, and disappointment?

"You're always mad!"

Christmas, after the presents. Sitting on the floor, playing on the new tom-tom. TAP taptap, TAP taptap. Head thrown back, laughing, rolling around on the rug in flannel PJs. Reach up a hand to bang out low chords on the piano. She comes in from the kitchen, singing. Lalala. A moment together.

C D E...F...G A B C

"Good. Do it again."

C D E...E... "Oops."

"Like this, remember? Reach farther with your thumb."

C D E...F G A B C

"The keys are big for you now, but your hands will grow. Do you like it?"

"Mmmm...I dunno." A pudgy, bare foot in each hand, trying to roll up like a potato bug on the bench.

"Do you like singing?"

Shy, sneaky smile. "Ay-eee dunnooo."

"Is there *anything* you know you like?"

Face down on the black leather, bashful. "Inaseeput."

"What?"

"It's a seeecret."

Strangely triumphant. A power in not telling—controlling, special, alone. The flicker of hurt and yearning in another's eyes: Excluded. Victim of the withholder.

"What do you mean, it's a secret? Why can't you tell me?"

That blank innocence, with a glint of challenge. Defensive, protecting. You want to know, but we won't tell, will we? Not until you do, and you won't until I...

Mummy's turn to go. She drops her purse down on the hall floor and puts her coat on.

"No, no, sweet potato. Not to the airport. That's tomorrow. I'm just going to see Lady Latidah for an hour and stop at the cleaners for my dress."

Mummy's teacher—Dohrayme Fasso Lahtido. Latidah.

"Do you want me to pick up something special for dinner tonight, have a little party before I go to Milan?"

Pizza. Baloney macaroni. Spaghetti. French toast.

"French toast!"

"Okay, I'll have to get more bread and syrup." Her quick glance. "Anything else you'll need right away?"

Aspirin. Hope. A different you. A different me. "Just some razor blades, please."

She pauses, smiles—warily? Facetiously? "No *real* close shaves, please."

Kiss-kiss. Every time could be the last. Well, go on then. Wherever it is you're really going. Bye-bye, bye-bye. Don't let's worry our pretty heads. It's safer in the dark. Play, let's play. Leave the curtains alone. Put a blanket over the table, we'll hide in the tent. Cards, panda bear, treasures.

"What's that in your tin?"

"Fedders."

"Good God, are those pigeon feathers? We must throw them out right now, they carry diseases. Come, we have to wash those hands."

"No! Pretty! Pretty! Mine!"

You want to throw the feathers out, the pretty feathers. And what should we keep instead? Empty jam jars? Newspaper clippings of glories past? A list of grievances, long and indelible?

Fierce eyes. "Not yours!"

Not mine. Is nothing to be? All the decisions already made and paths taken? Whoever you are, that's who I must be? Whatever you want, so I must choose? In your voice, the future, all that's necessary to know, all that's permitted to know. Safety first. Mind the gap, but ignore the sirens. Keep the giant fed and avoid his gaze. Our own appeasement policy. Right? Everybody learns to live with the fear.

Play house? Only for a short time, only ever for a short time. Daddies have important work to do. So who are we? Mummy and her little baby. Go to sleep, little baby. Mummy will hug you.

"Will she?"

"Daddy? Your eyes *red*."

Alone in the dark, "Lahfloor kuh tyoo mavay zhetay" beautifully leaking under the blanket edge. Strange dreams—strings of golden cherubs in the night sky, gently waved away by warm, unseen hands that bring me back to earth, hold me tight with an urgent strength.

"It's all right. It's all right. I'll try to wash the feathers for you. You can keep them."

XXII

They divorced before I started school.

Not the end of the world. I just thought it was at the time.

Our apartment became weirdly quiet—flat, in mood as well as layout. Like a war had ended, leaving everyone on the battlefield stunned and disoriented. All the drama and noise simply vanished, along with my father.

In a lot of ways, life was no different at all. He could just have been out of town, as he so often was, except for the fact that his things were gone too. And that they'd been replaced with lurking afterimages—like the glowing blotches you see after a flashbulb goes off—of everything as it had been, specters of a more colorful past faintly obscuring a duller, sadder now. Even though Mom allowed daylight to fill the place, even though she had the rooms redecorated and littered them with bright mementos of her travels and performances, I never really stopped feeling that we had traded electricity for candlepower.

She was seeing Georges by then, but he didn't live with us. He had dual citizenship—something that always sounded to me like the power buttons on a car window—so he was both French and American, as well as a doctor, and was something important at Sloan Kettering. They had met at a party held by a City Opera board member right after Daddy had moved into his own place on Central Park West. It was basically just around the corner from us, but going from two parents in the same house to one permanently sleeping elsewhere must be about the same as going from having all your arms and legs to being an amputee. Something's always missing, and you still feel pain in the limb that isn't there. From the moment he left, I no longer had a home. I had two bedrooms, instead.

He'd been leaving in stages for years, I think. I remember

once when I was very little, we were all sitting at the table having dinner—a rarity, I came to realize—talking about a big opera production that Mom had just heard she was going to be in. I remember it was in Vienna, because the name reminded me of these little pink sausages she liked to cook for breakfast. But Daddy wasn't proud of her. He was enraged.

He said, "You knew I wanted that job more than anything! You've known for years!" He said she should have turned the job down—called her a filthy sneak and something I didn't understand then that sounded to me like "opera tuna," which is funny now in a bitter sort of way. The real word must have been opportunist.

I remember she was about to take a bite, but put her spoon down and looked at him with a blank face. I knew even then it wasn't the way mommies were supposed to look at daddies. There was no love at all in her eyes, just this deadpan stare. She said to him, "We weren't up for the same part."

Then he yelled at her, which scared me. He stood up, knocking his chair over and throwing down his napkin, which landed in his soup. Mom suddenly started laughing and couldn't stop. She told him to keep going, maybe the ceiling would fall in on them again.

He packed a suitcase and left.

The two of them were seldom home together after that. They were very unhappy and I knew it in the vague, gut-level way that young children do. My father's voice seemed to get louder and louder—he fired Sam after a big shouting match over the phone and argued with David about what he should sing. He didn't like Mrs. Willis letting me watch TV or tear the labels off my crayons or run in the house and she would press her lips together so hard, they'd practically disappear when he was hectoring her about some transgression or other. He left once for a two-week job in London and came back two days later; Mom told me he'd left the production because he didn't think the director was doing a good job, but I overheard her telling Mrs. Willis later that he had made fun of the soprano for messing up her aria in rehearsal and when the director told him to stop, Daddy called him a brainless ox and the director fired him. When the phone rang, as time went on, it was almost always for my mother.

I woke up one night, very late, and heard low voices and sobbing; their fighting usually made me sick and frightened and I'd hide under the covers with my arms around my bear, but I remembered that Mom had gone to Houston, so I got up to see if she had come home again like Daddy had that time. I opened my door and was puzzled to discover that the house was dark except for the nightlight creating a faint glow in the bathroom, even though I could clearly hear someone in the living room.

It was winter and I was wearing fuzzy red pajamas with feet in them that made a plasticky whisking sound on the hall floor; I didn't want my parents to hear me out of bed, so I got down on my hands and knees and crawled as silently as I could until I got to the archway leading off the hall, then peeped around the wall. I saw the drapes were half open, letting in the strange orange light from outside. I could see the feet of someone long and dark and faceless lying on the couch. He was groaning and gasping out words I didn't understand, a terrifying sound that froze me into a lump of pure fear. I thought it was a monster.

I don't remember making any sound of my own, but I must have, because the thing gasped out my name, then again, louder, and I realized it was Daddy and I burst into tears. He was facing away from me and didn't get up, only wheezed out, "It's all right, come here," and held out a hand. I was still scared—what was wrong?—and crept toward him anxiously, not the least bit sure he wouldn't turn out to be a monster after all, but when I got near enough to see his face, he smiled painfully at me and wrapped his arm around my waist.

"Just give me a moment," he whispered, still struggling for air. I clambered over him onto the couch and curled up in his other arm, warm against his side. As my crying quieted, so did his labored breaths, and we lay there silent together for a long time. Though we said nothing, I felt he was glad I was there.

At last, he gave me a squeeze and asked, "Better?" I nodded. "I'm sorry I scared you. Sometimes, when I get upset about something, I feel as if I can't breathe properly and I have to lie down for a bit until the tightness here goes away." He put his hand on his chest.

"Why are you upset?"

"Well, it's rather hard to explain…"

He glanced down at me and I looked back up at him, waiting. His face was sweaty and mottled in weird colors by the streetlights.

He inhaled slowly and deeply. "I was sitting on the couch here after I tucked you in, thinking about my singing work and about your mother and her singing work. Success is very important to me, and though things have been going well for her lately, they haven't been going so well for me. That happens sometimes, when you're an artist—sometimes it feels as if you're doing your best work and everyone wants you to perform for them, and at other times, it seems as if you can't do anything right and everyone is against you."

He glanced at me again. He looked sad.

"Are *you* against me?" he asked.

I shook my head and burrowed more deeply into his side. He kissed the top of my head.

"Anyway, thinking about my work upset me, and so I lay down here to get my breath back."

"I thought you were talking to Mommy. I thought Mommy was home."

"No, pitch pipe, I was just talking to myself. The words to a sort of song. A French song I once sang to your mother: *Avec vous disparait tout l'eclat de la fete.*"

"What does that mean?"

"Just that I wish Mommy and I got along better."

"Does she know? You should tell her."

"You're a smart girl. That's something Mommy and I can agree on."

"Daddy?"

"Hmm?"

"Why does our house feel bad?"

A silence. He seemed startled.

"What do you mean?"

"It feels bad. When I'm at Maddie's or ballet or the store, it doesn't feel bad. It's fun. But when I come home, it does. Like something bad is going to happen."

"Like what?"

"I dunno. Yelling."

"Mommy and I don't yell much, surely?"

"But you're always mad. And Mommy's always mad. You just fight and fight and fight. It scares me. At Maddie's, everybody's laughing."

He didn't say anything.

"And I don't like the dark. I like to look out the window. You always close the curtains and Mommy has to open them again."

"I guess I like my privacy. Do you know what that is?"

"No."

"Privacy is being able to live and do things without anyone watching you or bothering you. I don't like the feeling of being watched. Except when I'm singing, I mean. When I'm not, I don't care to be around other people much." He kissed me again. "Except you."

"Not Mommy?"

"Your mother has other priorities. Come. Let's get you back to bed. It's very, very late and you need your sleep. I thought we could go to the zoo tomorrow, if it's not too cold. Would you like that?"

I just clung to his neck as he carried me to my room. I wasn't happy. There were things I didn't understand, things I had no words for. Somewhere in my stomach, I knew it must be me he didn't like watching him, because I always was, always watching him, watching for signs. Never sure when he would turn furious, or what would happen when he did, all of us together. I wanted to disappear, shrink into nothing when he raged at Mommy, get away from the terrible something that was always hanging in the air, waiting to happen. Waiting for things to go too far. I didn't know what.

I hated the zoo.

XXIII

I went to Britain with him once.

I often traveled with my mother to her gigs—when I was small, she had Mrs. Willis to come along and look after me and, by the time I was a teenager, Georges to keep me company and escort me to Mom's performances. And we spent as many holidays and summer vacations in Paris as she could manage.

But my father took me with him just that one time, when I was eleven. Part of it, I'm sure, was that he had no one to supervise me on his working trips: Mrs. Willis refused to go and none of his shadowy girlfriends ever lasted more than a few months. The other part was that he performed much less often than Mom as the years went on. She told me word had gotten around the industry that he was difficult to work with; only a few directors would give him roles, though he and Uncle Gunter had become a popular feature at festivals and on recital series and had made a good number of records together. He began teaching a couple of courses at Juilliard when I was in high school, I think mostly for the extra money. Teaching seemed to depress him.

We had been walking around the park one Saturday afternoon in March, on our way somewhere for what he still called tea—our usual weekend outing together—when he mentioned that he'd been picked to fill in on a Duruflé Requiem with the Birmingham, England, symphony in June. I'd be out of school for the summer by then.

"Not a fabulous travel destination, Birmingham. Sort of an industrial burg, but the orchestra is quite up-and-coming these days. I thought..."—his eyes flicked sideways at me and away again, with that reflexive stiffening of his back—"I thought perhaps you might like to come with me. The engagement's only two nights, with an afternoon rehearsal, so we won't have to be there long. We could tour Britain for a few days—see the Lake Country, Wales, maybe even pop up to Scotland, and then come back down to Oxford and London and Canterbury and all that."

He seemed to force himself to stop and face me.

"What d'you think? Does that sound like any fun, traipsing around over there with your old father?" His tight, bleak little smile lasted only for a second. "Of course, I know you've already seen some of London with your mother—"

"Yes!" I was astonished, both that he'd offered and that he thought I might not accept. "Are you kidding? I want to go!"

Relief and disapproval struggled for control of his face. "No, I'm not *kidding*. What a common thing to say," he scolded, and then gave me the first grin I'd seen from him since I was tiny. "So, you really would like to?"

I grabbed his hand and started dancing around him in circles, spinning him in place.

"All right, all right, take it easy." He laughed and tucked my arm around his. "But we should celebrate a *bit*. What would you say to catching a cab and going to Lindy's?"

"Oh boy!" I shouted and started pulling him in the direction of Columbus Circle and the stream of taxis heading downtown on Broadway. Then stopped dead.

"What about camp? Mom has me signed up to go to camp again!"

For years, as soon as school was out, my mother had sent me off to the North Carolina mountains for a month at the Explorer Camp near her family home, where Gramma and Grampa could be on call for emergencies and would show up for Family Visit every weekend with a basketful of barbecued chicken and banana pudding.

Daddy patted my hand. "I'll talk to her."

I must have looked doubtful. He frowned a little, but said only, "Stay here," and stepped into the street to hail us a cab.

Over dinner, we planned what we wanted to see.

"Castles!" I insisted, between bites of pot roast and cherry cheesecake.

"Castles...check. What else?"

"Armor and jewels and stuff. Gardens."

"All good—we can go to the Tower of London and Windsor and Hampton Court for a lot of that. And gardens are everywhere. How about cathedrals? Pretty villages? Museums?"

"What kind of museums?"

"Goodness—all sorts. The national galleries in London and Edinburgh have mostly paintings; the British Museum has ancient artifacts and sculpture, sort of like the Egyptian exhibit at the Metropolitan; the Victoria & Albert has endless, kitschy stuff..."

"What's 'kitschy'?"

"Not high art. More like slightly vulgar, souvenir-shop junk. Not that the V&A is vulgar, really, but it has mountains of ordinary, everyday things from long ago—furniture, clothing, figurines, ashtrays, toys...decorative arts, I guess you'd call it. Most of the castles are museums, too, essentially."

"Okay. I like paintings and the Egyptian stuff. And shopping!"

"Right. I figured that would start the minute we hit Gatwick. But what about Big Ben? And Buckingham Palace, with the changing of the guard?"

"Saw that with Mom." Why was that embarrassing?

"Oh. O...kay. Stonehenge?"

"Yes!"

"And what about scenery—hills and beaches and lakes? We'll want to see the ocean and the parks in Wales, and climb Arthur's Seat in Edinburgh and get up into the Highlands a bit..."

"Will the men be in kilts?"

"Mmmmmaybe. A few, no doubt, especially at Edinburgh Castle—I imagine the guides and guards are in costume... Have you had enough to eat? I see some untouched carrots in that dish."

"I ate most of them!"

"So you did. And tonight's special, so I won't make you polish your plate. Certainly, the *cheesecake's* all gone."

He made a sly, accusing face and signaled the waitress for the check. "Do you want to go anywhere else, or would you rather go home now?"

He meant to his apartment, where I spent weekend nights.

"Home. The wind's too cold to walk around anymore."

"You're right about that."

"Daddy?"

"What, pitch pipe?" he answered absently, filling in the tip and total on the bill.

I knew it was a mistake to ask, but I couldn't help myself. My voice ventured out, very small.

"When you talk to Mom, could you do it when I'm not there?"

The bitter look instantly darkened his eyes. I quailed.

"Why? Are you afraid we'll kill each other?"

"No."

"What, then?"

I didn't answer. His lips became a hard line.

"Come on. Finish what you started."

"I don't like the fighting," I whispered.

"And what makes you think there has to be a fight?"

I dared to look at him. "There's always a fight." And then quickly, pleadingly, "I could just talk to her myself?"

He stared at me coldly. "Well, that *is* how a female acts—so certain that a man is a clumsy brute and that she can do it better, whatever it is. You're quite like your mother, aren't you?"

Tears had started down my cheeks.

"Very well, you think you're such a diplomat, you're welcome to handle all the negotiations yourself. I bow to your superior skill. Just don't ask me for any help when she has a hundred silly objections."

He stood up. "I'm going home now. I can't leave you here, so you'll have to come along whether you like it or not."

He put on his coat and started walking out. I ran after him, openly crying.

"Daddy! Daddy!"

He paused on the sidewalk. "Oh, I'm good enough for you now, am I? Here, get in." And bundled me into the back of a cab. He sat up front, next to the driver.

Later that night, I tiptoed into the dark kitchen while my father was in his room with the door shut, and called my mother, weepily describing the trip Daddy wanted to take and begging her to let me go.

"Are you sure you want to, honey?" she asked. "Look how he's made you feel already. Wouldn't you have a better time at camp?"

"But h…he's never taken me anywhere big before. H…he wants me to come."

"Well, he has a fine way of showing it, doesn't he?" She sighed, with that sympathetic little chuckle I hated.

I hated them criticizing each other. He had asked me. It was special. She was spoiling it. Though I knew deep down, where I couldn't admit it, that he was spoiling it worse than she was. Why did I forgive him more readily than her?

"I want to go," I said, stubbornly. "I could still go to camp when I get back—we'd only be gone two weeks."

"I know you think you want to, sweet potato. But what if he's like this the whole time? And you know he probably will be."

"He isn't *always* like this." I felt inexplicably defiant. "Not with me."

In the silence, I felt her hurt and my own arrogance, but I didn't take it back. I didn't know how.

"All right, then." She sighed again. "I'll call camp and make sure this set-up is going to be okay. Gramma and Grampa,too. We can talk more about it tomorrow night. All right? Sweetie?"

"Mommy, why does he do it?" My voice was tinier than a mouse's.

"I wish I knew. In all the time I've known him, he's always seemed to want to punish everyone around him."

"For what?"

"For something I think he hates in himself, baby girl."

"But he always acts like he's right and everybody else is wrong!"

"I know. It's hard to explain. He doesn't love or even like very many people. But he loves you."

"He's never said so."

"I know. But he does."

I wanted to believe her, but I didn't. And yet, I wanted to go with my father on this trip more than anything.

We left in early evening, so we could sleep on the plane and feel sort of like it was really morning when we landed at six a.m. English time, instead of one a.m. our own time, but I was too excited to do more than doze a little. By the time we got into London on the train from the airport, I could barely stand, so Daddy got me some breakfast in the hotel restaurant and we sat on the couch in the lobby for two hours afterward, until our room was ready and we could lie down for a while. He had planned for us to spend one night there and then rent a car to go up to Birmingham the next day. That way, after Daddy's performances were over, we would be able to drive everywhere we wanted to visit and then end up back in London to sightsee and turn the car in before we flew home.

When we woke up from our nap, we were starving, but Daddy didn't want to eat in the hotel again. He said the best food in Britain was in pubs, so we went out looking for one. He was excited—it wasn't usually easy to tell but, that day, he strode along energetically, with the breeze blowing his hair back and his jacket flapping open, pointing out all kinds of things—the way the cars were driven on the opposite side of the street in Britain than they were in America (which I already knew) and the zillions of American stores and fast-food places, which he deplored, and funny signs, like "No Football Coaches" and "Have You Paid and Displayed?"—not mockingly or sourly, but as if he were pleased to be there, even if he didn't care for everything he saw.

We had passed a number of pubs that didn't suit him and he was starting to have to pull me away from the doors of American hamburger joints, when he noticed a sign down a side-street and hurried me toward it. "The Rose and Toad" it said, under a large painting of a knobbly, brown-and-green creature with a golden eye and a wide mouth in which it held a long-stemmed red flower. It sounded like a fairy tale to me, although the building itself looked shabby: cracked stucco and chipped black paint, with a faded strip of carpet in front of the grimy door. A hanging basket bursting with purple and pink blooms provided the only touch of magnificence. Inside, cigarette smoke created an unbreathable murk, which would ordinarily have sent my father right back out the door in a furious instant, but he chose to ignore it this time and found us a table where we sat side by side, with our backs to the wall, facing the room.

He went to the bar to order for us; I tried not to stare at the odd-looking people nearby, who all seemed to be either stubbly old men by themselves or pairs and threes of young people with nose studs and spiky hair, and gazed instead at the old photographs of racehorses and men in boxing gloves that lined the dark wood paneling.

Daddy came back. "Now, *this* is a real pub, just the old-fashioned kind I was looking for. We'll get a proper meal—no baked beans on toast here."

"Baked beans on *toast*?"

"Sounds dreadful, doesn't it? Ah, here they come already."

And the barman and a waitress were there at the table with two beautiful, hot little pies that turned out to have chicken and mushrooms in them, with baby carrots on the side, and lemonade for me and what Daddy called a pint for himself, a big glass of foamy, mud-colored stuff that he claimed was beer. He actually laughed at my expression. But the pies were amazing and so was the apple tart we had for dessert, which came with a wedge of cheese—I was so hungry, I practically choked, rushing to get it all in my mouth. Daddy exclaimed over everything and tried to explain British things to me while we ate: what schools were like, what all the different coins were worth, why you had to ask for a glass of water in a restaurant and couldn't expect it to come with any ice.

He was wearing a dark-green polo shirt. There was a paper-covered bottle of something I'd never heard of and couldn't pronounce called Worcestershire Sauce sitting on the table, along with a tiny gold-colored metal ashtray. The lumpy carpeting was a dirty red. And I had brought my first-ever purse, a little tan shoulder bag with white top-stitching that Mom had bought for me before I left and that held my comb, a tube of lip balm, the pack of playing cards I'd brought to amuse myself with on the plane, and my palm-sized troll doll with the cranberry-colored hair, which was my favorite.

It was the happiest time I ever had with my father.

It was a short day—I was still so tired that we had to come back to the hotel after two or three hours of seeing Trafalgar Square and Hyde Park and Harrods, for an early dinner and an early bedtime. But it was long enough for me to see what our family could have been, if only he had had the courage to accept what we wanted to give.

XXIV

We went for a boat ride in Birmingham. It wasn't memorable for sightseeing reasons, not compared to the many stunning things we saw elsewhere—just a tame little float down a canal lined, as I recall, by a few wildflowers, tangles of rusted metal, and a lot of industrial buildings. We went on the afternoon of our last day there.

I'd had to sit through rehearsal right after we arrived, because there was nowhere else I could go by myself. I hadn't seen my father perform very many times, mostly just at outdoor places like Tanglewood and Wolf Trap and Ravinia, where children were tolerated along with picnic baskets. So I watched curiously as the conductor led Daddy and the other soloist, a mezzo, through their pieces. I was proud of his voice. It was clear and strong, but also very smooth and beautiful, like a thick sheet of water flowing over polished marble—not like other classical singers I'd heard, whose big, throaty voices vibrated so wildly, you couldn't even hear the melody. On the other hand, watching him perform made me cringe. It was just too weird to see my own, everyday father up there making dramatic faces and gestures, so I covered my eyes to listen and fell in love with the music. It sounded like sun sparkling on the Hudson River in some places, and like dark, medieval mysteries in others.

And then everybody left the stage but the chorus, whose cranky director kept stopping them every three notes, over and over again, until I couldn't stand it anymore but, luckily, Daddy was ready to go by then and so we left. We poked around the huge new center the hall was in, had an early dinner at a nearby café because Daddy didn't want to eat anything but a small salad before his performance that night, and then went back to the hotel so he could rest. I tried to watch TV, but all the shows seemed strange or stupid to me, so I ended up reading

and playing solitaire and giving my troll doll different hairstyles
for two solid hours. Being an international singer didn't seem
too glamorous to me if it meant having to take naps in your
underwear instead of dressing up and going to parties.

But then it was seven o'clock and we did get dressed up, and
a big car came to take us to the hall. Daddy took me backstage
to meet the maestro, who was fun, and the mezzo, who wasn't.
I stayed with him for the first piece, a short thing that was only
for piano and strings; at the break, Daddy handed me over to
the hall manager, who looked like Santa Claus. He kindly took
me to my seat, giving me a program and making a little show
of glancing over first one shoulder and then the other before
sneaking me two chocolate drops, with a wink.

The place sparkled. The chandeliers, the stage lights, the
gowned ladies in the audience—they looked like diamonds
stored in a polished wooden jewel box. The whole orchestra
came on and started making noise with their instruments, to
tune up, and the chorus filed in and sat. The oboist played a
note for all the musicians to tune by, led from the front of the
stage by the concertmaster, and then there was a deep, breathless silence that seemed to grow and grow like an expanding
balloon until the mezzo and Daddy and the conductor walked
out to take their places. Then it popped with a loud explosion
of applause.

Daddy was seated near the podium. He caught my eye and
smiled briefly when I waved, but then resumed his dignified
expression and didn't look at me again.

The maestro shook back his hair and raised his baton. The
hall fell silent once more, and then his arm came down, releas-
ing the sunny, watery music as if the baton had been an electric
switch. The sound rippled around me, wordless voices and
liquid strings; I felt as if I were on a raft, moving with it. When
the shining, stormy third part began, Daddy stood to sing. His
voice rose and fell, dark silver-gold like the gleaming outline
of a mighty thundercloud with sunlight behind it—elemental,
iridescent, I would say now, part of a magnificence I hadn't

expected. It overwhelmed me, moved me to tears. He was part of this power, one with this astonishing sound that could crack mountainsides, fling everything earthly heavenward, and soothe it all to sleep again like a gentle twilight. A sound that came, in part, directly from him, from his flesh and bones and breath. Transfixed, I suddenly understood what must have made my father want to sing.

I had never thought about it before. It was just what he and my mother did, the way my friends' parents were lawyers and TV producers and business people. My parents didn't seem famous to me. Why would they? None of my friends or their families really knew or cared about classical music. I never had, either.

And yet, when the last note drifted away and the conductor dropped his arms, I burst from my seat with the rest of the audience, standing and cheering as Daddy and the others took bow after bow. Someone came out of the wings with flowers for the mezzo; the next moment, the hall manager appeared at my side with a single red rose and asked me if I'd like to give it to my father. I stared at him and he took my hand, leading me up the stairs to the stage and gently pushing me toward Daddy. I walked forward two steps and thrust the flower at my father, and he took it and kissed my cheek while the audience roared. Then the manager led me off and I waited backstage with him until Daddy joined us.

"Bravo!" the manager said to him. "And a lovely young lady you have here. Bravo, again."

"Thank you, yes, she quite upstaged me," he replied coolly, turning to me with that tight little smile, and I realized with alarm that he wasn't pleased with me, in spite of the kiss. He hadn't liked me coming onstage at all.

The manager looked from him to me and back. "I thought the gesture might mean more, coming from your daughter," he said with a face half sad, half contemptuous. Then he took my hand and shook it, giving me a warm smile. "A pleasure to meet you," he said, and walked away.

The lump of misery that had dissipated over these first two happy days of our trip returned painfully to its accustomed place in my stomach.

"Shall we go?" Daddy said.

I dragged my gaze from the floor to his unwelcoming eyes. "Why are you mad?"

He raised an eyebrow. "I'm disappointed at the way things ended here tonight and annoyed at that man for meddling. It wasn't his place to invite you up without asking me in advance and it wasn't your place to be there at all. Curtain calls are for honoring the performers—it's a strictly professional moment and family have no business there. He should have known that, and now you do."

He put a hand on the back of my neck and steered me toward the door.

"It's late. Time to go back and get some sleep."

"But I thought there was a party!"

"And so there is, but I'm in no mood now. Bed for you and some peace for me."

"But why?" I was suddenly angry. "You promised we'd go, it was part of our trip! He was a nice man and he did a nice thing and you were mean! Why do you always have to spoil everything? You spoil *everything*!"

I broke away from him and ran, dodging through the tuxedoed crowds of musicians and choristers coming offstage. I heard him calling my name, furiously, but I just wanted to be far away from him, and so darted out the stage door, tore through the green room and out the other side. I saw a women's bathroom down the corridor; it was the only place I knew he couldn't come in to look for me.

It was empty. I went into the farthest stall and locked the door, sobbing. I hated him. I hated him and I wanted him to love me and he didn't. Why? What did he have to be so nasty and angry about? Nothing pleased him for long—as if happiness for us and him were an unstable state that inevitably decayed into solid, lasting strife. All it took was a moment of pique over something—anything—that didn't happen according to his plan. Whatever that plan was.

It felt like a long time had gone by. I'd cried into so much paper that I had to flush the toilet twice to get rid of it. I'd just come out to wash my face at the sink when I heard voices at the door and one of the lady ushers came in and saw me. She leaned back out the door and said, "Here she is," and was immediately pushed out of the way by my father, who strode in and grabbed me by the arms. His chalk-white face turned scarlet.

"You wretched little devil! How dare you hide like that? I've had to look everywhere for you! What *were* you thinking?"

Terrified, I began to cry again. The hall manager, who had followed Daddy into the restroom, put a hand on his shoulder and said, "Why don't you come across to the library, where you can sit and talk to her?"

Daddy threw the man's hand off. "I'll thank you not to touch me or tell me what to do! This entire situation is your fault—if you hadn't interfered with my daughter, encouraging her to make an embarrassing display of herself, none of this would have happened! Now step aside and let us through!"

"Very gladly." He was clearly outraged, but spoke quietly. "But for God's sake, calm down and stop frightening the child."

"I don't do anything for God's sake," Daddy spat back at him. He seized my hand and gave me a ferocious glare, hissing, "Come. Now," and pulled me out of the room. We went down the stairs to the lobby and out the main doors to the street nearly at a run. Daddy started down the sidewalk, still tugging me. I was bewildered.

"Where's the car? D…don't we get to ride in the car?"

"We're walking, as you see."

"I w…wanted to ride in the car!"

And as if losing the car ride were more than I could bear, I sat right down on the pavement in my good dress, buried my head in my arms and wailed.

He ordered me to stop at once and get up, but I was past caring what he did to me. I wanted to go home and never see him again, and the thought made me cry so hard that he finally knelt down and held me until I was wept out and limp.

"Come. Can you walk now?"

I shook my head, weakly.

"All right, then."

He awkwardly gathered me up in his arms and carried me, staggering a bit, the remaining few blocks to the hotel.

The doorman ran up. "Is she hurt, sir? Is she ill? I'll call—"

"No, no, thank you. She's just exhausted—needs to go to bed. I think you can stand now," he said to me and put me down.

We rode the elevator up without speaking. He told me to get into my PJs, then paused.

"I expect you're pretty hungry, aren't you?"

I just nodded.

"Let's see what's on the room-service menu."

In the end, he let me order a big hamburger with fries and a dish of chocolate ice cream, and let me eat it watching American cartoons he found on some cable channel. He wasn't angry anymore and it seemed as if everything should have been fine again, healed.

But it wasn't. All his anger seemed to have entered me.

His kiss goodnight felt as much like a lie as his kiss onstage had turned out to be. He was so exacting about how people should treat him—so touchy, so mocking, so vicious when crossed or affronted, and yet he felt supremely entitled to be unfair himself. He had punished me for something that wasn't my idea, and worse: for something that should have pleased him, that should have pleased any reasonable, normal father. But he was seldom reasonable. And while I'd always feared him when he wasn't, now I was learning not to trust him when he was.

And so, the next day, we took a boat ride. I wouldn't say much to him that morning and maybe it was the only thing he could think of to do with me. We sat at a little table under an arched roof made of glass and gazed out at the light-gray sky and the dark-gray water, sipping lemonade and listening to the guide. I avoided Daddy's eyes. I didn't want him to see the disillusionment in mine.

XXV

Uneasiness hovered over us. After a day or so in which we silently toured the villages and countryside of the Midlands, I realized that one of us was going to have to unbend and reestablish something like a normal speaking relationship. And judging by what had happened to my parents' marriage, I figured it was going to have to be me. So I became polite, as if he were the father of some friend I happened to be traveling with—made conversation of a sort about whatever we were looking at, asked his permission for things as only a guest would. We were civil. It wasn't fun, but it was an improvement.

In this fragile state of truce, we wandered through Coventry and Warwick Castle and Stratford-upon-Avon. Finally—Daddy having ruled out Scotland for lack of time—we went to Wales.

Something strange happened in Wales. I still can't explain it.

We had come down the M50 to Gloucestershire and crossed into Gwent at Monmouth around lunchtime. I'd started keeping a little travel journal after Birmingham, mostly because I was entranced with all the storybook-sounding place names and wanted to keep a record of them, but also because writing gave me an excuse not to talk. When we got off the highway and stopped at a sort of bistro to eat, I busied myself listing the latest odd locations in my notebook and looking at the map to see what was coming next.

One intrigued me enough to break the silence.

"What's Tintern?" I asked Daddy, who had put down his menu and was glancing around the room with a scowl, obviously annoyed that no one was coming to take our order.

"Little town with an abbey nearby. A ruined abbey."

"What's an abbey?"

"A building where members of a religious order live and work, like a monastery for monks or a convent for nuns, with rooms to sleep in, and a kitchen and a church and probably vegetable gardens and such. For people who want to be loomed over by God twenty-four hours a day." He grimaced. "Actually, Tintern Abbey is quite old and famous. A poet named Words-worth visited it and wrote a poem that most people have to study in school, sooner or later. I suppose we ought to go see it—you can impress your teacher with a first-hand account, when the time comes."

"Okay." I didn't mind. Tintern sounded like lantern and I saw in my head a great, castle-like place aglow with magical light. But I was surprised that Daddy would volunteer to go anywhere religious after Coventry: When we'd parked outside the cathedral there, he had taken one look at the grim brick-and-concrete hulk they'd put up to replace the original that had been destroyed by bombs in the war, and refused to go in. Said God was enough of a monstrosity himself without people constructing hideous piles in his honor. He'd stayed in the car, moodily, while I explored by myself for a few minutes. It was undeniably ugly—almost brutish, inside and out, with none of the grace the old part had, even in its wrecked state. But except that the bombs falling on it was sad, I wasn't bothered by it. A church was just a building to me.

When I got back in the car, Daddy started to pull out of the space, but then jammed the brakes on and turned to me, as if he couldn't help himself.

"So what did you think?"

I was surprised. "I don't know," I said, honestly. "The old part was a lot nicer than the new part, though there isn't much left of it."

He put the car in park again. "Didn't give you the creeps?"

I shrugged. "Not really. I don't *get* church. Maddie has to go every Sunday and she always acts like it's a big pain, and her parents always make her have fish when they take us out on Fridays and she always has a fit because she wants a hamburger. Why can't she just have a hamburger? Church just seems like a lot of weird rules you have to worry about not breaking so you won't go to hell. And Maddie doesn't even believe in hell, so what's the point?"

"That's a very good question."

"Do you believe in God?"

A look I'd never seen before took over his face, a bitter, closed-up kind of look that wasn't so much angry as unnerved, as if he wanted to say no, but was afraid to. He shook his head slightly and put the car in reverse again.

"God is nothing but a bad idea that people with power over others use to get what they want. Don't let them use it on you," he said curtly, and stepped hard on the accelerator.

So going to Tintern made no sense to me, from his point of view, but I wasn't about to pry at him. I just looked out the window as we drove through the lush countryside, taking in the hedgerowed fields and the rare, brilliant yellow slopes of feathery rapeseed that yielded to stands of tall trees. The sun had fully come out for the first time in days, which cheered me up a lot and turned the road we were on—hardly more than a shady lane—into a river of shifting pools, hazy with bubbles of light here, sharply black there, all overarched by a gorgeous, green-gold canopy. Even Daddy seemed happier; I'd always half-consciously wondered why sun in the house bothered him so much, but sun outdoors didn't—as if home were a place to be afraid, but being in public made him brave.

We parked near the abbey and stood looking at it a long time before going into the visitor's center to get guide-maps. It gave me a different sensation than Coventry. No rebuilding had interfered with the tumbled walls and gray, eroded stones and it seemed more at peace with itself and its tragedy, as if its skeletal remains, broken though they were, were quite beautiful enough.

We didn't walk around together: Daddy got a headset for the audio tour, but I didn't want one, so we made our own ways through the ruins and grounds. We ended up together in a grassy area that made a sort of courtyard; he took off his earphones with a tentative smile.

"Rather striking, isn't it?"

"I like it. It looks almost more like a sculpture than a building."

"So it does."

"But"—I winced inside at asking what I couldn't suppress—"I thought you hated churches."

He looked at me thoughtfully, without irritation. "I *don't* like churches, though some are worth seeing for architectural or historical reasons. And they're often marvelous to sing in, particularly the ancient ones. But I think I like this place because it doesn't feel like a church at all, just a very interesting relic of a lost civilization. There's very little of humans and their twisted beliefs left here, and a great deal of nature. I'd say it's a better balance."

I wanted to ask more about the twisted beliefs, but thought better of it.

We took snapshots of each other in front of a great, empty window whose stone tracery was thought to have held stained-glass pictures in rich reds and blues, but that now framed only grass and trees in natural greens. Mine shows me, a stick child in loose shorts, as overpowered by the huge, vacant archway as a buttercup by an oak tree, tightly clutching the strap of my purse with both hands, one arm folded vertically and the other pressed hard across my pink T-shirted stomach, as if the bag were a balloon likely to carry me off. The wind has blown my short hair over one eye, but the uncovered one stares directly at the camera, its frankness belied by the misgiving in the smile. My father's image records his practiced performer's pose—three-quarter view, arms at sides—whose rigid lines form a cage that his oblique glance escapes, refusing to be met or known, or to reveal anything.

Like hurt or guilt. Like the truth. Like tenderness.

Unconfessed.

We stayed the night at a nearby bed-and-breakfast that luckily had a vacancy; Daddy had made a reservation for us in Cardiff the day before, but Tintern had slowed us down and neither of us wanted to drive farther that night. Not that we were all that enthusiastic about the B&B—for two people used to gleaming, modern hotels and sophisticated service, the lace-curtain-and-quilt homeliness of the place felt...well, not shabby, exactly, but *unprofessional.* I knew Daddy was dreading having to make conversation with the family, but they must have sensed this because, after the necessary chitchat about the room and our bags and what there was to do and the full English breakfast, they left us alone.

We left early the next morning, while the mist was still sitting like topping on the oxbow of river across the road. Daddy wanted to follow the coastline southwest along the Bristol Channel for a way, then cross the river Usk (another excellent name, mastodonish, like musk and tusk) and swing up to Caerphilly before ending in Cardiff that night. Caerphilly. I'd written it in my notebook the moment I'd discovered it on the map. It sounded like horses, like "kerfuffle," like "filigree"—another impossibly whimsical British name, a place where gnomes and fairies should gather for tea parties. Daddy had seemed reluctant to consider going there, at first—asked me if I wouldn't rather tour Chepstow Castle and its town, as they were right there by Tintern, but the word Chepstow had no melody to it. I wanted Caerphilly, and so, as he had about most things since that night in Birmingham, he let me have my way.

It was a day of pale, watery sunlight that erased the line between sea and sky. We followed local roads as close to the rocky, muddy shore as we could, stopping once in a while to walk out on a seawall or a bit of beach and look at the shallow water of the channel. I got bored, then hungry; we crossed the M4 and stopped for a snack. By the time we parked on the drive leading to the castle, the sky was overcast and I was full, sleepy and whiny about having to walk around anymore. The look on my father's face reminded me why I had been so carefully polite to him for a week. I forced myself out of the car.

And then I saw the castle.

It rose from its lake like the black core of a volcano rising from a crater: stark and grim, unlovely, and yet possessed of some fierce solitude, some brooding, primeval power that gave it beauty.

I had never seen anything like it.

Wide-eyed, I grabbed Daddy's hand and dragged him up the walk—a stuttering progress, as I became immobilized every ten seconds by some new view of the bare towers against the sky or reflected in the moat or pushing up from steep patches of emerald grass within the walls. It was nothing but stones— stones arranged for defense and shelter, now worn and streaked or overgrown—and even so, what they made became a sort of being, with mood and presence, with *effect*, the way notes become, not just music, but a living experience of music. I didn't use such words, then—I just knew that the harsh purity of the place spoke to me as if we shared something I hadn't known was mine, spoke in a soundless tongue that described the dark, shapeless things I felt, that pulled me. And I under- stood it because the castle *was* those things.

There was little in it, just a few heraldic shields hanging in the Great Hall and a few plain tables and chairs. Someone had had the good sense not to spoil it with exhibits and animatronic mannequins. It was only itself: the bones of the earth, reordered by ancient human intelligence for a clear and simple purpose. And in the reordering, they had, through a kind of alchemy, taken on their manipulators' essence, a nobility not of privilege, but of brilliance and severity, of secrecy, resilience, and blunt expectation, so that the walls into which they were made cap- tured the dark and light of mankind's hooded complexity and naked, relentless will.

I climbed every slope and parapet, peered into every corner. I liked it empty. It didn't occur to me to imagine it peopled with knights and ladies: Weighty as it was, it belonged to the air, to wraiths and mists and echoes—to feelings, not to rational thought, and certainly not to work. A place only of sensations and the subconscious.

I realized after a while that Daddy wasn't nearby and went

searching for him. I finally noticed him sitting on the grass with his back against the wall of the big round tower. He had folded his arms across his raised knees and put his head down on them as if he were sleeping. But at my tentative tap on his shoulder, he looked up immediately. His eyes were red.

"Have you seen enough?" he asked.

I slowly shook my head. "Could we stay here? Is there a hotel?"

He rubbed his eyes. "No, we really can't. We have that reservation in Cardiff and we've already had to pay for one night we didn't even stay there. I suppose we could get lunch here, but then we must be off."

"Don't you like it?"

"I didn't say that," he replied, sharply. "It's just not as new to me as it is to you. I've been here before."

"You didn't tell me that. When?"

He studied me. "Before you were born," he said, unwillingly. "Your mother and I came here before you were born."

"Why didn't you say so?"

"It hardly seemed likely to be of any interest to you, nor was it properly any of your concern."

"But it's about *us*, our family!"

"We haven't been a family for a long time."

He pressed his lips together and stared at the crushed grass under his feet.

"*I'm* your family, and I'm Mom's family too!"

I waited. He had never told me much about his life, not about meeting Mom, not about growing up. That's how I knew when something mattered: it was never discussed.

He took a crumpled tissue from his pocket and briskly scrubbed at his nose with it. At last, "Caerphilly is where I asked your mother to marry me," he said. "We were going to come back here together one day. But we didn't, and now we won't. *Diwedd y gân yw'r geiniog.*"

"What does *that* mean?"

"Just something my father used to say as a joke. 'At the end

of the song comes the payment.'" He shrugged. "I never actually wanted to see Caerphilly again."

He put his sunglasses on and leaned back against the wall
again. "You go on and look around a while longer, if you like.
I'm going to stay here."

I stood there a moment or two longer, but he didn't say
anything else. I wandered down to the curtain wall and gazed
over it at the lake and the crowds of people walking around it
without really seeing them. This is where their marriage had
truly started, where I had started, in a way. Our family had been
born here—a family that died in infancy a few years later and
thousands of miles away. I imagined I saw them together, on
the sidewalk or on top of a tower, laughing together as I was
sure they had, but couldn't remember when. Ghosts of a dead
love. Unresurrectably dead.

I hadn't realized that I'd held a hope that they would get back
together one day. Until that second, I'd have said I was glad to
keep them apart, to keep the peace, that I hated the fighting
and the sarcasm and the constant fear of trouble. It would have
been true. He was a terror and she provoked him. They were a
disaster together. And yet I knew right then that something was
abruptly gone that had always been there, and it would never
come back. We would never be a real family again, the three of
us—forever only two at a time, with a recurring blank space in
the rhythm of our lives, like a skipped heartbeat.

And that's when the strange thing happened. The desolation
of the vanished hope that left me empty somehow collided with
the desolation of this somber fortress that filled me up, and an
odd intoxication seized me as I looked at the dark towers and
the green hills, a kind of recklessness I had never experienced
before and never would again—a wild euphoria of grief, like
the flaring of a star before it collapses into dense, black nothing.

Weirdly, I seemed to rise and expand, as if I were drifting
an inch or two above the ground. I circumnavigated the castle,
ecstatically running up every slope and stairway as if I would fly

off the top of it, in soaring love with this black mass of stones, and in despair. I sailed back to my father on these wings of wax and pulled him along with me toward the town, chattering and dancing around him, every sense elevated, every perception as vivid as if it had been outlined. The small patches of flowers, the chimneyed rooftops, his mystified smile, each quaint or drab shop window—every sight was beautiful and the beauty was sharpened by the buried ache at the core of me.

I floated up a hill on a narrow, winding street, blithe to my father's resisting steps, and found at the top, as if I had known it was there, a low, rambling lodge, white with green shutters, and a broad green garden in back with a few picnic tables scattered over it. The front door opened on a fantasy of rose-printed sofas and lamplight, of black-lacquered captain's chairs full of bristly old men who grinned sweetly and winked from under their cloth caps like the golden lights in the bottles on the mirrored wall behind them. Every silver hair of their chins glimmered, every banknote crackled like butcher paper as it moved from pocket to bar, and we filled our hands with baskets of hot, richly oily fish and chips and cold bottles of lemonade, before gliding outdoors to spread it like a feast on the farthest table at the highest point on the rim of the hill, overlooking the castle below. Music popped in electronic spangles from the inn loudspeaker, and we sang and crunched our steaming fish and joked and uproariously swilled down our biting, bittersweet drinks, and it was a party—a party, and I abandoned myself to it, looking on through the faraway clear lens of my odd rapture at a wake attended only by me and my father, and I keened inside over the corpse of our family and the loss of the love that had made us one.

A faint sun appeared from behind the clouds, modest and misty as a bride's face behind her veil of tulle. It was late. We gathered the remains of our meal and took them inside, coasting slowly out the door to the street on an ebb tide of fatigue and the old men's farewells. Subdued, we descended the hill and turned in the direction of the car. My father strolled quietly, an abstracted look in his eyes; I gazed indifferently at signs and stores.

"Daddy, look. Daddy."

He wasn't paying attention.

"Daddy, there's our name."

"What?"

"On that shop over there. That one."

He had been startled out of his thoughts; now, his look of confused surprise gave way to wariness.

"Yes, I see…"

"Isn't that amazing?" Our last name wasn't common. I pulled on him. "Let's go in!"

"No." He said it flatly, leaving no keyhole of indecision into which I could insinuate myself and wheedle until I'd unlocked his resolve: he'd used his no-appeal tone.

"But why? I've never met anyone else with our last name. Maybe we're related!"

"That's precisely the problem," he muttered. "We probably are."

"We—wait…"

He turned the corner, hardly even slowed by the drag of my heels.

"We're related to them? How? Who are they?"

I let go and stood there as he walked on. "Are they another one of your secrets?"

He stopped as if I'd speared him to the ground.

Passersby turned their heads, but I didn't care. Of course, he did.

He was back beside me in two good strides, grabbing my hand and tugging me forward with him.

"Don't think embarrassing me by making a scene will get you what you want," he hissed.

"All I want is to find out if I have a bigger family and who they are. Why can't I know about them? Is there something wrong with them? Or is there something wrong with me?"

I pulled my hand out of his.

"Why can't I ever know about *anything* to do with you? It's like you want to keep your whole life in a dark room, including me!"

Without warning, he confronted me, hands clenched, and I backed away a step as he roared, "I've tried to protect you and your mother from..." The words hung there as he seemed to hear them. He went white and clapped his hand over his mouth, bending over as if he were going to be sick.

"Daddy? Daddy? Protect us from what?"

He finally straightened a little, haggard and diminished as if something inside had stopped supporting him. He reached for my hand, gently this time, kissed it and let it go.

"From me," he said. "From me."

He nodded toward the parking area down the street and we walked.

"My father grew up here," he said, almost to himself.

I thought he was changing the subject. He took in deep, ragged breaths.

"All of my own family are long dead, including my father's brother, and I was an only child, like you. But my grandfather had a brother, and the person who owns that store may be related to him. May be our cousin."

"This is where we're from?" I stared at him.

"Where part of our family is from, yes."

"And that thing you said at the castle, before, that I didn't understand—that was in Welsh?"

"Yes."

"So you and Mom *didn't* just happen to come here?"

"We didn't come to see any cousins, if that's what you mean. I've never met them. I don't want to meet them. But I wanted to see my father's hometown, and so your mother and I decided to stop in while we were on vacation. We spent a couple of nights in Cardiff and came out here on the bus one afternoon. So there's your story."

"And you both liked it?"

"Yes, we both liked it."

I stopped. He stopped, too, wearily, hands on hips.

"What?"

"Did you plan it all out, asking her? Did you give her a ring?"

"No." He half-spun away, abrupt, edgy. "No. Nothing at all like that. I'd had no thought of getting married, none, and neither had she. I thought marriage was... I just wanted to be with her, and there was something about this place, the way she was, here. I didn't mean to ask her to marry me. I just did. I just..."

He walked away, over to the railing of a lookout over the gray-brown lake and stood there with his hands in his pockets. I followed him and tried to take his arm, but he shrugged me off.

"I know that's not what you wanted to hear," he said, stiffly. "I expect you wanted it to be quite different, for me to have been sure. I was never sure of anything about us, about her. No surprise that it didn't last, I suppose."

He flicked his eyes in my direction. "I know you wish it had."

"Don't you?"

The question startled him. "We were miserable, all of us."

"Are we happy now?"

He didn't answer right away, just stared across the lake at the bleak crags of the castle.

"I imagine your mother is," he said at last, bitterly. "She's always looked out for herself quite nicely."

My eyes suddenly overflowed.

"You hate her, don't you? And you hate me, too!"

We stood face to face. I saw tears in his eyes. I had never seen him cry. Not ever.

"Hate you? Why would you say that?"

"You never let me get close to you." My voice broke. "Everything I do makes you angry, like you wish I'd never been born."

Something shifted behind his eyes.

"That's not true."

"Yes, it is. Yes, it is!" I was sobbing. "You never say you love me. You've never said it. You don't love her, and I'm her daughter and you don't love me, either."

"My mother never said it to me, either."

He wiped his eyes on his shirt sleeve. "I'm glad you were born. Very glad. And I don't hate your mum. I didn't want to be divorced. But I couldn't help feeling afraid, deep down, that she didn't really care for me. And I suppose I made sure of it."

And that's all he said.

We walked to the car and got in, driving away in silence. All the way to Cardiff, I saw, as if they were signposts along the twilight road, the long and ghostly line of my family—me, my parents, all the unmet and never-to-be-known relatives of my father's past—each an arm's length from the other, never connecting, never speaking, all of us fading away to the horizon in our isolation from one another, visible only for the fear in which each of us was darkly wrapped, waiting for the single touch, those few reassuring words that would link us all, and dispel our loneliness and self-doubt in comforting, endless waves of sweet sound and light.

I was sure now that my father had loved my mother, that he still did. And that she would have loved him, if he had let her.

Diwedd y gan yw'r geiniog. I made up a little tune for the whispering syllables and hummed it to myself as we followed the river Taff toward the sea.

XXVI

And so we went back to our semi-separate lives, he to who knew what, I to something like normal with my cheerful, busy, often-away mother.

She was part of the regular world. At home, she wore jeans and no makeup, and matter-of-factly cooked and cleaned when the housekeeper was away. She liked diners and bargain-hunting and walking around New York; her favorite thing was to make a vat of macaroni or fried chicken for us and eat it in front of the TV. Except for being witty, beautiful, and an international star, she was an entirely ordinary and reliable woman, always ready with a hug, always available by phone. She gave my life a foundation of security and sanity. Consequently, I undervalued her.

It was my father I wanted and missed, his attention and approval I could never fully win, his affection that was always just out of reach. I kept holding out my hand, but the distance never completely closed. And yet, it grew less, very slowly. He could not say he loved me, but he called more often for conversations in which it stayed unspoken, his careful briskness nearly masking the hint of something else, something wistful, in his tone, especially after my children were born. His career dwindled as mine grew until we were even, he teaching more—and more resignedly—and singing less, but no less brilliantly, sticking to the recitals and small productions that removed him from the circles in which my mother reigned.

I saw him often—never for long—and learned to listen, when he came to dinner and to play with his grandsons or to walk with me in the park as we had of old, for any vague comment, any scrap of reminiscence that might emerge on purpose or not, camouflaged by talk of other things like a password by random letters, that would unlock more of what he was and why.

I lurked on his peripheries, a gleaner. And though he never let me see behind the covered windows of his memory, he opened doors, instead, through the boxes of keepsakes and letters, photos and books for which he claimed to have no room and gave to me to store, in the ties he worked with such feigned indifference to foster for me with Uncle Gunter and Aunt Debbie, Rob, and his old teacher, Brownlea, on the pretext of helping me with my career as a composer.

Only ego, perhaps—the lure of legacy. But I believe it is an oblique sort of bravery, this surreptitious leaving of clues for me to find and follow out of the dark. He and his mother and father, my earlier selves—I am learning them bit by bit and turning them to music, teaching my children the words and notes as I go. Together, we turn my father's story into songs for him to sing and be silent no more.

Borne on Waves (Song for My Father)

Enter here.
At last, the crashing pain is smashed and spent.
It hisses and recoils into the main
to seethe and brood.
You're left marooned,
ringing like an echo on the shingle
of this shore,
near-drowned and torn.
Pursued and preyed upon by light of day,
rebuked and bruised by stony, silent night.
Twisted and swayed.
Alive by chance, delivered into hell,
hungry and afraid to test the firmness
of the sand.
A lonely man.
Stretch out your arms and grasp the reaching vines.

With fingers laced in deep-connected roots
be fixed and held,
embraced. And meld
with all the rest like you, of atoms made,
borne here on waves of light and sound and storm
that fall and rise,
to this isle of tides—
anchorless and cast away, but yearning
for a berth.
Of Earth.

Acknowledgments

In the long lines of people who help authors survive and succeed, life partners are often saved until the end, for the greatest, final thanks. But my husband, Jean Dubail, must come first here as well as last, and in all the tough middle sections, because there has never been a moment when he wasn't there listening and holding out his hand to help me steady myself, get back up and keep going when continuing to try seemed pointless. The trek through the writing and publishing of a novel is a hard one and, in my case, took many years. Without him, I might not have reached this destination at all, much less so joyfully. This book is not only for him, but also of him and what he has shown me of love that lasts.

Right behind him stand many family members and dear friends whose constant moral support has meant everything: Diana Jack and Evan Dubail; Susan and Don Shuttleworth; Roger Kirkman; Björn Hennings; Kasumi; Caitlin Brady; Anne Nipper; Susan Russell; Supipi Weerasooriya; Christopher Breuer; Mark Tietig; Morgan Howell; Priscilla and Scott Wallace; Richard Jack; Tom Sowa; Dan Baumgarten; Jenifer Ward; Debi Kops; Jeffrey James Patton; Elaine Rooney; Mark Gillispie; and Rob Jackson. I add a salute to Rossie Starr, with fond appreciation.

A number of special people have not only been caring and encouraging comrades, but also irreplaceable sources of advice, information and validation, especially my longtime friend, colleague and double-checker of musical facts, Donald Rosenberg. Thanks to him and to Terry Hawkins, Chip Cox, John Grogan, Naheed Patel, Amanda Dennis, Aaron Poochigian, Mark Dawidziak, Amy Ralston Seife, Ernest F. Suarez, Ryan Wilson, and Lee Oser.

And my deep gratitude to all of those whose professional

assistance has led to this published book and its future: Jaynie Royal and Pam Van Dyk of Regal House; Laura Marie; Ira Silverberg; Benjamin Taylor; Elissa Schappell; Heidi Julavits; Justin Taylor; Umair Kazi and the staff and members of the Authors Guild; and—always my first, best editor—Jean Dubail.

BOOK CLUB QUESTIONS

1. What role do you think location plays in this novel and how does it affect and/or reflect the male narrator's character development and choices?
2. What does music represent to each of the major characters?
3. What purpose does it serve in the story as a whole?
4. Why do you think the author changes the novel's narrative voice from the man to his daughter? How does this change relate to the story's main themes?
5. What forces cause relationships to suffer in each of this family's generations? How are these forces perpetuated or dispelled?
6. What do you think the author is trying to show and say about families? What purpose do the secondary characters—Mr. Brownlea, Gunter, Debbie, Donna—have in conveying that message?